THE MUSEUM OF ALL THINGS LOST & FORGOTTEN

ORDINARY SORCERY
BOOK II

ALEA HENLE

ISBNS: 978-1-952735-04-2 (e-book), 978-1-952735-23-3 (as by Alea Henle), 978-1-952735-05-9 (inactive print, as by A.R. Henle)

Published by Crabgrass Publishing

Editing by Rare Bird Editing

Cover design by Augusta Scarlett

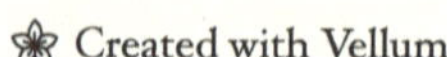 Created with Vellum

LOST

A text message from the future arrived on my phone around noon.

My sneakers' rubber soles squeaked against the slick, polychrome marble floor, mostly muffling the arrival ding. The elaborately decorated stairway before me used to be a bit slick, but otherwise a piece of cake. No more. A layer of dust blurred the intricate figures inlaid in the marble—circles, diamonds, and suns. More flecks drifted in the air, collecting on my uniform shirt and shorts and graying the dark green. The grime coated my tongue, tasting disgusting and making me sneeze.

Rather than pulling my phone out, I grabbed the gilded wood railing tight to keep from slipping and falling. Although steady, no guarantee it would support my weight. Better to use it for balance. I inched forward. Broke into a sweat when my feet slid to the side. My hair stuck to the sides of my head.

Bell-shaped earrings pealed with every shallow breath—not a good sign. The other times I'd climbed or descended the stairway, water chimed in the fountain at the very center, but it had ceased to flow. The vaulted glass ceiling overhead clouded over, filling the hall with a gray gloom.

Everything had an aura of dullness and dilapidation, from the floor to the frescoes and intricate trompe l'oeil tapestries lining the walls of the upper level, to the bust of Louis XIV of France positioned directly above the fountain. Even the gilt bronze dolphins supporting the red marble fountain basin seemed to spit dust.

The last time I'd passed this way, the chamber gleamed with newness and the fragrant scent of cleaning oils rubbed into the marble to make it gleam. What a difference a week made!

The railing creaked and swayed. I loosened my hold and scooted until I reached the flight of steps. Step by step I descended to the fountain's landing. Instead of taking the wide array of steps leading to the ground floor and the vestibule beyond, I ascended the matching flight up the far side.

The Grand Escalier of Versailles, also known as the Ambassador's Staircase, had existed for less than a hundred years, between the Sun King and his successor, Louis XV. It manifested as part of the D.C.-based Museum of All Things Lost and Forgotten a month or so ago, and based on its increasing decrepitude wouldn't last much longer before it returned to storage in the virtual vaults or wherever lost and forgotten places and things went when they weren't readily accessible from the museum. They shuffled around, some staying in one place for a long time and others appearing then disappearing.

Some other chamber would manifest here instead. Perhaps the replacement would be less dangerous.

I questioned my decision to take the year-long internship at least once a week, sometimes as often as three. Then I'd turn a corner and find a treasure long lost to war or modernity.

Chichen-Itza when new-built.

Nebuchadnezzar II and Amytis's Hanging Gardens in full flower.

The Buddhas of Bamiyan.

Employees regularly witnessed such sights. Few other people saw them. Then again, most visitors came in through the front doors of the museum and never made it past the superficial display rooms, cafe, or shop.

I'd shared a photo of the staircase with my sisters and friends when it first showed up, fresh and beautiful.

The sorcerers among them believed it a magical shadow of the real thing.

The mundanes asked about the museum's finances and how it survived since it kept making expensive replicas of famous lost places. When I replied that the museum ran on lost and forgotten monies, they laughed and assumed I jested.

Not true, but not worth convincing them otherwise either.

Before going through the wide door into another hall, I sneezed on a fresh mouthful of dust. Then pulled out my phone and turned to take a photo of the decaying version.

The newest text flashed onto the screen—listed as being sent by Beatrice Portia Williams aka Bea aka me with a send-date one week into the future. The text message came from me—or rather, I'd send it to myself in about a week.

Messages from the future constituted the magical equivalent of mundane fortune tellers and fortune cookies. The Webmasters of Fate offered the service for people requesting advice from a future self. The notes arrived without anything to indicate whether the advice came from a future self who wanted the future she lived in to become real or hated it and sought to ward it off.

At least this was simple and direct.

<<Run>>

Not on this slippery floor I wasn't.

Unlocking my phone, I deleted the message. Turned off notifications for texts. Then snapped a photo of the stairway in all its faded glory.

The big ornate doors stuck in place. Bits of gold leaf and enamel flaked off as I pushed the handle. Tucking the phone back in my pocket, I threw myself into the task.

The doors swung open, hinges creaking as they rotated.

I hustled through before the doors shut, glancing ahead only to check whether the surface on the other side required stepping up or down.

And wound up under a full moon. Fallen leaves and twigs crunched beneath my shoes. Tall trees soared to either side, the source of a fresh, crisp scent. Branches and full foliage arched and obliterated the sky except for small, scattered patches of midnight blue and the stark white of the moon.

A forest?

Wavering, I leaned against the nearest tree. My fingers dug into scaly bark and thick branches covered in long needles. The moon turned the world into harsh contrasts of shadow and light.

Lost again! Not my fault this time.

Everything in the museum moved but followed certain rules. One of the most reliable specified all interior doors— i.e. any door that, back when it existed in the outside world aka mundane reality, had not opened to the outside—would only open onto interior spaces. The same wasn't true of exterior doors. They opened anywhere.

If I'd left the Grande Escalier by the doors on the lower level, where ambassadors once entered, I might wind up anywhere.

But I'd stayed on the upper floor. The door *should* have led to another inside space or one of the halls in the very real building connecting the museum to the mundane world.

My phone still registered eastern daylight time, showing early afternoon despite the dark night surrounding me. Perhaps I'd leapt across far distances and arrived in a landscape tied to one of the museum's other outposts—Beijing or Sydney.

Or someone had gone awry and I unknowingly retraced their steps.

Goose bumps covered my forearms no matter how I rubbed them with my cooling hands. A chill wind blew through the branches, carrying a hint of snow mixed with the stench of fresh droppings.

A pile of dark scat lay only inches away. Damp mud preserved a couple of paw prints. Bits of bone protruded from the droppings. It probably wasn't human bone.

Opening the mapping app on my phone, I noted the deteriorating condition of the Grande Escalier and documented the shift from hall to forest, and day to night.

Anyone else who passed this way would be forewarned—as long as they checked the map first. We had to keep sweeping through the halls, chambers, and natural environments closest to the museum proper because they changed on an irregular and unpredictable schedule.

The doors I'd passed through vanished. No matter. One of the highly recommended suggestions—in other words an unofficial rule—involved never retracing one's steps. Circling back worked, as long as one took a different way and always moved forward or sideways.

I just had to figure out a convenient exit point.

Then a loud sniff broke the silence.

No sign of any creature or being, but a sob followed the sniff.

"Hello? Is anyone there?" I stepped over the scat.

"Papa?" A child's voice rang out, high-pitched with an edge of hysteria. "Papa!"

Hoofing over damp ground, I nearly slipped more than once on muddy spots covered with damp leaves. Stray branches brushed my shorts, leaving bits of bracken behind. A couple minutes run, then I stumbled to a halt.

A *young* child stood in the clearing—four or five years old at best. They wore dark sneakers with red flashing lights around the heels, knee-length light-colored shorts, and a short-sleeve shirt. Both shirt and shorts had mud stains, as did one of the child's hands. Their fine black hair was short, no longer than the tips of their ears. A bracelet of big, plastic beads encircled one wrist in bright primary colors against light-brown skin. Tears trickled down round cheeks.

No parents or other adults anywhere. Trees in view aplenty, but no humans. Not even shoe marks or footprints in the mud or on the fallen leaves.

Nimur, the spirit of memory to whom everything in the museum—the House of Memory—belonged, had a hard and fast rule about no unattended minors allowed whether they came through one of the front doors or the back ways. If they said it once they said it a hundred thousand times: *"Children do not belong among the Lost and Forgotten."*

So much worse than the Grande Escalier leading to a forest.

There had to be an adult around.

Sweat moistened my forehead and the small of my back. My chest grew tight and my breathing shallowed. Heartbeat sped up.

What if I scared the child, being the stranger in a dark wood? Or they might refuse to talk to me, leaving me to carry them back, possibly screaming, or have to summon help. If they ran way and got hurt. Their parent or guardian or whoever might show up and misinterpret me as a would-be child thief, or . . .

Moving fast meant making mistakes meant being wrong. Pinching my arm helped me focus and fall back on my four step method of making decisions.

First: breathe.

Next: break the problem into smaller, component pieces.

Third: pick whatever piece seemed most manageable and work through it.

Then tackle the rest of the pieces one at a time.

"Hi. I'm B-bea." I waved. "I work here. Are you lost?"

The child stuffed a fist into their mouth, muffling the sobs. Tears kept rolling along their cheeks, and their shoulders shook.

I dropped to my knees.

The child smelled of baby powder and peanut butter. This close, the stains had a faint whiff of iron. They'd gotten something on their hands and tried wiping it off. Paint maybe?

Anything but blood.

"It'll b-be all right. We'll g-get you help and find your father. Okay?"

Big eyes watched me. After a long moment, the child nodded.

"All right." I pulled out my phone. "D-do you know your father's number?"

The child removed their fist from their mouth and extended it, covered with drool. The bracelet around their wrist jangled as the beads shifted back and forth. The black on red and yellow resolved into letters and numbers, clear and big and easy to see.

"May I?" I moved slow, giving ample opportunity for them to draw back. Their shoulders hunched up to their ears, but they let me turn the bracelet.

"So, you're Cindy? A lovely name."

Cindy watched me place the call, teeth chattering. The sound stopped when she stuck her fingers back in her mouth. She leaned against me, skin cool to the touch and studded with goose bumps. Children's clothing acceptable for summer in the District of Columbia didn't pass muster in an autumnal forest at night. I wrapped an arm around her, loose but sharing body heat.

The phone kept ringing.

No one answered. A man's voice, no name but crisp and at the lower end of the tenor range, told me to leave a message and he'd get back to me as soon as possible.

"This is B-bea at the Museum of All Things Lost and Forgotten in D.C. I'm with your d-daughter Cindy. P-please call me at this number so we can reunite you with her. If I d-don't hear from you soon, I'll lead her to the v-visitor's station on the first floor, near the main entrance."

I hit redial, just in case.

As the phone rang again, Cindy shifted. Pushed back against my arm around her shoulder. I let go, hand flopping against my side.

She stopped staring at my phone. Her gaze moved up, angled above and behind me.

A crunch broke the silence between dings.

Rising, I turned and set my body in front of Cindy.

A woman stood there, as short as I and with a similarly solid build. A glimmer of warm sunlight hung around her. Lengths of cloth pulled thick, wavy hair back from a round face with deep-set eyes and skin the color of beach sand undershot with gold tones. A thick, dark tattoo around her mouth made it twice the normal size.

A quilted robe in dark shades covered her from neck to ankles, a sash at the waist keeping the fabric closed. She wore wooden sandals raising her a good inch or two off the ground.

A Rolex wristwatch glittered at one wrist. Despite the cool woods around us, a hint of fish or salty ocean air clung to her.

She blinked a couple of times, giving off a whiff of somnolence, but scarcely had Cindy and I noticed her than she dropped down to kneel next to the girl. Glanced back and forth between us, lines furrowing her brow.

"I'm Bea, this is Cindy." My phone rang over to voicemail again, and I ended the call.

The woman's mouth shaped our names without speaking them.

"English?" she asked.

"Yes. American English. Early twenty-first century,"

"You may call me Haru." She didn't say it was her name, which marked her as one of the Forgotten, the beings who never left the museum. "You have stumbled into my homelands. From where did you come?"

"I'm from D.C., in the United States." I said.

"Does it hurt?" Cindy pointed at Haru's mouth, rubbing her own with the back of a hand.

"Not at all. It was done long ago." Haru shook her head—then glanced over at me. "Do you belong together?"

"No. Cindy's lost."

"Papa lost." Cindy stamped a foot. Sniffed. Stuffed her hand back in her mouth.

"I'm working to g-get hold of him. Unfortunately, he's not answering." I jerked an elbow at the stains on Cindy's clothes.

For the third time, I dialed his number only to go to voicemail.

Haru didn't blink at the cell phone. A good sign, along with her watch, suggesting she got around enough to be aware of modern technology. Some of the older Forgotten didn't like anything newer than a couple hundred years.

"I will find your father, if you give me your hand." She

offered Cindy hers. The child sucked at her fingers, then put her other hand out.

Haru tilted her head back, nostrils flaring as she sniffed the wind.

A few snowflakes danced on the breeze, sparkling in the light.

For a woman walking on sandals with inch-high soles and trailing a child, Haru moved fast. She led the way around a rocky outcropping. An archway formed in the empty air. Carefully set silver-gray stones curved inward to meet at the keystone.

The air within the arch quivered, blurring the other side. Warm reds and oranges shone through. The red resolved into damask wallpaper lining the walls from waist-high up to the vaulted ceiling. The orange turned into mahogany panels covering from floor to chair railing. Matching wood formed the floor, except where thick rush carpets stretched nearly wall to wall. Candelabras hung from the ceiling, casting warm yellow light throughout the room. Sundials lined up under windows.

A dozen or more side tables, all different woods and styles, lined the corridor. Each bore an array of timepieces. Chrome alarm clocks. Old combination clock-radios. Elaborate mantelpiece clocks with painted faces. Pocket watches both with and without chains. Wristwatches likewise with and without bands. Cuckoo clocks hung above the tables, with grandfather and grandmother clocks my height or taller interspersed between.

No protective glass or security system or anything to keep people from touching or taking. If a visitor snatched something of value and managed to walk out the door with it, it rightfully belonged to them.

Cindy gave a cry rather like a seagull in full flight. Her legs pumped, pulling Haru along. She zigged and zagged, heading for a wide doorway about two-thirds of the way down.

In contrast to the hall, uniform pale gray covered the room from floor tiles to ceiling. Discreet florescent light fixtures filled the space with white light brighter than the moon in the forest. Video displays covered nearly every inch of wall space. Usually they showed split screens. One half displayed what someone present in the room had done at some point in the past. The other played how the watcher might have spent their time instead. The two views always differed.

This time every screen displayed a single image: a man with a pool of blood under his face. Rusty red marks marred his shirt.

The man lay in the center of the room. His jean-covered legs sprawled apart. One arm spread wide, light brown skin and green shirt bright against the gray tiles; the other arm lay tucked under his torso. His head turned to the side.

Nothing else in the room except the screens, a round sofa at the center, a stroller pushed into one corner, and him.

My heartbeat sped up, temples throbbing with pressure. Sweat oozed from every pore, and I flashed between too hot and too cold. A sour taste bloomed at the back of my throat.

Cindy ran toward the man only to hang back at the end. She stuffed her right hand back in her mouth, left clinging to Haru.

The other woman wrapped an arm around the child. Fixed her eyes on me and jerked her head at the body.

I rushed over and knelt at the man's side. Blood stained both nostrils, and he had a gash across one temple. Drops welled along the wound, oozing down both sides of his head to fall onto the floor.

"Medical assistance. Lost T-t-time. Urgent." I'd never used the panic app before and had no idea how long it would take for help to arrive. What could I do? Moving him might be bad. He'd clearly hurt his head, maybe his neck as well.

"D-do you know anything . . ." I waved at the man.

"No, I've not had much to do with healing." Haru drew Cindy closer, rocking in place. "I track other Forgotten. Wanderers, Sleepers, Destroyers."

His breathing came to a rattling halt for a moment. I froze. So did Haru and Cindy, cutting her sob half-way. I subsided into a messy pile when he drew in a shaky breath on the count of five.

My phone glowed and pulsed through my shirt pocket, but it made no noise.

I laid a trembling hand against the cool floor tiles.

"Help!"

A grinding noise shattered the quiet. My bones and teeth reverberated as a big metal box painted white with green snakes coiled on the sides rose through the floor tiles. A light mist bloomed around it, carrying an antiseptic scent.

The top burst open, cover recoiling back with a twang. A thin shelf popped up holding a small gold-toned bottle. Trays below held bandages galore in all sizes, bottles with liquids and pills, a stethoscope sitting next to a sharp knife in a red sheath, tongue depressors and medicine injectors and assorted face masks.

The bottle at the top twitched, scraping against the metal shelf. A heart-shaped white label glowed against the warm glass. Big black letters spelled out *Water of Life* with smaller print reading *use me first*.

No instructions provided. Should I pour it down his throat and make him drink or douse his skin?

More words appeared below the first set: *apply externally or internally*.

Squares of clean white cloth—swabs of some kind—manifested next to the bottle.

Biting my lip, I grabbed the top swab—got two. Both crumpled in my fingers, soft and light as cobweb. The bottle cap practically leapt off the instant I touched it. A sweet odor filled the air, reminiscent of mint and grapefruit.

I soaked the swabs in an instant, spilling several pale green drops in the process, then dabbed at the wound on the man's temple.

He took a deep breath and gave a long sigh. Although his skin exuded heat the first time I swabbed the gash, it cooled by the second. The flow of blood slowed.

"Papa getting better?" Cindy lunged toward her father.

"Bea's taking care of him." Haru wrapped an arm around Cindy's middle and slowed her approach so she didn't plunge into him.

Tiy rushed in a few moments later. After one all-encompassing glance around the chamber, she dropped to her knees and slid to the other side of the fallen man regardless of any damage to the midnight-blue jumpsuit covering her tall figure. Her arms and shoulders were bare, showing dark skin with russet undertones. Bobbed black hair gave her long, narrow face a resemblance to drawings of women from ancient Egypt before the Ptolemies and Cleopatras.

"Allow me." Polite, but her steady alto had an insistent note.

She snatched the soaked swabs from my hands, then set to cleaning him.

A few breaths later, Silvestre and Liam bustled in. They elbowed me away with quick glances of apology. I scrambled backward, gulping in air.

Silvestre's black robes formed a half-circle shadow against the gray floor, covering all but the tips of his matching boots. His shaven head gleamed warm beige under the bright ceiling lights. A heavy gold cross dangled from a cord around his neck, swaying with every movement. He interspersed rapid-fire orders in English with lengthy passages in Latin uttered in a wonderful, sonorous baritone. He touched the fallen man gently as he treated the wounds.

Liam hovered nearby, as always. Pale-skinned with light blonde hair cut short, he wore plain sandals and a brown robe cinched at the waist with a length of hemp rope. Whirling back and forth between Silvestre and the medical kit, he passed over instrument after instrument and bandage after bandage, all without speaking above a whisper.

Antiseptic smells filled the air. So too did Tiy's interruptions of Silvestre's praying, something he didn't appreciate given the way his eyes narrowed. He turned up the volume.

The injured man made grunts and moans. In a movie, this would mean he'd wake soon.

My shoes squeaked on the tiles as I slipped backward over to Cindy and Haru.

Then I burst into a fit of coughing, throat dry and sore.

"Toss Beatrice a lozenge," Silvestre snuck in between lines of Latin. As always, he insisted on using my full name and gave it a decided Italian pronunciation.

Liam turned and dipped his hand into the medical kit. With only a single word of warning, "catch," he lofted it my way.

I tucked the wrapper in my pocket and popped the sweet into my mouth. A burst of strawberry lubricated my throat.

"They'll help your father recover and heal." I bent down to Cindy's level.

Cindy sucked on her hand, glancing between me and the three working on her father. After a minute or two, she nodded. Pulled her hand out of her mouth and bit her lip. "What about baby?"

"B-baby?" I glanced at Haru, who shook her head.

"Baby brother. Jose." Cindy pointed at a stroller in the far corner.

Unseen, unnoticed. The stroller faced outward, with the straps to hold a child in hanging loose. A length of dark-gray plasticized fabric stretched over the seat, offering shade from sun or rain—and with two separate parts. One protected a seated child, while the other attached not to the stroller but to a basinet. Below lay a bag quilted in red and green, overflowing with wipes, baby bottles, and toys. The smell of baby powder—and poop—overrode the coppery taste in my mouth.

The sunshade squeaked as I pushed it down,. Only a pacifier with a blue and white handle rested within the bassinet. No baby.

I wiped sweaty hands against my jeans.

"Is baby okay?" Cindy pressed against my side, rising to peer in.

Haru laid hands on her shoulders and encouraged her to settle back down.

"B-baby isn't here." I squatted down next to her, thigh muscles protesting.

Cindy stuffed her wet hand back in her mouth. Eyes big, she mumbled something around her hand.

"What d-did you say?"

"Mean lady took him?" She slipped her fingers out long enough to speak more clearly, then sucked all the harder.

"Mean lady." I repeated.

More people began to fill the rooms—mostly Forgotten, but also a few other interns and employees. One had the sense to set the room offline for visitors. Three went over to the biggest monitor and restarted it, setting it to display the events of the past hours. The rest went to help Tiy and Silvestre with the groggy man starting to sit up.

Cindy squeaked at the sight. Pulling out of my grasp, she ran over and threw herself at her father. Silvestre caught her in time to ease her down. She snuggled against her father's side, picking up one loose hand and holding it against her chest.

"One of the Forgotten touched this." Haru picked up the pacifier and sniffed it. "I don't recognize who."

Maybe she smelled some special fragrance, but I only got dirty diaper.

"Can you find the baby?"

"Track the infant no, but the woman who took him yes." She took a second whiff of the pacifier. Her lips tightened, sorrow clear on her face. "I hunt and bring to reconciliation any Forgotten who break Nimur's laws."

"You did well, he will live and recover." Liam said.

I jumped several inches off the ground, having missed his approach. He patted my back and flashed a sweet smile.

A moment later, he blinked and stared over my shoulder. "Haru?"

"Liam, good to see you again." She nodded and bowed, pacifier still tucked in one hand.

"Oh, this is excellent timing." Liam returned the bow. "I hadn't seen or heard of you in so long I thought you might be Sleeping."

"I only rested a little while." Haru gestured at the empty bassinet. "We have a renegade, a baby-thief. Are you set for a hunt?"

"Of course." Frowning, he swept a hand across the cloth bottom of the bassinet. Sniffed his fingers and grunted. "But we'll be needing a host. This is not the kind of act easily forgiven. It means an enforced period of Sleep at the least. It's your lead. I'll stand witness. Bea, you'll come, won't you? In case you're needed?"

I shrugged, turning out my hands. A hunt, for a Forgotten and a stolen baby. Nothing in the training manual covered this. Even the unofficial information-sharing website fellow interns had created lacked instructions about what to do when called into a hunt.

"Excellent." He nodded, then turned and scanned the room. "As for a host . . ."

Liam dived off into the cluster of watchers, vanishing except for the top of his head bobbing. Haru cupped her hands around the pacifier and went in the other direction, shifting the stroller away from the wall and running her hands along the smooth surface.

I wiped a hand across my forehead, then rubbed my heated cheeks.

At least Cindy's father improved. Blinking his eyes, he laid a shaky arm around his daughter's shoulder and held her close.

Liam managed to sneak up on me again, this time with a young, gaunt woman with tawny skin shambling in his wake. Jagged short blue-black hair showed off silver hoop earrings and a nose-ring. A big, black X crossed over the heart on her *I love N.Y.* T-shirt and she'd wrapped an eye-blinding neon pink-and-green chiffon scarf around her neck. Her jeans had so many rips she likely relied on a spell to ensure they didn't fall off her legs. She scowled and hunched her shoulders as she stuck her hands in her pockets, standing with bare feet shoulder-length apart.

"Do you know each other?" Liam waved a hand, continuing without bothering to wait for an answer. "Jay Doe, meet Beatrice. Bea, Jay Doe. She's the newest of our Forgotten,"— he pointed at her then me—"and she's one of the newest interns."

She jerked her chin at me in an approximation of a nod.

I licked the residue of the strawberry lozenge from my suddenly dry lips. "Pleased to meet you."

She nodded again, but nothing else.

"Are you ready?" Liam hovering around her.

"I know what to do." She said, chin raised high.

"Very well then. We're going on a hunt." The skirts of his robe swirled around his legs and his sandals slapped the floor as he strode off.

I stumbled after.

Haru and Liam tapped knuckles against the smooth surface around one of the mounted screens, which showed Cindy and her father on one half side. Tiy, Silvestre, and others surrounded them. The other half displayed Cindy running along the path around the Tidal Basin. Her father followed behind, pushing the stroller. The sun shone overhead, reflecting off the waters. Verdant green leaves arched across the path as the cherry trees soaked in the hot summer weather.

Alternate possibilities. No doubt Cindy's father now wished he'd taken the children to the Basin rather than visited the museum.

"Ah!" Haru stood back, brushing her hands against each other.

A hairline crack manifested, dark against the gray paint. It ran up and down, stopping below the screen. A second line appeared perpendicular, then a third down on the far side.

"How did you find it?" Liam gave the surface a light push. With a low screech, the door rolled inward. A gust of dusty air puffed out, making me sneeze but no one else. Darkness loomed beyond, and a dusty floor with a few clear footprints. About my size, but narrower.

"I've seen such as this on other occasions." Haru rapped her fingers against the wall. The door opened further.

"Before you or after?" Liam waved at the passage. "Hunter's choice."

"After me, all three of you." Haru tilted her head to the side as she inspected him over, gaze moving on to Jay Doe and myself. Ducking, she stuck her head into the hole.

"Dark as can be." She snapped her fingers and golden luminescence surrounded her hand, hard to see in the room but quite evident when Haru entered the passage.

Liam created light as well, tinged silver rather than gold, then followed Haru. Jay Doe made a pinkish illumination, but hesitated. Arms tight against her body and jaw set, she drew in a deep breath and went next. I came last, my spell creating a greenish glow. All of us had to duck to pass through the four-and-a-half-feet-tall by two-feet-wide space. Fortunately, the passageway beyond extended higher—much, much higher. Ten or twelve feet. Thick, rough stones formed the far wall, cool to the touch and with a hint of moisture.

The door swung, hinges creaking. Jay Doe squeaked. I whirled and stuck out a foot to hold it open.

Too late. It latched with a soft snick.

"Never mind." Liam called from down the passage. "We'll get out another way."

He and Haru had gone several feet. Their feet disturbed the dust, kicking it up. Thick, heavy, and tasting of book paste. I covered my mouth and nose with my free hand.

Neither Haru nor Liam reacted to the dust, but Jay Doe adjusted her scarf to cover her mouth and nose. Her breath still came in fits and jerks as her shoulders hunched even further inward. At least once she cast a nervous glance at the narrow hall.

I magicked the fabric of my shirt to stretch and pulled the top up over my nose and mouth. Instead of dust, I smelled lavender-scented deodorant and my own sweat.

"You okay?" I asked as we lingered behind.

"I'll be well enough." Her eyes flickered in the light, shifting in jerky circles. She cupped her light close against her chest and headed off.

Holding my light hand high, I followed behind.

We caught up to Haru and Liam when they reached an

intersection with another passage. The sections to the left and right stretched off into darkness with no signs anyone had been by recently. Distinct footprints stood out amidst the layers of dust.

"It's too easy a chase." Liam squatted and laid a hand against one print. "Perhaps whoever it is wants to be found."

"We can ask when we catch up." Haru took a few steps down, one hand trailing against the stone wall. "The footprints tell no lie. She passed this way."

"She?" Jay Doe edged around Liam into the intersection. Some of the tension in her shoulders drained out once she stood in the wider expanse, with corridors to all sides. Perhaps the cleaner air helped, as a light breeze wafted through the crossing passage.

I stayed back in the archway.

"There's a familiar flavor to the air. If I'm right, I've met her on occasion, though not to see and be seen in a long time." A slow, whistling sigh escaped Haru. "She always had a fascination for babies."

The slap of Liam's sandals overrode the softer scuff of Jay Doe's feet and my shoes as we followed Haru down the passageway. We all had dust up to our knees. A particularly large patch clung to the front of Liam's robes from when he'd knelt down. Haru's elevated shoes reduced the amount of dust on her.

The track took many twists and turns, but always footprints stood out against the dust. Haru tested the air at each intersection with other passageways, but followed the prints every time.

The walls and floor shifted. Coarse stone gave way to brick, which in turn became finely hewn and polished marble. For a short stretch, the ceiling lowered to five and a half feet, and the whole of the tunnel became earthen. Roots wiggled above our heads, brushing my hair when I failed to duck low enough. Dampness filled the air, accompanied by a hint of mold.

Jay Doe waited until both Haru and Liam had cleared the section before darting through. Rather than rushing hot on her heels, I held back but ran as well in turn.

Even with my mouth and nose covered by my shirt, I breathed a lot easier when we emerged into a narrow hall of whitewashed stone on one side and unpainted paneled walls on the other.

My footsteps echoed in my ears and reverberated along my legs as I marched ever faster.

The wooden walls changed after a couple of yards. Round holes marred the panels at regular intervals.

"Peep holes!" Liam's whisper whistled up the hall. He hushed and checked through them, then sighed. "No one there to hear."

Haru slipped into his place as he moved on to another set of holes, then Jay Doe.

When my turn came, I rose up on my tiptoes to get high enough to peek. My hands braced against cool, smooth wood.

The holes themselves constituted small circles offering a narrow view straight ahead. In this room, an immense jade vase took pride of place. Everything else faded into background noise compared to the smooth sides and delicate figures engraved on the sides. It stood alone atop a block of stone, although faint glimmers to either side suggested the room held other objects as well. The wall contained a residual aroma of sandalwood, which lingered in my nostrils even after I stepped back.

Taking turns, we popped around each other to gaze through each set of peep holes. Although none sat farther than six feet apart, all offered glimpses of rooms from very different times and places.

A bathing room lined with intricate wood screens, and a hint of sulfur in the steam rising from the waters.

A dimly lit space no more than five feet by five feet stank.

An elegant dining room featured walls covered with lush gold-and-green cloth, a glossy mahogany table, matching chairs, and a dozen place settings all gleaming with silverware next to delicate blue-and-white china. Except, several of the chairs had unsteady legs. The china bore signs of breakage and repair. Hints of copper shone underneath the silver—silver plate, not solid. The wall hangings had tears, all repaired with varying degrees of skill.

No sign of people whatsoever.

As I pulled away from the decaying dining room, a faint cry echoed down the hall.

Liam skipped several sets of peep holes to try one further down. A moment later, he drew back and waved his hands to get our attention. Then crossed his lips with a finger to be sure we kept quiet.

Haru peered through next, then Jay Doe, and last me.

The wall creaked under my hands as I strained to see through the holes.

"Careful," Liam whispered, "there's a door there."

I lifted my palms from the wall, using only my fingers for balance. My feet ached from arching high,.

An immense fireplace lay directly opposite, surrounded by white-washed walls. At least six feet long, the fireplace had bread ovens built into one angled side. Various iron and brass implements depended from hooks embedded in the stone—ladles, pokers, and more. A small fire burned at the center, logs resting on thick iron bars raised the flames above the brick floor. Directly above hung a large copper pot from a metal contraption, and something within burbled and emitted wafts of onion-scented smoke.

A long wooden trestle table stretched along the side, almost out of sight, supporting several candles.

A low-backed wooden rocking chair near the fire creaked as the woman seated in it rocked back and forth. She wore a bodice of some type and skirts once plum-colored but stained with soot or mud. Likewise streaks of ash and dirt marred her cream-colored apron. Her white blouse had slipped on one side, so the candlelight highlighted the resonant terra cotta undertones of her shoulder. Dark brown curls fell loose around her face, mostly concealing her features.

An air of bliss hung around her despite the fussy baby cradled in her arms. Small fists waved in the air. A mix of sniffs and soft cries indicated the infant did not appreciate his surroundings.

She smiled nevertheless. Stroked the child's cheeks. Cooed. Uttered soft words and phrases, then shifted into singing a lullaby in French.

"It's Madeline." Haru slipped over to take my place for a second check before pulling away.

"I get the door open in two shakes of a lamb's tail, then we rush her." Liam did a few knee bends.

"No, surprising her is not the best way." Haru waved at the vacant peep holes. "She cares for the child as though her own. She may have convinced herself she holds her lost son. Let us try a more peaceful way."

"It's risky. There's fire there, and too many things useful as weapons." Liam paced across the corridor, skirts swishing about his ankles.

"I'll go around and approach her direct. Convince her to give herself up and return the baby." Haru dusted her hands.

"Very well, though on your head be it all if aught goes ill and demons get loose." Liam ran a shaky hand across his skull, leaving his short hair in disarray and a third of the strands sticking out at all angles. "I'll crack the door to the passage when you start talking to her, distracting her. If there's any sign Madeline will resist or fight, we can trap her between us."

"Fair enough, but do not run in at the first shout or curse." Haru headed down the hallway. Only the softest shuffling sound marked her passage into the dim distance. A few minutes later, light spilled into the hall. The brightness outlined her form until she passed through a door.

Liam positioned himself in front of the peep holes, hand poised to open the door to Madeline's room.

Jay Doe retreated to the far wall, arms crossed over her chest and fingers rubbing her elbows.

The strange vibrations in the air made my teeth and toe bones quiver. I slipped over to lean against the wall near Jay Doe.

My phone beeped, announcing a new text.

Liam glared, and all the whirling energy focused on me.

Whipping around, I hustled farther away. Silenced the phone, but couldn't miss the message.

<<Run.>>

Jay Doe seemed to be breathing easier. She stared at Liam with a wrinkled brow. He'd pressed an ear against a hole.

"Is there anything I should be doing?" I grimaced. "I've never been on a hunt before."

"No, nothing yet." Jay Doe waved a hand. "*You* might not be needed. It depends on what outcome is to be required, Sleep or remembrance."

"But you will be?"

"When Nimur is." A shudder, and her voice dropped even lower.

"What does the one have to do with the other?"

"You don't know Nimur?" She turned to face me head on, eyes wide and incredulous.

"I've met them a handful of times. At my interview, orientation, and once when a couple of fate webmasters stopped by for a tour." I ticked the times off on my fingers. "At the interview, they asked me some questions and stared at me for a couple of minutes. Orientation—they gave a speech welcoming the new interns and said they hoped to see us around and enjoying our work, then left. And the last time, I happened to be in the foyer when they came to meet some visiting webmasters."

Each time they'd appeared different save for the rainbow-colored light blazing in their eyes.

"Nothing more?"

"Yeah, I guess. I mean, Silvestre basically told me I'm better off if I don't see them much." He'd glared at me and the other new intern, bare moments after Nimur arrived to welcome us. "They're the spirit who powers the museum, the angel of memory, and very busy keeping everything running. They don't have a body and only manifest when they're needed."

"True they don't have a body, or if they do it is this entire space within which we walk and speak and breathe." Jay Doe tipped her head up, throat muscles flexing. "For them to be present in a way the living can interact with them, they need a host."

"So a host literally serves as the body for . . ." My mouth snapped shut.

"Yes. Hosts are always among the youngest of the Forgotten, under a hundred." She stared at the far wall, a muscle twitching in the corner of her jaw. "Any of us can serve, but always three to five of us host more than others. We anchor them. It is a trade. We grow in power and immortality faster as we host. This requires they take us over. The more they are present, the less we are aware."

"Thank you for telling me." I twiddled my thumbs, toes twitching. "I'm sorry for any discomfort I caused you."

"I understood there to be costs when I took their offer."

"Urk." Across the corridor, Liam pushed the door wide. The hinges creaked. He didn't pass through, but stood ready to enter room.

His body blocked everything but bits of whitewashed bricks along the ledge over the fireplace. Smoke sifted in through crack, making the light limning his body against the frame fuzzy.

Haru spoke, low and musical, in French. Another voice replied. Madeline, no doubt, but her tone bobbled back and forth from high to low without any rhythm. Squeak to boom and back, sometimes in the same word. Very different from when she'd been singing.

I crept around Jay Doe and Liam to the peep holes. Madeline stood up to show Haru the baby. The chair rocked back hard, without her weight, and hit the edge of the table with a hard thwack.

Liam shoved the door open, knocking me out of the way. I reeled backward. Stumbled against the far wall. No blood, no cut, no concussion, just bruises.

Thuds and cries filled the air as Liam rushed into the room. Wood hitting wood. A screech.

The scuffling ended, leaving only the high, thin wail of an inconsolable baby.

Jay Doe glanced my way. The light wafting up from her hand showed indecision on her face, whether to come and check on me. Then she followed Liam through the doorway.

A minute or two later I barged in after, by which time Liam had the baby in his arms. He rocked the small body. Cooed over the waving fists. Tried to soothe the wails, which faded as they kept being interrupted by hiccups.

Madeline struggled, pleading or cursing. Fought to free her arms, which Haru pinned behind her back. Shoes scuffed against the floor. Although a head shorter, Haru had too good a hold. Nevertheless, Madeline fought on, her upper body canting towards Liam and the baby.

"I have her name, but we need Nimur to give the judgment." Haru nodded at Jay Doe, sympathy warm in her eyes.

Jay Doe drew in a deep breath, head lifting.

The smoke from the fire suddenly formed a thin rope twining around the room. The fire itself went out. The candle snuffed.

Then the fire reappeared with full flames scorching the bottom of the pot hanging over it. Every candle in the room burst into light, from the tallow stick on the table to sconces I'd missed along the wall and a great iron wheel overhead.

Warm light filled the chamber, turning even the white-washed walls orange-yellow.

But Jay Doe's eyes glowed with all the colors of the rainbow. These seeped from her pupils and irises as her body reshaped into Nimur.

Their body compacted and shrank from Jay Doe's height to something closer to Haru's and mine. Hair stayed black, acquiring green highlights despite the yellow glare of fire and candles. Forehead broadened, chin extended, skin color and nose remained the same. Jay Doe's clothes pulled taut across a chest and belly grown broad and keg-like.

Nimur resembled a composite image of all manner of people. Their appearance and voice differed every time, though they always appeared and sounded familiar.

"What need have you for me?" The words had a harsh edge.

English, or so it seemed. Yet when Liam response, Latin fell on my ears while a shadow of his voice rang out in my head in English simultaneously.

"She stole a child, a baby, from its father's arms." Liam jerked his head at Madeline.

"Is this true?" Nimur shifted to face Madeline.

"My baby. I want my baby back." Madeline leaned toward Liam and the infant. Writhing, she strained to escape Haru. The shorter woman gritted her jaw and held fast.

"Confession is good for the soul." Liam addressed Madeline straight on. He cradled the baby, who still sniffed but whose cries had subsided. "Admit what you have done, and find release."

"Give me my child!" As with Liam, Madeline's voice had two layers: French in my ears and English in my head. "They took him and laughed as they dashed him against the wall. I screamed, but they kept laughing. They hurt me and left me. I tried to crawl over, but couldn't find him. They keep laughing and laughing, and he's screaming for me to find him. Today, I saw . . ." She redoubled her efforts to escape. Managed to drag Haru two steps closer to Liam and the child. "Give me my baby! Don't hurt him! Give him back to me!"

Haru pulled Madeline back, setting her head against the other woman's and whispering in her ears.

"How far has this gone?" Nimur glanced back and forth between Liam, Madeline, and Haru.

Liam tilted his arms so the baby's head emerged from the swaddling blanket. Small, round, with a good-sized tuft of black hair atop. Tears gleamed on the soft skin. "She attacked the father and stole the baby. Haru tracked her here."

Nimur touched the baby's forehead with one finger. He stopped crying. Blinked. Beamed at them. A moment later his face twisted into a series of grimaces and he grunted. The smell of fresh baby poop filled the room.

"I'll take him back to his father." Liam scrunched up his face, clearly trying not to breathe through his nose. His throat sounded thick. "Then send more help. Return if I can."

"That will be well." Nimur nodded.

"Repent." Liam swung around the table in a wide arc bringing him close to Madeline, though not enough for her to reach him or the child. "It's time to Sleep. You'll feel better when you wake."

Madeline redoubled her struggles and wails as he left with the baby.

"Child."

Madeline stopped struggling at Nimur's soft word. Her body wavered. She shook her head once, then slipped to her knees. Haru bent, still pinning the other woman's arms behind her back, but Madeline had begun to shake and sob.

"Do you wish to Sleep?" Nimur knelt next to her. "Or is it time for your remembrance?"

"Will I be with my child if I am remembered?" Madeline lifted a wet face, features slack and empty of near all expression.

"I make no promises." Nimur laid a hand on Madeline's head, stroking disheveled brown hair. "I have no dominion anywhere but here, but I believe you will find peace."

Madeline slumped further, then drew in a deep breath and sat back against Haru. Lifted her head and shoulders high. "Then let me be remembered."

"Very well."

Nimur crooked a finger to summon me.

I stumbled to their side.

"Are you here of your own volition?" Rainbow eyes fixed on me.

"Yeah."

"Do you consent to remember this person, and ensure they are remembered in the world through your self and your actions, should their talisman not be found and brought outside?"

They spoke slowly, enunciating each word.

Too late to run away. Only Haru and I remained, and

whatever they needed me for, she wouldn't suffice. Which meant Nimur required an intern, because by any other criteria Haru would be preferable. More powerful, knowledgeable—she showed no confusion as to what Nimur asked of me.

"You may decline." Nimur lowered their head, eyes still fixed on me but the whirling colors gentle rather than brightly contrasting. "In which event we will summon another, and another, until one is found who is willing."

I sucked in a deep breath and entwined my fingers to stop them twitching.

"I'll do it. Yes."

"Beatrice Portia Williams, hear and stand witness." Nimur's eyes flashed through the full rainbow spectrum, then they turned back to Madeline. "What is your talisman?"

"My baby's cap." Madeline's eyes flickered shut. A smile played over her mouth, though tears trickled down her cheeks. A faint tang of blood tainted the air, and a few drops rolled from where she'd bitten through her lip. "I sewed it myself, with scraps of wool and linen, before the night *they* came to arrest the lord and burned the house. All white and blue, with blessings embroidered, and he wore it until they killed him. No matter how I washed it, I never got the stains out."

"Do you know where it is?" Haru let go, rising and stepping back though she remained watchful.

"It's not here." Madeline shook her head, eyes still closed and arms held tight against her sides. "I kept it near, though hidden. I last saw . . . when I heard my baby crying."

No baby's cap anywhere in sight. Not under the table. Or with any of the implements hanging from the walls or around the fireplace. No drawers anywhere, but plates and bowls and jars in various sizes filled a cabinet along the wall with the peep holes. The doors creaked as they opened and shut.

Peering into the pot over the fire resulted in an overpowering whiff of boiled onion.

"It's not here." I backed away, coughing.

"We will have to do this the harder way, with name alone." Nimur summoned me back to their side with another crooked finger. "Listen," they said, then faced Madeline again. "What is your true name?"

Madeline swayed. Her mouth opened and closed several times. After a minute or two, her deep, guttural tone registered in my ears and not my head.

An instant after she said it, the words became a heavy weight in my mind. I clapped my hands to either side, massaging my skull and trying to keep my head upright.

The weight in my head belonged to her and no one else.

Nothing of Jay Doe remained about Nimur, only a strange force with rainbow eyes.

"You will be remembered." Nimur laid both hands on Madeline's head. Twisting their head, their eyes blazed with command. "Go. Get outside as quick as you can. All the way outside, and let no one stop you on the way. If they try, tell them remembrance.

"When you get there,"—their voice softened—"say Madeline's true name. We will know when it is done. Remember her, and see she is remembered."

My head swam. Knees trembled.

Haru had to tell me to run.

※ 2 ※

REMEMBERED

Sweat dripped down my back, making my shirt stick. More poured down my face, oozing into my eyes so they stung and went blurry. I blundered into doors and furniture several times. Every forehead wipe earned little more than a few seconds grace before sweat seeped into my eyes again.

The muscles along my legs strained and ached from the exertion and from propelling my solid, heavy frame forward. Even my jaw ached from jouncing every couple of strides when I mistimed a step or slid sideways.

My feet slipped on a thin carpet with a busy red-and-blue-and-gold pattern. I latched onto a nearby doorway and digging my fingers into the wood frame despite the hazard of splinters.

For all I walked mapping routes every couple of days, I recognized nothing of my whereabouts.

I ran all right—away.

I slowed down to a swift jog, more conducive to figuring out how to get out.

This particular room triggered no memory flags. Long

and rectangular and lacking in windows or skylights, it didn't stand out in any way—probably stitched together from several hotel ballrooms. Standard-issue wallpaper changing every few feet: gray for one section then pale blue then pale gold. Elaborate sconces, all electric, marked the walls at regular intervals. The styles matched the color of the wallpaper: brass to copper to gold-washed. Likewise the carpet shifted patterns.

An assortment of display cases stood along the walls between doors and archways leading off to other exhibit spaces. No glass cases, so all the artifacts lay out and open to view under the late-twentieth-century fluorescent lights.

All kitchen wares, from early pots and pans up to the latest and greatest stoneware. One section of wall boasted an assortment of ladles. Another held a dozen different designs of frying pans. Different illustrations of cooking, from a crude sketch replicated from a cave wall somewhere to a brightly colored oil painting of a troop of chefs preparing an elaborate feast, the work of one of any of a number of top name artists or forgotten masters.

An old exhibit hall, no doubt. Possibly abandoned, but not to the extent it had dissolved into the ether or wherever lost things and places went when they weren't part of the museum.

Lacking any better idea, I hustled down and pushed open the door at the far end. It clattered as it swung on rusty hinges and opened on the kitchen of some long-dead restaurant.

Deservedly destroyed, for every inch of it had a tinge of neglect. Rust on the old-fashioned light fixtures, and half the bulbous light bulbs broken. Brown-green crud growing on the long grill. Patchy linoleum underfoot that might once have had a pattern in yellow or orange, but had worn down to a dusty cream. Boards covered the counter over which hands had once no doubt passed plates of burgers and fries, or other fast-cooked food.

The name pressed on my brain. Sinking, seeping into my blood and bone. Pushing me onward, forward, and outward.

The kitchen had only one other door. Fingers slipping on greasy streaks, I turned the handle and jogged out onto the midway of some long-gone amusement park. A breeze carried the scent of the sea, tasting of brine. A rusty, half-decayed roller-coaster reared up directly in front of me.

I needed to be inside running through rooms and corridors to get outside.

Whirling around, I dashed to the building next to the old burger shack. Pushed through a set of saloon-type swinging doors. They slammed against my body from thigh to throat.

Then I raced into a fun house complete with a full set of mirrors reflecting me every which way. Tall and thin. Shorter and squatter. Green-faced. Upside down. Ducking my head to ignore the mirrors, except for flickers in the corners of my eyes, I hustled on.

The floor moved under me. Rippled and rocked. I lurched, stumbling at an angle . . . but instead of slapping into a wall, I tripped into a room filled with ornate mirrors. Caught my balance and rushed across it into a long, industrial corridor featuring case after case filled with lost books of all ages. The original map to Treasure Island, lost in the mail before the initial publication. A sampling of lost books, most destroyed in the outside world from fires at the libraries of Nalanda, the Moscow Tzars, and the Duchess Anna Amalia, among others.

I helped set up this display a month ago. I paused to catch my breath next to my favorite table. Round and beveled along the edges, the warm maple planks held illuminated manuscripts bright with vibrant reds, purples, greens, and golds. One so big two people had to carry it. Another small enough to fit in the palm of my hand. Two boasted precious metals and jewels decorating their covers. Others sat in cradles, open to pages showcasing equally brilliant colors within.

Madeline's true name filled my brain. Pain sparked and lights flashed in my eyes as I stood still. Only movement eased them, so I started shuffling, jogging, and worked back up to running again. Wheezing, my lungs gasped for every mote of oxygen.

Rounding a corner, I nearly slammed into a knot of visitors. A group of white teenagers laughing and joking and texting away.

"Sorry, sorry, sorry." I managed to keep on my feet. "G-gotta g-go."

"Where's the fire?" One of them slapped the air, face twisting in a snarl.

"No fire. P-personal emergency. Sorry, sorry." I caught sight of Liam at the periphery. "Fastest way out?"

He smiled and pointed, stopping to help the two who'd fallen get back to their feet.

The name filled my brain. Nothing mattered but getting outside and ridding myself of the heaviness. My head hurt worse than any other part of my body, with sharp flares slashing right and left, up and down.

Crowds everywhere I went. Many folk took refuge in the museum on Saturdays to get away from the horrid heat and humidity, mingling with all the day trippers and tourists come to cram in visits to as many of the other museums on or near the Mall.

Slowing down didn't work. The name pulsed more as I eased up. Rainbow flickers surrounded every speck of light. Pushing hard, I quickened my pace. My thighs and calves ached and no matter how deep I dragged in air I failed to bring in enough oxygen to spark any thought in my brain beyond the desperate need to escape and let the name loose.

The soles of my shoes started wearing through, letting nearly every crack in the floor or dip in the lines of grout between tiles make a double impact on the balls of my feet.

The name sank down from the top of my head to the middle, heading towards the stem of my brain.

My mouth remained dry as heck, no matter how I swallowed. I ran my tongue around, but lacked much spit. The moisture in my body as good as turned to sweat instead. I only tasted my own desperation.

The name started to lodge at the back of my mouth, at the top of my throat. If I didn't say it soon, I'd choke.

But I hadn't reached the outside.

Angling to the side, I headed for the less-popular closed stairwell rather than the wide, formal stairway leading from the entry foyer and main hall to the second-floor exhibits. The carpet turned black and red, and discreet signs denoted the door into the administrative offices on one side; the balustrade overlooking the hall below lined the other side. The hallway stretched wide enough for six to walk abreast— but people clogged it and blocked the way.

Cindy stood there, one hand tight around her father's. He cradled his son close in the other. A white bandage stood out against his dark hair at one temple. The baby carriage sat parked right where I'd have otherwise tried to dart through.

Tiy accompanied them, but Silvestre had vanished.

Half-dozen others crowded around them including the official museum director, a sorcerer rather than a Forgotten. A tall, stout Black man in a crisply tailored gray suit, he had one hand on the door to the admin suite, as he made a full apology, assuring the family he understood the museum's responsibility for endangering them and would make full restitution and compensation and take action to prevent any recurrence.

All very well and good—they'd be taken care of—but all the people left no space for me to get through except at the very end next to the balustrade.

Shifting back to block the way, Tiy stood akimbo, her blue jumpsuit giving the pose a superhero gloss. She only needed a cape fluttering behind her to complete the archetype.

"Is it taken care of?"

A word dripped from the weight of the name and spilled out of my throat lower than my usual voice.

"Remembrance."

Tiy's hands dropped from her hips. Her chin rose and her eyes flashed. "Follow me, I'll clear the way."

The director said something too, but I didn't make out the words as I lurched back into action.

Run ... run ... run.

Tiy not only ensured I had space to run, she rearranged the museum. Even as we bucketed down the hallway beyond the admin suite, it moved from the second floor to the first, down behind the gift shop and near the restrooms. Sweat beaded her forehead as she shifted things. Nevertheless, she kept pace with me and remained a few steps ahead. Any and all crowds parted before her.

She gave me a clear shot down one hall, around a corner, and then out the nearest of the bank of glass doors. She even pushed the button to swing it open, then stepped out of my way.

The automated opener whined and moved the door inch by inch, too slow. Throwing my body against the lever, I pushed it wide enough to slip through.

Only to stand, wavering, at the top of a bank of stairs. A ramp sloped down to my left. Others entering or leaving walked up and down to my right. Below lay the sidewalk and crowds heading to or from the Mall and its many museums.

Hot, humid air assaulted my lungs, so thick I nearly choked after the cool air conditioning inside. The heat strengthened the usual smells of the city, not least the overflowing trash can at the far end of the plaza in front of the museum. Rotting food made my stomach turn.

Hot sun shone down. Shadows flickered, but remained too small to offer much relief. Sweat from the heat quickly replaced sweat from the run, keeping me warm and damp.

A harsh rapping made me jump. I whirled around.

Tiy remained inside, not putting so much as the tip of her finger outside. She knocked on the metal door frame and glared at me.

"Say the name!" Lifting her hands, she waved at me. "Remember and make the world remember too!"

The syllables filled my brain, leaving only room enough for automatic actions such as breathing.

I opened my mouth, lips and tongue dry, and a croak emerged. But on the second try, hoarse sounds emerged.

"Jeanne de Paris."

Every muscle in my body seized. My eyes spasmed. The same rainbow light in Nimur's eyes filled me. A thousand, million, billion sensations flooded my body. Screams rang through my head. Images flashed before my eyes with whirling colors. Every cell in my body shrieked in pain.

Next thing, I lay flat on my back on the ramp, head lower than my feet. Blood rushed to my cheeks or I got sunburnt or both.

The sun overhead shone way too bright. Colors seemed stronger—the blue of the sky bluer, brown-gray of the concrete walls lining the ramp more intense.

A horrid taste coated my mouth as though something

crawled in there and died or I'd swallowed the contents of a garbage can.

I dry heaved, because nothing remained in me but equally foul-smelling air.

The creak of wheels and whir of a motor alerted me someone had started up the ramp.

Rolling to the side, I pressed back against the concrete block wall. Caught a little shade.

Not one but two interns hove into sight.

Yolanda rounded the corner to head up first, setting the pace in her motorized wheelchair. It really zoomed when she let it out. She had one hand wrapped around her smart phone to work the controls, the other held a bag on her lap. A half-dozen copper and bronze bangles chimed around each wrist.

A sweet set of thick, blue-black box braids shimmering with random copper beads swung from the copper ribbon binding them at the nape of her neck. The beads and ribbon exactly matched her big, round earrings *and* the thread used to embroider the museum insignia on our uniform shirts, and she refused to tell anyone where she sourced it though she handed out lengths to anyone who wanted one. The uniform shirt bagged and sagged on her almost as much as it did everyone. Waist down, she wore a short black skirt and knee-high black boots, showing a smidgeon of dark skin between the two.

She sat high as she rode, and didn't have to crick her neck looking up at people when she rolled along next to them. I'd always thought of the chair as a whole as a big contraption of black faux leather and black plastic and metal on rubber wheels. Plus a touch of purple plastic here and there. From a lying-on-the-ground perspective, gold pieces in the front caught the light and the wheels appeared dusty brown rather than black. She kicked up a dust cloud before and aft as she drove it up.

Some of the dust reached me ahead of her and I sneezed. This only made my head hurt all the more. By the time I stopped sneezing, Yolanda stopped and frowned down her long, steep nose at me. Mirrored sunglasses masked her eyes.

A moment later, Paulo appeared next to Yolanda towering high. Tall and thin, he had a lithe build still filling out. At twenty, he ranked as the youngest of us. The uniform shirt complemented the warm copper undertones in his skin. He wore jeans and thick-strapped sandals. Running one hand down his long, black braid, he peered down at me through wire-framed glasses.

The tang of barbecue from the recyclable container perched on Yolanda's lap pointed to their having gone for a late lunch and returned in time to find me in the way even after I rolled over, with accompanying aches and pains.

"Flushed, shivering, and heaving." Yolanda clicked her tongue at me, her classic New Jersey accent sharp on my ears. "What the blue blazes happened?"

I managed a croak.

"Do you need help getting up?" Paulo's soft, high tenor and Texan accent reverberated above the last remnant sounds echoing in my head. He squatted next to me. Smiled, concern clear in his eyes.

I lifted my arms.

Paulo reached down and grabbed hold. My legs turned weak as wet noodles, so he wound up dragging me to my feet. Then kept hold as I wavered. Drew me in to lean against him, but I pushed away. Better to lean on something than someone.

I flailed, reaching out. My fingers wrapped around faux leather. Dug in. I stared down, realizing I grasped the back to Yolanda's chair, a major no-no.

"Excusez-moi. P-pardon." The words scraped my sore throat as they emerged.

I let go. Shifted sideways until I managed to grab onto the sun-warmed concrete wall lining the ramp. By this time my leg muscles started behaving as they should, giving me some support. Enough, barely, to stand on my own.

Again, Paulo braced me, hands firm on my shoulder and side.

I smiled at him, sort of. Shaky. Mustered the energy to thank him, although it emerged as "merci b-beaucoup."

"Lord, what's up with you?" Yolanda moved a few inches closer.

The whine of the motor mingled with the creak of the automatic door opening behind us. A blast of cool air escaped, nearly softening my legs right back up.

Tiy stood just inside the doorway.

"I'm sorry, Bea, but you can't come back in today. Tomorrow yes, but . . ." Tiy smiled at the others. "Yolanda and Paulo, I need you to take Bea back to the Quarters. But first, Yolanda if you will keep watch over her, and Paulo, may I borrow your phone?"

The bright sunlight dazzled my eyes. My body didn't fit around me as it should. Some part of my brain thought I should be taller. Dizzy, I slipped to one side and grabbed hold of the closest thing to brace myself. Alas, this proved to be Yolanda's chair again. Rearing back I swayed again and nearly fell.

Yolanda grabbed me as I did an inelegant swirl. I landed back against the concrete wall.

She talked. My ears heard. My brain processed. Yet somehow I understood nothing. Not her nor Tiy and Paulo's muttered conversation, either. No words made sense, not yet.

Digging into the chair's built-in storage unit, Yolanda pulled out a full reusable water bottle.

My hand-eye coordination stank. I took three tries to grab it and two to unscrew the top.

"Merci." In a moment I drained it half dry. Spilled some, but the water cooled my chin and shoulders.

"Truly, what've you been up to?"

This time her words came through clear enough for me to understand. Taking a deep breath, I did my best to offer a coherent response.

"Le souvenir." Not what I'd planned to say. I didn't sound like me even to my ears, but rather as though I pretended to have a French accent. Finally I managed the right word: "Remembrance."

A mix of delight and horror mingled on Yolanda's expression. Her turn to struggle to decide what to say. Or, more likely, what to ask.

"You didn't! You have to report on this for the website. Who, what, where, when, how . . ." She leaned forward. The leftovers started slipping off her lap, but she caught the container before it spilled.

I shook my head, whole body shivering. Nearly lost hold of the wall and slipped sideways a step, scraping against the rough surface, before I caught myself. The water bottle wound up pinned between my belly and concrete blocks. I nabbed it with one hand and took another swallow.

Her mind had jumped to the website she and Paulo were developing, an informal exchange of information among interns to address the gaps left by the haphazard apprenticeship training, also known as learning by doing, that the Forgotten provided.

The whole adventure still stunned me, too complex to be reduced to any kind of quick answer, or a too-long-didn't-read version. Even the first query—who—had multiple answers. I'd said Madeline's true name once, let the weight fall, but bits of it seemed to sink ever further into my blood and bone.

Would saying it again risk more danger or change anything?

The door swung open and Paulo emerged, his stunned expression very close to Yolanda's.

"We're to take her home," he said to Yolanda, then tilted his head sideways and frowned at me. "You'll need help. Can you even walk?"

"Yeah. I think so. If I lean on you." I failed to stand fully upright, much less walk a straight line. At least my head had settled back into a closer approximation of normal. I understood English and spoke it.

Home. Someplace more comfortable to subside into a heap. Worth accepting a little assistance getting there. Or more than a little.

Paulo quirked an eyebrow at me. With gentle hands, he peeled one of my arms away from wall and wrapped it around his waist. A good choice, since my arm barely reached up to his shoulders. I tucked my fingers around the leather belt holding up his jeans and let go of the wall. My legs wobbled and held—mostly. I flopped against him and he grabbed my shoulders to brace my other side.

"Did Tiy give you any details?" Yolanda snatched her water bottle from my hand.

"Nope." Paulo squeezed my shoulder. "She needed my cell phone to call for help for Bea." He inched us back against the door, out of the way so Yolanda had room to turn around and head back down the ramp.

"Forgotten d-don't use cell phones." I'd never seen any carry one with them. Not even when Silvestre allowed me to help take down an exhibit of lost or missed conversations, which included several bins of lost cell phones.

"They can't have any of their own, since they don't exist in the mundane world, but they can use prepaid lost ones—burners with minutes remaining." Paulo squeezed my shoulder in reassurance. "But Tiy didn't have one on her and wanted to make a call. She says someone will be coming to help us with you shortly and to hang tight."

"Oh." A series of warm fuzzy feelings wiggled through me, followed by puzzlement "Who?"

"She didn't say."

Yolanda breezed past us and started down the ramp at a slow but steady clip.

"Ready?"

Not hardly. All the same, I gritted my teeth and wrapped my fingers tighter on his belt until the edges dug into my skin.

My first step lurched to the side. Mistimed, with him moving before me and taking a longer stride. I slipped, but he slapped both hands around my shoulders and held me up.

"Your legs are t-too long," I said.

"Or yours too short." He flashed a smile. Ran a hand across my back in encouragement, stooping to get closer to my height. "Try again?"

"Thanks." We both adjusted our stride, but it still took the whole length of the ramp before we managed to get in sync. He adjusted to my inconsistent pace quicker than I to him.

My walking improved with every step. The dizziness faded, although the flashes at the corners of my eyes persisted. All the same, I clung to Paulo, apologizing all the while until he bopped me on the head and told me to cut it out. "You'd do the same for me."

I ducked my head to hide my cheeks flushing and teeth grinding.

We met up with Yolanda where the ramp met the side-walk. She inspected us and gave a snort. "I'll clear the way, you follow. Got it?"

Summer tourists were out in enough force on the side-walk. Far easier to walk in her wake than forge our way through clumps of people holding phones and jabbering about which way to get to wherever they headed.

The Museum of All Things Lost and Forgotten owned the whole block. Most of it held the building itself, or at least the part physically residing in Washington versus the portions physically located in other cities, or the vast virtual environs. The building ranked as a proper hodge-podge, taking design elements from different eras and parts of the globe. A turret here, a dome painted celestial blue there, a slanted wall formed of perfectly carved rectangular granite stones on this side. It never appeared the same twice, although mundanes rarely noticed.

Back when whoever designed and built it, they developed a small section of land separately. A modest, unassuming brick building stood there: the four-story communal living facilities where most of the interns lived, which everyone called the Quarters.

Two feet of air and nothingness separated the Quarters from the museum. Unless an intern had local family to live with or lots of money, most of us ended up here. We received multiple warnings when we signed up that the two buildings had no physical connection whatsoever.

It lay two sides of a block away. Nothing more.

Once upon a time, I could walk it in my sleep. This time I managed the first block, but only because I didn't let go of Paulo or he of me.

As we turned the corner, pressure pulsed at my temples. A concrete sidewalk and assorted tourists in shorts and T-shirts lay ahead of me, complete with a trashcan overflowing at the far corner. A cracked street crowded with cars. The side of the museum with the Quarters in the distance.

Then my eyesight flipped. Another view layered over or beneath reality. Cobblestones and piles of muck overlaid the sidewalk and part of the street. Low buildings rose up to either side, caked with spattered dust and clumps of greenish-brown things. Mold, perhaps. A sewer smell clogged my airways.

Instead of the afternoon sun shining overhead, only a few sources of light broke the darkness. Lanterns and fires in the distance. Cats howled in the distance. Yellow eyes glittered in the occasional spot of moonlight.

Every moment a different set of smells assaulted me. First trash and barbecue leftovers and sweat, the usual effluvia of summer in the city. Then a dank combination of urine and feces. Back and forth, back and forth.

Paulo and Yolanda's voices no longer rang in my ears, replaced by the harsh laughter of men talking. The sharp, acrid smell of spilled wine going bad encouraged me to speed up. A chill breeze blew about, frosting my ears.

The men's voices grew louder, closer. They spoke in French. I shouldn't understand and I didn't.

Yet I also did. Fear seeped into my bones and nipped at my heels.

I pulled my shawl around my shoulders. Patted my skirts for the slit offering access to the knife in my pocket.

My fingers closed on empty air. It had vanished!

Except . . . I almost never wore skirts, nor did I carry a knife.

Blinking hard dispelled the narrow night scape of streets and terror. The phantom image dissipated into the low ramp leading up to the front door of the Quarters. Yolanda zoomed ahead of us, triggering the automatic opener from her phone. The arched double doors opened inward to let out a blast of cool air.

The air conditioning completed banishment of the strange visions. After the hot, humid street, the wonderful cool raised goose bumps head to toe.

I lurched forward—and toppled one step inside as the cold

shocked my exhausted leg muscles into unexpected stiffness. Paulo saved me from face-planting on the floor. Half-carried me into the common living room and laid me out on the overstuffed sofa upholstered in a newish red-and-purple flower pattern. Only a two-seater, so even an adult as short as I couldn't lie flat. My upper body reclined against the equally overstuffed arm cushions.

Yolanda parked next to the sofa. Unlaced my shoes and pulled them off, dropping them onto the floor with two solid thuds, but left my pink anklet socks alone.

A high ceiling with the pressed-tin squares painted white soared over a mishmash of chairs in different styles, assorted side tables, and a single, solitary bookshelf with whatever reading matter or other trinkets had been left in the room the last time anyone cleaned—this time including two stray, mismatched socks at least one of which needed to go into the laundry. Plus someone's unclaimed vape equipment despite how many of us complained whenever anyone used it because the smells gave us headaches.

I sank into the cushions and my eyes fluttered closed.

Solid footsteps thumped against the ancient Persian carpet covering the wood floor. A moment later, someone pressed a cold bottle into my hands and gave a comforting squeeze.

"Drink." Paulo kept his hands around mine until my hold steadied. "Let me know if you need help getting it down your throat. You need to keep awake until help comes, got it?"

"Thanks." My new favorite word. The fortified water or a power drink of some kind had an artificial strawberry aftertaste. The sugar and flavor helped ground me and give me strength to face two interns intensely interested in learning about remembrance.

"So, you okay? You need anything?" Yolanda sank to rest more level with me.

"I'm okay, thanks." On second thought, I drew in a deep breath and took twice as long as usual to pick words I wouldn't stumble over. "How's Cindy and her family?"

"Cindy who?" Yolanda exchanged puzzled glances with Paulo.

Evidently Tiy hadn't caught Paulo up on everything. Had any of the other interns been around? I couldn't remember who all I'd seen or not seen when running through the museum, apart from a few familiar faces.

"K-kid lost. Father attacked. Infant stolen. Returned. They okay?"

Big double takes on both their faces. Next thing they whipped out their phones and started texting away.

Threw a bunch of comments at me, too, making a game of seeing who discovered what detail first, and ensure it was preserved on their website. Nothing stuck with me except relief at hearing Cindy and her father and brother were all right and being taken care of.

Except, even as they spoke other voices overlaid theirs, deeper and speaking in French.

In the blink of an eye, I ran through narrow streets at night. Dodged holes and uneven cobbles. My stained, plum-colored linen skirt bore a long tear and the hem was coming loose. The matching bodice had jagged rips. No cap covered my head. Hanks of brown hair blew around me. Uncomfortable shoes pinched at my toes despite the quarter-sized hole at the tip of the right shoe.

Men followed in hot pursuit. All wearing dark trousers and lighter-colored shirts and jackets with tails. Their hats glinted red when they passed by a smoke torch fastened to a rough stone wall. Wavering light obscured their faces, but not their voices. They yelled, calling me names or words that boiled down to whore.

The same street as before? The same men?

Or different. The scene kept changing, with only a few constants: me running and men chasing.

Stains on the walls or road. Blood. Urine. Feces. Bodies.

Stenches beyond anything I'd ever experienced in my life.

Always so quiet. Why didn't anyone come to investigate? Intervene? Did anyone even care?

With each new variation on the theme my clothes became more tattered and torn. More stained. I grew sore in places I shouldn't be, and more desperate to escape.

A harsh buzzing sound blared, completely out of keeping with everything else. The men didn't react.

An instant later the scene shifted. The vague outlines of the common room reappeared, but hazy and indistinct. Instead of a street scene, an elaborately decorated room manifested around me. Intricate wallpaper with white floral images on blue covered the walls. The street stenches vanished under a heady aroma of iris and sandalwood.

My clothes lost their stains and reformed into a simple, dark ankle-length skirt, red blouse, and creamy apron covering from the middle of my chest to right above my skirt hem. A cap of some sort kept my hair from my eyes. My body swelled in the middle, with the skirt and apron protruding over a definite bump. Something—or rather someone—kicked me from under my skin.

Twice.

I'd never been pregnant or particularly wanted to be. The sudden sensation of having something living within me did nothing to change my mind.

One hand held a long strand of blonde-brown hair and the other an enameled wooden hairbrush. With slow, steady strokes, I brushed powder from a woman's hair. She sat in a gilded chair, clad in a long satin dressing gown decorated with bouquets of pink and blue flowers.

Loud voices sounded in the distance. Shouting, yelling.

Greasy yellow light flickered through the windows despite thick curtains. The woman's hands clenched around the chair arms, knuckles growing white.

My hands shook, but I kept brushing hair. The same locks. Over and over.

A crash followed by the tinkling of glass breaking made me break into a billion shivers.

The shouts drew nearer. Footsteps thundered down the corridor. Or in a street outside? . . . Men's hands grabbed me, fingers digging into my shoulders, legs, breasts. I thrashed, but couldn't get away. Yelled, screamed, pleaded, but they cursed and grunted louder.

Lower, calmer voices mixed with the shouts. English words reached my ears alongside French, though neither made any sense.

But the voices speaking in English, those I recognized.

Paulo.

Yolanda.

Calling for me? Saying my name.

A hand gripped my shoulder, fingers digging in.

I jerked.

The world around me changed again. My vision tripled. Three sights assaulted me: the elaborate room with candles and shadows, a dark twisted street on a moonless night, and the common room with three people in it hovering over me.

I curled into a ball. Closed my eyes and clamped hands over my ears to keep from the dizzying sights. A welcome darkness enfolded me, except every other sense grew stronger. Hands touched me no matter how I fought. The stench of sweat and alcohol made me want to puke, especially mixed with lavender hair powder—and strawberry-flavored water. Rocks broke more windows, shattering glass until shards covered me and sliced my skin.

Amidst all the chaos, a new voice spoke in English. Deep

and resonant—and strange. "No, don't touch her. We need something else. Strong smells. Cold or heat or something sharp, prickly, or soft."

"How about an ice pack?" A whirring mixed with more glass breaking, and fists smacking against walls or flesh.

I concentrated on those hints of the world I belonged to.

"Why should we trust you?" Paulo's voice, closer to me than the stranger.

"I've been where she is, or as good as, and I know how to get her out."

A long pause.

"What's her name?" The strange voice came closer.

The worlds around me reduced from three to two. No more softness of hair in my hands, or crash of broken glass. But I trembled all the same. Something hit my head. Hands grabbed me, dragging me against a bumpy, stony surface. Men laughed, calling me bad names and joking about what they meant to do with me.

Then something cold in my hand made me jerk.

An instant later, the sudden sharp stench of coffee-flavored vapor filled my nostrils.

"Bea, listen. We put an ice pack in your hand. There's a vape pipe near. If you can hear my voice, find the cold, the smoke. Feel the ice. Smell the vapor. Focus on those. Ignore everything else. You're safe, at home. Push away everything except the cold and our voices."

The deep, strange voice described the common room. The short, overstuffed sofa on which I lay. The bookcase with assorted books and stale-smelling socks. The pressed tin ceiling overhead. "This is where you really are. Anything else is not real. Push it away. Focus on what's around you. Your eyes are open, but you don't seem to see us. Try blinking."

The smoke alarm went off, high-pitched and so sharp my jawbone reverberated. The awful flavoring in the smoke made my nose itch. Hands on my shoulder or not, I sneezed once. Twice.

The ugly words in my ears faded away.

Instead, I huddled against the sofa cushions. A stranger crouched in front of me holding an icepack against my hand. Warm brown eyes watched me close from a long, narrow face. He had black hair kept very short, tawny skin, and laugh lines around his eyes. His clothes had started out nice—white button-down shirt, gray slacks, and black shoes, but big sweat stains under the arms and across the chest made the shirt cling his chest and show the lines of his undershirt. His lips curved in a tired smile when my gaze met his.

Paulo cursed under his breath as he put out the vape pipe. Waved his hands trying to keep the vapor from reaching the smoke detector. It gave a few more shrieks, then stopped whining.

My water bottle rested on the sofa cushions nearby. I drained it to the dregs to get my throat working more than a croak.

"Thanks." I'd leap up and hug them all, but lacked the strength. "I . . . Thanks. Really."

"So, what gives?" Yolanda moved back a foot, giving her a good vantage point to watch me and the stranger. "Is this going to be a regular occurrence? Bea collapsing at a moment's notice and mumbling in a language she doesn't know?"

"I what?" I straightened so that I sat on the sofa with one leg dangling off and the other tucked under. Better than squinched into a ball against the cushioned back.

"You babbled in French." She crossed her arms over her chest. "Since when did you learn to speak it?"

"I d-don't . . . What did I say?"

She let loose a variety of liquid syllables. Then shrugged one shoulder. "Translated, you went back and forth between pleading for mercy, praying for help, and asking how did your lady want her hair styled. Oh and cursing men to be eaten by dogs."

Paulo gave a choked laugh or grunt.

I glanced his way, but he threw his hands out.

"I don't speak French, don't ask me what you said." He stayed standing, but leaned against the wall. "It didn't seem much, but you repeated the words and got pretty loud about it."

"I did catch the line about the dogs." The smile on the stranger's face grew broader. He stood and stretched, then settled onto wooden chair nearby. "You named, ah, rather specifically the parts of men you particularly wanted to become dog food."

"You speak French?"

"Not as well as I read it, but yes."

"Which still doesn't answer the question of what happened to Bea, and whether it will repeat." Yolanda gave him a level stare.

"The answer to the latter is yes, barring extreme good fortune." He nodded at her, then turned his attention back to me. Entwined his fingers together into a church-and-steeple and pressed his paired pointer fingers against his lips. "How much do you want to share?"

"Hey, we're the ones who got you here." Yolanda banged a fist against the arm of her chair.

"And she is the one who will have to live with you after." He flashed a rueful grin at Yolanda, then Paulo. "It's farther in the past for the rest of us, although it never goes away completely. We have basically one rule: whoever is currently remembering makes the rules."

"Who is we and us?" I asked.

He didn't speak at first. Glanced and nodded at Yolanda and Paulo, then lifted an eyebrow my way.

"It's all right, speak in front of them." I shifted my seat, sinking further into the cushions. "They'll have t-to know something sooner or later, or they'll make my life a misery with their q-questions."

"There are ways to avert undesired sharing." The stranger cast less friendly glances at my fellow interns.

"No, everything's okay. I made a bad joke." I waved a hand. "I'm all right with it."

"Very well." He gave kinder nods at Paulo and Yolanda.

By this time they had their arms crossed over their chests and jaws tight as they glared at him.

"But is it okay if they take notes? For the website?"

He frowned, turning his hands out. "I'm not familiar with that."

"It's new. Meant to consolidate what interns know about the museum and Forgotten, and organize it for easy access across languages and around the world."

"We're bringing together previous attempts. It's intended to supplement the apprenticeship model most Forgotten favor." Yolanda's arms remained crossed and her jaw tight but she inclined her head. "I"ll be happy to show you it —later."

After a few moments' thought, he nodded. "Might as well include this, then."

Yolanda and Paulo both instantly reached for their phones, thumbs poised to take notes.

"I represent a group of former interns and others, all of whom remember—in the fullest sense of the word—at least one Forgotten. The unlucky ones, sadly a majority of us, remember more than one." He flexed his fingers and shook them. Drew a deep breath and puffed his cheeks as he blew it out. "Basically, we're a support group. Call on each other when nightmares threaten and no one else answers, because one of us always will. We even have our own helpline. Tiy called it earlier. It's spelled to route any call to whoever's nearest and available. This time me."

"And you are?" Some tension drained from my aching muscles. Others had remembered Forgotten and survived.

"Diego Rodriguez Sanchez at your service." He gave a slight bow. "An intern five years ago. Now I'm a special collections librarian at Arden College. Fortunately, in town attending the American Library Association meeting over at the convention center."

"Close." Yolanda rapped her knuckles together, lips pursed.

"A good thing, too." Paulo gave a small grin. "I'm Paulo and this is Yolanda, both interns as well. I had to help Bea get back from the Museum here. She barely walked on her own."

"And why's she speaking French when she doesn't know the language?" Yolanda asked.

Diego listened to them and nodded, but kept his gaze fixed on me. "What do you want to know?"

"Everything." I shuddered and drew in a deep breath. "No, I know I need to be more specific. But I . . . It's only, what, an hour? T-two? Since Nimur asked if I would remember and I said yes."

"It's hard to say no to them." Diego glanced around the room. His expression shifted from calm to puzzlement and concern. "Where's the talisman?"

"The what?" The word struck a chord.

"You brought something out of the museum, a talisman, did you not?" He sat up straighter, eyes growing wide.

"No . . ." I winced, head aching in residual echo of the pain and pressure of carrying the weighted syllables. "Only her name."

Diego cursed in Spanish, mostly words I didn't recognize, unlike Paulo who snorted then gave a strangled exclamation.

"Why is it so important?" Paulo asked.

"Talismans document the existence of the Forgotten. Each has one. Bring their talisman into the world, and it becomes physical proof they once existed. Discovering it ranks as your first priority." Diego slammed a hand down against the arm of the chair. "Find it and bring it outside, whatever it is."

"Why?" Memories shifted in my head, bringing to the fore scattered shards of Nimur asking Madeline about her talisman. A baby cap, she'd said, but disclaimed any knowledge of where to find it.

"Here's the short answer: until you do, you'll be plagued by foreign memories. What happened when I arrived—shards of whoever-you're-remembering's memories had you trapped. Sometimes you'll relive scenes entire, others you'll only get fragments." He leaned forward, eyes shadowed and expression turned gaunt. "Either way, your life will be hell."

"I brought her memories with me?" I asked.

"You brought her into the world to be remembered." Diego turned his hands out. "It starts and ends with you, until you find a way for others to remember her as well."

"Is there no other way?"

"Bringing out the talisman is the simplest." Diego shrugged, grimacing. "Do you know what it is at least?"

"Yes." My hands drew together and curved, as though soft fabric lay within my grasp. "A baby's cap. Pieces of blue and white fabric, wool and linen. Quilted together and stuffed with rags to make a roll around the edges, to cushion him. It's been washed but there are still bloodstains on it from when they snatched him from my arms and dashed his body against the wall."

The cap slowly manifested within my hold. First as I'd described it, with faded stains. Then, as though time ran backward, the stains grew dark. Turned a bitter, burnt brown-red of dried blood. Back further to fresh red.

My lungs seized, breathing shallowed, and a red haze crept over my eyes. Every mote of my body shivered, chill seeping in.

Warm hands wrapped around mine. Fingers gentle as they pried my cupped hands apart. Another hand stroked my back.

I jerked and nearly bumped heads with Diego as the image shattered into a million pieces.

"Better?" Diego crouched before me on his heels, hands still holding mine.

I nodded and swallowed, lips nearly numb.

Paulo perched on the arm rest, bracing me. He pulled his hand away from my back, leaving a cool spot. "Will we need to break Bea out of trances over and over? Until we find the talisman?"

"Maybe," Diego sighed and shrugged. "Try different sensory stimuli. You may find it harder at first, until you make peace with everything. Experience helps."

"*We* find?" I sank against the soft cushions as my chest heaved and lungs gasped in air.

"On it." Yolanda waved her hand between rapid-fire taps against her phone. "The description's out to every intern, flagged top priority." She paused for a moment, glancing away and not meeting my eyes. "Do you know who it belonged to? Any information helps."

"Madeline, t-true name Jeanne de Paris." So easy to say the second time. The words tripped off my tongue. But Diego still held my hands. The warm press of his skin kept back any memory surges.

"I know her!" Yolanda drew in a jagged breath. "She's been hanging around the main halls for months. Helped out with a couple exhibits. A bit flaky, but has a good eye for design and layout. She's gone?"

"She's being remembered." Diego corrected with a gentle shake of his head.

"Is that a euphemism for she's dead?" My hands shook, drops of water flicking off the rim of the almost-empty bottle. Every nerve in my body jangled. Goose bumps popped out all over. "If she's dead, did my saying her name kill her?"

"No," he wrapped his hands around mine, steadying me. "You brought her out of the museum and into the world to be remembered when you spoke her name. Her body couldn't make the transition, but her spirit did. You got her name from her, right? She couldn't leave to return to the world until you helped her."

Diego didn't say anymore. He waited with my hands in his. Paulo and Yolanda remained quiet, other than tapping away at their phones. The familiar sound soothed me. Helped ground me in the Quarters.

"You d-didn't answer my q-question." I found a couple drops of fortified water left to swallow. "You know, about another way t-to stop my reliving her memories?"

"Memorialize her somehow, in writing or painting or sculpture or whatever." His phone dinged, but he tucked a hand in his pocket and silenced it.

"What?" Write or paint or sculpt?

"What do you know about the Forgotten?" Diego settled back in his seat and twiddled his thumbs.

"They're former humans who took Nimur's offer to live in the museum, which they often call the House of Memory, and become immortal," I said.

"They're not immortal. They don't die as long as they're in the museum." Paulo made a chuffing sound.

"But they aren't able to leave," Yolanda said, "which sort of equals immortality."

"Take a step back. When the Forgotten enter the museum,

the world outside forgets them. There's nothing anywhere in the world to indicate they ever existed. No bodies, artifacts, or tools for archaeologists or anthropologists. Not even stories." Diego braced his clasped hands against his chest. "For the Forgotten to leave the museum, they have to return to the world and be remembered some way. Simplest is to bring out their talisman. Those are usually given to a museum or library, or cultural center, or descendant peoples as appropriate. Or you can write a poem, novel, song, or story. Draw or paint or sculpt her. Somehow make it so others also remember her. The more others do, the less the burden on you."

"You mean I have to write or d-draw?" I licked dry, strawberry-water flavored lips. "I c-can't. Not happening."

"Then find her talisman and bring it out." Diego leaned forward, staring right at me. "Until then you'll keep having flashes of her memories as bad as the one you went through, or worse. There are ways to keep them minor, reduce their effects. Keep aware of yourself and your surroundings, so there's always something you can search for and focus on, even in the middle of a remembered nightmare. Something in your hand, or a taste or smell, or keep favorite playlists on repeat on your phone."

He went on at length suggesting things to do, of which only one registered: to be conscious of where I stood at any given time and what I wore. Focus on what I *should* be seeing and feeling until the memories faded away.

Paulo took notes on his phone. Yolanda tapped away at her phone, but a sideways glance showed she too kept notes as well as texting.

After a point it all blurred together. My head drooped on my neck. No more memories haunting me yet—except the occasional unexplainable smell. Or the weird taste of something buttery and slippery in my mouth.

Everything boiled down to one thing: find the talisman ASAP.

Find, find, find.

Paulo and Yolanda pledged to search for it every free minute, as did every other intern as they trickled back to the Quarters when the museum closed. Even many of the Forgotten had gone out looking for Madeline's talisman, they assured me.

Part of me wanted to run back and start scouring the rooms myself.

But not yet.

Diego advised against my going back to the museum that day.

"Rest," he said as we stood between the front door and the stairway, Paulo watching from the living room. Diego texted me to make sure I had the support line in my phone, and his direct number as well. "Call when you need someone to talk to. We know what it is like."

After he left, I went straight to my bedroom. One of the smallest in the building, it had room only for a single bed, dresser, and combination bookcase-desk with chair. All solid wood, a bit beaten up but still good.

My grandma's old rainbow-colored quilt covered the bed. The bookcase-desk held my computer, e-reader, and assorted knickknacks. My posters of ancient places as they existed in the last decade or so—versus the versions I'd seen in the museum—hung on the wall.

Home sweet home.

After getting ready for bed, I set my iPhone to play music to sleep to, soundtracks to favorite games and movies, at a volume I'd hear but wouldn't annoy my nearest neighbors . . . much.

Put my phone on the end of the desk closest to the bed,

then wrapped the thick, soft belt to my bathrobe around my hand as something to hold onto.

I slipped into bed too wrung out from the day's events to do even so little as text or call my sisters or closest sorcerous friends. Especially since I lacked words to describe what had happened. Diego probably had it right when he said some things, such as remembrances, could only be understood by someone who'd gone through it.

Though I'd grown up in a family that didn't go to church often, basically only the big Christian services for Easter and Christmas, my mother raised me and my sisters to pray every night. To God, the universe, and the wonder of it all. I didn't know if my sisters kept it up or not; we talked about a lot of things but rarely religion. I, however, never failed. In part from habit, but also because it offered me ease. The worst nights of my life aligned exactly with the rare times I forgot.

So as I lay on my side, I brought my palms together and prayed for Cindy and Jose and their father. And for help in times of need.

It would be nice if I never had to move so fast again, too.

My phone dinged with the text from the future showing up again.

<<Run!!>>

✿ 3 ✿

ADRIFT

Rather than running back to the museum the next morning, I trudged. The chemical chocolate taste of my protein shake breakfast lingered in my mouth as I left the Quarters to retrace my steps around the block.

My legs ached from yesterday's jolting bolt. Although lightweight, my uniform shirt and gray sweatpants pressed against sore skin with every step. My black Teva sandals had good, thick treads and stood up to shuffling across cracked concrete.

Although early in the morning, the air already had the consistency of warmed-up pea soup. Little traffic filled the streets and sidewalks, on Sunday mornings. Except for stray tourists wandering around with coffee cups while weltering in the heat and waiting for attractions and amusements to open, which they wouldn't for another hour.

Yolanda sat tall and focused ahead of me. Her matching green uniform shirt gleamed with few wrinkles. She paired it with black trousers complete with crisp pleat in front and tucked into her trademark knee-high boots. A faint aura of honeysuckle perfume hung about her; she wore wooden dangle earrings and a quartet of matching wrist bracelets etched with geometric patterns.

At her insistence, we held either end of a short length of bright turquoise plastic rope someone had exhumed from the utility closet.

"Something for you to use to hold onto this reality." She flashed a warning glare as she handed over one end. "I'll notice if you keel over or run off."

Part of me scoffed at the notion of failing to navigate the simple L-shaped path back to the museum; yesterday's disaster resulted from the recent shock of remembrance but nearly a day later I'd recovered. Mostly. The other side of my head doubted and preferred to the old adage better safe than sorry.

Besides, arguing with Yolanda rarely worked out for me. She made no bones about aiming to be a director of a museum someday, possibly this one, and had already made a good start on developing supervisory skills. In particular, she had a knack for incentivizing into action less ambitious staff members such as myself, who'd be happy to someday be a cog in a research mill somewhere or maybe a coder improving geo-mapping applications.

Within a few steps, I plotted to ditch the rope, though, for something else on the return trip. Anything softer, for a start. The plastic had begun to disintegrate. Bits of twine or whatever poked out of it, all short and sharp and impossible to avoid. Both hands bore ample scratches by the time we made it to halfway around the block.

Alas, she'd guessed right. I did need something to hold on to.

For which I blamed not sleeping well the night before. Not due to the aches in my legs, though those didn't help.

Nor thanks to my favorite playlists repeating music on my phone all night, and bathrobe sash tied around my hand.

Nothing worked well enough to keep me from nightmares. Getting chased and having stones thrown at me. Listening to screams and yells and the tramp of feet alongside marching torches whose flames crackled and stank of grease. Crouching in a far corner of a stinking prison trying to pretend I had a future beyond the dark, gloomy walls. Standing on the railing of an old stone bridge trying to decide whether or not to leap into the river below, knowing I couldn't swim.

Cradling the broken body of a small baby in my arms.

With a whole body shiver, I picked up my feet and slipped past Yolanda to lead the way. Hands and feet fairly vibrating with eagerness to get to the museum and get some answers.

Then the street shifted to one far narrower. Cobblestones formed beneath my feet, half missing. I darted this way and that to avoid setting bare feet into oozing pits of muck. The same scene as yesterday? My clothes seemed similar, familiar, but nicer. No knife hidden through a slit in my clothes.

Instead, it weighed down my hand. The worn wooden handle proved lighter than the long, dull blade.

NO! I had rope twisted around my fingers. Sandals on my feet protecting me from the sidewalk, not bare soles on cobblestone. Sweatpants instead of skirts. A uniform shirt. Yolanda hot on my heels.

Rope in my hand. Stiff. Prickly.

Slowing, I stared at my hands. Willed away the knife. The blade wavered, then vanished. The rope appeared instead, utterly artificial turquoise bright against my pale, sweaty skin.

"Keep going, a little further." Yolanda yanked on the length binding us.

The bits of plastic twine twisting off the rope bit into my

skin and left scratches. I adjusted my pace accordingly, and the tension eased.

I flashed her a grin, hopefully not too shaky. "I know, I know, skip the steps. Ramps are where it's at."

"You got it." Yolanda buzzed into the lead.

Gritting my teeth, I picked up the pace. I got to the ramp first though I only beat Yolanda because she let me. All the same, momentum kept me going. I stretched the rope almost taut and reached the door first.

Swiped in, while smiling at the couple of people hanging out and shooting the breeze on the front steps. Promised the museum would open at ten on the dot, as it did every day. The accessible door swung open as Yolanda triggered it from a distance with her phone.

I stepped inside and moved over to the side to leave room for Yolanda.

A nice mix of vegetation perfumed the museum air—plus a blast of warm, artificial-lavender-scented dryer sheets. A special exhibit of "Lost Clothes" occupied the center of the foyer. A dryer sat on a raised pedestal at the center of a round depression in the floor. Laundry baskets—wicker, wood, plastic, and every other type known to humankind—rotated around the dryer, which regularly burped odd socks and pieces of clothing. Most fell into the baskets, some into the cracks between them.

In the space of a minute, three unmatched socks, one pair of blue-and-white striped boxers, a pink-and-green scarf, and a Mariners baseball cap arced from the machine into different baskets.

A big sign next to the display encouraged visitors to grab and take with them anything they recognized and thought might belong to them.

Something about the display caught my eye. I studied the baskets for a few moments, then shrugged and gave up.

All at once, the scene changed. I stood atop the upper-most balcony, far removed from the foyer floor. A hint of snow tinged the air. Many of the people below wore winter coats or stood at the coat check with heavy garments. Thick wool skirts swirled around my ankles, and a scratchy blue-and-white shawl half-covered a blouse with a tight, high neck that nearly choked me.

The railing pressed into my belly, as I scanned the crowd. Man, woman, and two young children here. Woman, woman, and three stair-step kids plus a little fist waving from a baby carriage there. An infant's high-pitched wail echoed and re-echoed as it drifted up.

Heat poured off a body near me although no one stood near. A low voice whispered in my ears and heart. "A baby's crying. Where's your baby? Who took the baby?"

A slapping noise broke my reverie. The flash of pain on my arm shattered it completely.

Returned to myself, I shook like a rain-soaked dog ridding itself of water. Yolanda sat before me, tapping the toe of one boot. She'd pulled the plastic rope binding us nearly taut. This left her with a long enough length to whirl as if a lariat.

"You c-couldn't have p-pulled the rope t-tight?" I glared at her and touched the long pink weal marring my arm.

"Tried it. Didn't work." She glared back, pulling the rope to and fro through her fingers. "You back?"

"Yeah." I shook again and gave a huff, then turned away and muttered over my shoulder. "Thanks. I owe you one. You know, for g-getting me out. Not for the injury."

"Let's track the talisman down and get it out of here." She kept hold of the end but let the rest of the rope go slack. "You get real weird and loopy when you're not here."

I wrinkled my nose and grimaced at her, receiving an eye-roll in response.

She took the lead. My hands grew tender from holding

the prickly length as I followed across the great hall to the staff elevator tucked behind the coat check.

Unlike the public and freight elevators, the staff lift didn't exist in the original building. It alternated between different elevators no longer in existence in the humdrum world, and occasionally dropped riders in the wrong place entirely. My eighth day on the job, I got off on an unfamiliar floor, walked for ages, then wound up nearly exiting through a side-door in the Natural History Museum and Botanical Garden in Belo Horizonte—in Brazil. The Forgotten living there found me, but declined to escort me back and put me to work sorting items lost to the mundane world in a fire. In the end, Silvestre came down to retrieve me. He lectured the whole way back.

Two weeks later, a second accident with the elevator sent me into pre-destruction Volubilis. From there, I slipped sideways into an old souk in Marrakesh where the mundanes weren't sure what to make of me. Liam escorted me home, several hours later.

This time the staff elevator presented a modern appearance, comprising a fancy rectangular box with paneling on the bottom half and blue silk wallpaper above. Heavy perfumes—rose and jasmine and some kind of musk—wafted from the curved light fixture. I sneezed every couple of breaths.

The doors whined as they shut. The button for the second floor lit when Yolanda pressed it. The gears grunted and groaned, as they raised the cage up at a moderate pace.

Yolanda got off first. The instant she cleared enough space, I leapt off to sag against nicely boring beige walls. They probably belonged originally to some mid-century low- or mid-rise torn down in the name of progress and higher real estate. Perfect for displaying glorious works of art. The narrow wall facing the elevator held two paintings. A shield bearing the snake-haired face of Medusa on one, and gritty, grimy laborers clearing rocks from along a road on the other.

Nearby a much larger wall currently featured Diego Rivera's original "Man at the Crossroads."

Free from the narrow confines of the elevator cage, I drew in a glorious, perfume-free breath.

A fetid stench choked me, making my belly roil. The neutral, light brown carpet vanished. The light from the fluorescent fixtures overhead dimmed into a thick haze pierced in the distance by thin rays of sunlight falling through narrow openings in a barred window. I curled in a ball. Rocked against stone walls, the rough surface scratching my skin through my clothes. Splotches of rusty brown clung to the fabric of my skirts.

More rust-colored stains marred my baby's cap. All I had left of him. Nothing remained of anyone else I'd loved or cared for. With ragged fingernails, I picked every mote of dried material from the soft cloth. Used saliva to moisten and cleanse it.

A tightness grew in my belly. The coils of a great serpent named hate had me in its grip.

Or, rather, a plastic rope wrapped around my waist pulling tight.

I coughed and let go of my end of the rope. The tautness around my midsection eased as the twine loosened then dropped to the floor.

"I'm back."

"You better be." The turquoise rope twitched and jerked against the bland carpet with a shushing sound as though a snake as Yolanda coiled it. She handed the loose end out to me.

Huffing, I wrapped the rough strand around my hand.

"You need a keeper." Yolanda shook her head. "And I'm not volunteering."

"Got it." I shivered and ran a hand through my hair. Tucked strands behind my ears and out of the way. Then repeated both motions, over and over because they were the kind of gesture *I* did regularly, not Madeline-Jeanne. "D-don't g-get sucked into a remembrance. This stinks b-big t-time."

"I'll keep that in mind, and add it to the website list of top recommendations." She pulled me along in her wake down to the glass doors leading into the admin suite.

This early on a Sunday there wasn't a receptionist on staff although the museum itself never truly closed, only this particular way in. Hundreds of outposts around the world made it a true 24/7 operation. After all, people who got lost stumbled in all the time, closed or open, and had to be dealt with.

Today, Tiy had turned on the lights in the admin suite, but left the door locked. She paced around the reception desk and waiting area. She'd changed from yesterday's midnight-blue jumpsuit to jeans and a scoop-necked pale blue top with wide sleeves billowing around her arms. Blue gems and silver sparkled at her ears. Sandals with matching crystals inset into the straps flashed from her feet.

Her right hand held an old cordless phone, a big brick thing.

She caught sight of me gazing through one door and Yolanda the other. Acknowledged us with a nod and a wave, but signaled for us to wait.

As long as we had to wait for Tiy to let us in, I pulled out my phone and texted Diego.

<<Need practical advice on handling memories.>>

<<Senses are the key.>> He texted back. <<Find the talisman.>>

<<Got it. But keep getting lost in memories. Need help.>>

<<Don't let Madeleine's memories sweep through you. Pick and choose.>>

The line swam as I read it time after time, but never

changed. How long since he'd been part of a remembrance? My hands tightened around the phone, the dratted rope scratching the back of the case.

<<Right—how???>>

<<Make friends with her.>>

A muffled grrr escaped my gritted teeth.

"Who're you texting?" Yolanda nudged me.

"Diego." I sank down against the wall and sat on the floor. Angled my phone to show the screen even as I texted back <<Huh?>>

<<Until she's remembered in the world, she's remembered in you. Make friends with her.

<<If you can.

<<If you want to.

<<Or at least fake it enough to gain some control over their flow.

<<Holding them back builds up a flood.

<<More later.>>

Then nothing.

"Make friends with her?" Yolanda shook her head, giving me a side-eye. "She's dead, isn't she? Isn't that the point?"

"Maybe he meant she's alive in me, as long as I've got her memories."

The possibility made my fingers twitch.

I texted back asking if she lived on in me.

No answer.

Rather than give up, I texted a brief overview and the question to the helpline instead. Maybe someone else who'd participated in a remembrance would be more available?

<<Define alive.>>

<<Big help. Not.>> I replied.

<<Be careful what you ask.>>

<<Could she take me over?>> I asked

<<Her memories live in you—don't let them rule you.

What would you be willing to remember? Start small. Ease the adjustment. Not all memories are heavy.>>

"What does that mean?"

"No, it makes sense." The copper beads in Yolanda's braids clacked as she nodded. "When I get a new wheelchair, I can't shift over and zoom off on the spot. I can only sit in it for a little bit at a time at first. It takes lots of adjustment, to reshape it to fit me. Pick something little. You're still you, with something changed. Added."

"Right."

Start small. Okay. Feet. Didn't figure there'd be anything off there. Nice to be proven right. My feet hadn't changed. Legs same. Torso, arms, neck, head.

Except, when I held my arms and hands in front of me with my eyes closed, all at once they shimmered into view. Faint light outlined muscles and sinews as though phosphorescence covered my skin or something luminescent ran in my veins.

My hands started remembering. Physical memory. Actions.

Threading a needle.

Inserting it into fabric just-so. Pulling through. Starting the next stitch in the blink of an eye.

The best way sew a fine seam with neat, even stitches as small as a staple. Embroider flowers on a hem or ribbon.

When I ripped clothes, they went into a bag for the next time Mom or one of my sisters visited, or into the trash. No matter how many times I watched friends whip off a spell to mend clothes, I failed to manage the sorcery myself. Belief mattered in magic, after all, and a sorcerer only succeeded with spells she believed she had the ability to cast.

Yet if I'd had a needle and thread in my hand . . . unexpected confidence bloomed in me about my ability not only to mend but cut and sew my own clothes.

Opening my eyes didn't change a thing. A glance down at my shirt showed loose threads in the insignia.

My fingers rubbed together. Without consciously intending, I manifested a needle. A couple of quick flicks, and the needle flashed in the light as I tacked the loose threads back into place.

Snapping my fingers sent the needle back to wherever it came from.

My hands dropped to rest in my lap, fingers twitching.

"Now that was interesting." Yolanda leaned over to inspect my shirt. More than half her body canted beyond the frame of her chair, though one hand gripped the armrest pretty tight.

"Interesting."

The door to the admin suite swung open and knocked against the far wall with a solid thud. The wall behind me vibrated.

Tiy stepped out. Her sandaled feet, toenails decked with dark blue polish, made no sound against the thin carpet. She nodded at Yolanda, then turned her full attention on me.

"I thought you'd fetch up here sooner than later. Come on in." Tiy raised one eyebrow, lips quirking. "Lay out your questions."

I lumbered to my feet, but stood aside to let Yolanda enter the admin suite first.

Tiy studied me, head tilted and asking without words if I wanted to share this with Yolanda.

I nodded, fingers rapping against my legs.

Yolanda and I had a bargain. She probably would've escorted me over anyway; she regularly worked the opening shift on Sundays. All the same, she'd taken extra care. My turn to pay up—with information for the website and her future. Sitting in and learning more about remembrances would give her added familiarity with the operations, and help position her for the next full-time job opening. Depending on how much I got out of Tiy—or, more accurately, how much Tiy decided to share—Yolanda might even owe me another favor.

The door closed behind Tiy with a click. She gestured for me to take a seat on one of the couches and chairs lining the waiting area. An overstuffed couch covered in thick fabric with immense purple roses rested against the far wall. An ovoid form chair upholstered in a brilliant shade of pink sat side-by-side with the roses, although the shades clashed horribly. Another sofa sat opposite in zebra-striped leather that gave me the willies.

Most notable among the miscellany: an actual throne of gilded wood with blood-red cushions. Torturous carved layers of wood formed the back and arms. On first, second, and third glance the wooden panels appeared to portray sweet domestic scenes of shepherds and shepherdesses frolicking innocently in fields full of flowers and sheep. Until and unless someone dropped the right hint, people considered it a mild offense to comfortable furniture. Yet pressing a lever shifted the arrangement of panels, after which the frolics became much less innocent and the sheep had decidedly shocked expressions.

I settled in a bland but sane armchair covered in blonde silk that likely once graced a dining room somewhere before being lost or forgotten. A quick adjustment spell made it sink a couple of inches and the contours shift to adapt to my proportions.

"I'm sorry to say no one has found Madeline's talisman yet. How are you doing?" Tiy leaned back against the reception desk, a simple maple affair standing about three feet high.

"Not g-good."

"Understatement." Yolanda rolled her eyes as she shifted

to have plain views of both of us. "We're talking a minimum of three incidents of one kind or another getting here from the Quarters. Under twenty minutes, tops."

"There's no standard, no studies, but three in such a short time does seem a bit excessive." Pushing off the desk, Tiy walked a circle around me.

"Especially since I had no idea this might happen. G-getting her memories, that is. Living them." I wrapped my fingers around the armrests, digging deep. "Since I had no clue what remembrance involved in the first place. It's not exactly covered much in the orientation materials, is it?"

"Most never need to know." Tiy laid a hand over mine and gave a gentle squeeze, then returned to the desk. Hefting up, she sat with legs dangling and jeans dark blue against the polished wood.

"What about those of us who d-do?"

"We don't know who you'll be in advance. I don't." Tiy crossed her arms over her chest. "Perhaps Nimur has some notion, but they've never shared so much as a hint with me."

"Would've been nice to have had some clue what I said yes to when Nimur asked." I mirrored the arms-over-chest stance.

"They asked?" Yolanda's head whipped my way, eyes narrowing.

"Yeah. I don't remember the exact words," I said.

"Are you here of your own volition." Tiy delivered with Nimur's intonation. "Do you consent to remember this person, and ensure they are remembered in the world through your self and your actions, should their talisman not be found and brought outside."

"Yeah."

Yolanda blinked. "Hmm . . . Compact and comprehensive. How long did it take to come up with the wording?"

"Who g-gives a flying F about the wording, what was I

supposed to do, say no? T-to Nimur?" I leaned forward. "And sure, maybe I'd have forgotten if Silvestre covered it in orientation and wound up saying yes without understanding. All the same, at least I'd have had a chance t-to think about it."

"We have tried addressing the matter up front in the past, and it had a deleterious effect on some interns." Tiy dropped a hand and rapped her fingers against the desk. "There are those who seem to want the experience. Consider it a challenge, and try to extract the true names of Forgotten from them. No matter how we change the selection process, we still end up hiring more of those than we'd like."

"You still should've t-told us more. More knowledge b-beats none." Unwilling to remain one down in the physical sense, I leapt out of the chair and paced the length of the room. Arms wrapped over my chest again.

A whiff of smoke from a wood fire made my eyes smart. Nothing in the admin suite explained it. Even if I'd smelt cigarette or cigar or pipe smoke, local laws and customs banned smoking in the museum proper.

But wood smoke? Had to be another of Madeline-Jeanne's memories threatening. I grabbed tight hold of myself and focused on my surroundings so as not to slip back into her past.

"Truly, this is a rare occurrence." Tiy watched, pity clear on her face. "I know this museum matters to you, both of you, but we're a backwater. Most traffic comes in elsewhere on the globe."

"Not much c-comfort. It's my life flipping upside down." Reaching the end of the room, I pivoted and kept going. The movement helped keep back unwanted memories. Maybe. "It wouldn't seem so awful, maybe, if the memories weren't horrid. There hasn't b-been one happy so far."

"Madeline . . ." Tiy sighed and rubbed her temples. "A misfortunate woman, and ill-suited to life among the

Forgotten though she lasted a long while. Over two centuries."

"Why did she become one of the Forgotten if such a bad match?" Yolanda knocked her water bottle against the arm of her chair in emphasis, then took the top off and drank deep.

I nodded, dropping back into the chair.

"She fit the criteria." Tiy kicked her legs, heels knocking against the desk. The hollow beats emphasized her words. "What do you remember about how Forgotten come to be?"

"A person has to be dying with no chance they'll be found or rescued in time. They have to be over the age of consent, as defined by their people and culture." Yolanda ticked off items on her fingers one by one. "Nimur's appearance and offer must not violate any beliefs they hold."

Tiy glanced at her, then me, eyebrows raised as if expecting either add something.

I shrugged. Yolanda'd covered what I remembered. She frowned, but didn't add anything more.

Except Tiy kept glancing back and forth between us. One heel kicking against the desk a hair faster each time, as a tic twitched in her cheek.

Maybe Yolanda had skipped something . . . or considered it so basic it went without saying.

Basic.

"They're lost and forgotten," I said.

"Lost *and* forgotten." Tiy nodded, slipping off the desk to lean against it again, head bowed. "To belong in the museum, in the House of Memory, things and places must only be lost *or* forgotten. People must be both. Lost—no one knows where we are when Nimur comes to us. And Forgotten—no one cares."

Her head remained low, shoulders slumped.

Something deep within me responded.

Cold wrapped around me from toes to head. Bitter,

freezing chill fit to make my teeth rattle in my head. Damp cold. Wet, as though I'd broken through the top of an ice-covered lake and swam until I reached land. Or maybe I hadn't made it and floated in chilly, sluggish water.

Ice formed on my body. Turned every limb into a leaden weight too heavy to lift. White crystals lined my eyelids, making them droop. Cutting off my vision bit by bit.

With each breath, I exhaled less warmth. Ever smaller clouds formed above my mouth. Couldn't feel my feet, hands, legs, arms.

Then a stranger appeared. Tall and lithe, maybe six feet. A thick orange-gold swathe of hair cascaded halfway down their back. They had skin of burnished gold, with a broad face and steep nose. Rainbow eyes glowed with light. A fine robe of creamy silk embroidered with fanciful birds appliquéd along the front and across the shoulders flowed from shoulders to toes. Heat rolled off them in waves, making the air vibrate and forming an aura.

An angel. Strange and bearing little resemblance to paintings I'd seen. What else explained such a visitation? Not that I deserved their attention, yet they manifested out of thin air for *me*. They knelt on the cold, icy surface and took my face between their hands. Such warmth against the deathly cold rattling in my throat.

"Child, this is the end of your life. You will not survive. Are you ready to face Death and take their hand, or will you consider another offer? If you take my hand, we will pass from this world into the place where those such as you cherish things lost and forgotten. Tend them. Care for them. If you come with me, I promise you will be remembered."

Beloved faces flashed before my eyes. A woman with dark eyes and a care-worn smile: my mother. Children running laughing through a fallow field, thorns and briars catching at the ragged hems of their shifts: my brothers and sisters. A young man of lithe limbs covered in warm brown skin, first seen in livery of blue and gold and then unclad.

Last and longest the vision of a baby, all big eyes and button nose and smiles, and a distinct resemblance to the young man.

And all the faces tinged with pain and loss. Gone too soon, ripped away by sickness or raised swords.

I fought to hold the images, not let them go. Yet even as I did, I realized this time I hadn't slipped quite so deep into Madeline-Jeanne's memories. Moreover, this particular recollection actually connected to what Tiy and Yolanda and I discussed.

Madeline-Jeanne whispered yes, accepting Nimur's offer, and I returned to myself.

Maybe Diego and whomever staffed the hotline offered good advice about making friends with the spirit in my head. Sitting and exploring Madeline's muscle memories left me with a useful skill. Perhaps even led to the relevant memory shard, and contributed to it ending quite logically and without me doing much of anything.

How long had the memory taken me? Neither Yolanda nor Tiy seemed to have noticed anything off about me so it must've been short.

"Madeline may have misinterpreted some or most of Nimur's offer when she accepted it." Tiy stood straight, one hand braced on the desk and head still bowed. "The first days, years, decades she spent here searching for her baby no matter how often we told her she wouldn't find him. No one so cherished by the living joins the Forgotten, even if he'd survived to reach the age of consent."

"Makes sense." I coughed, clearing my throat. "Nimur told her if she took their hand she'd go where people like her cherished things lost and forgotten. Madeline-Jeanne believed her baby counted." His smiling visage came to mind easily.

"She certainly thought about him, as well as other loved ones."

Tiy frowned. Pushing away from the desk, she took a turn around the room. Her sandals made soft shushing noises against the carpet. Her eyes narrowed as she stared long at me and Yolanda before speaking.

"Heka—Mneme—Nimur—used other words with me." She pressed her palms together before her chest. "It's been so long since I was a host, I'd forgotten they don't say the same thing."

I froze. Leg muscles tightened, lifting my feet an inch or so off the ground. Arms rigid at my side. Dared shift my head only the slightest to the side and glanced at Yolanda, who'd gone stiff and silent.

No one ever asked the Forgotten about their past. Some of Silvestre's history became general knowledge. He confided bits on a regular basis, that added up into a slightly-confused whole. After getting kicked out of Genoa and wandering around Italy and southern France, he ended up convicted of heresy in Milan in the early seventeenth century. His enemies locked him in an isolated prison cell. Except everyone who kept the prison functioning, or remembered him, died of the plague leaving him to starve in his cell until Nimur, whom he sometimes called Moneta, came and made him an offer he couldn't—and didn't—refuse.

Alternatively, instead of starving, Silvestre caught the plague too and the prison authorities dragged him out into the wilderness where they abandoned him. The circumstances under which he'd become Forgotten never came across quite as clearly as his loud and frequent assertions about having been wrongly convicted. He took great satisfaction in outliving his enemies, sure and certain this proved he had the right of whatever philosophy he'd advocated. He never explained that point in much detail either.

Liam hadn't ever said anything to me or any interns and staff members I'd met. At some point he'd spoken of a prior life as a scribe in a monastery somewhere on the coast of the British Isles. Ireland or Wales or England. Exactly where he'd lived varied depending on which intern told the tale of having heard it from someone who heard it from Liam a couple dozen months or years ago.

His accent seemed sort of Irish, but also not, which didn't help figure out where he'd come from. Wherever he hailed from lay on a coast somewhere, remote and vulnerable to Viking raids. The lone survivor of one such raid, he took sufficient injuries he wouldn't have survived without Nimur, who he referred to sometimes as Ge-mimor or Mis-gemynd.

Although Tiy said less, interns generally agreed she predated most of the other Forgotten we interacted with regularly. Maybe some older Forgotten Slept, or worked elsewhere. She came from Egypt when Pharaohs ruled, exactly which we speculated about on occasion. According to Yolanda's website, Tiy's village perished when the Nile floods failed for years in a row.

"So, Nimur customizes what they offer? Or their host does?" Yolanda asked. She'd surely noticed the name slip as well, but took care not to repeat it.

"Nimur makes the offer, not the hosts. They told me if I took their hand I would learn to read and write, and help preserve knowledge and other things from otherwise being lost and forgotten." Her face softened, taking on a distant, almost wistful expression. "A potent lure, for I'd always envied scribes."

Without warning, the walls and faces melted into a formal garden. Moisture-laden air surrounded me. Hot, but not so thick as D.C., thanks to a lovely breeze.

Flowers and trees surrounded me, All ornamental and laid out in carefully tended beds. Shrubbery walls at least six feet tall enclosed a wide rectangular space. Brightly colored blooms filled the air with sweet scents. Roses flourished in profusion in every shade from white to red. So too did bulbous orange-red flowers sprouting atop long, thick stalks. A circular bed overflowed with purply blue petals.

Big bees hummed as they bumbled from one blossom to another. Wings briefly shadowed parts of walkways laid out in irregular stepping stones as birds twisted and soared high overhead.

A lightweight linen cap kept my hair out of my face. The breeze made the ends of the ties dangle against the nape of my neck until I tucked them back under. I wore a thin cotton chemise, cream-colored and a soft contrast to the pale blue bodice pinned over my chest and back. A white apron, a frilly thing with an inch of lace all around, hung from my waist over my darker blue skirts. The heels of the black clogs covering my feet clopped against the gravel.

A thick line of sweat traced the length of my spine, making my chemise stick there.

Not for the surroundings, but the company.

Two men accompanied me, both swathed in monks' robes. One in black, whose long black hair, liberally salted with gray, fell about a long-nosed face shifting from beige to tan under the sun. The other, paler and clad in gray, boasted a clean-shaven face and skin already starting to redden, especially where a long healing cut slashed across one cheek.

The long-haired monk spoke, loud and often; the pale almost never.

Wonder of wonders, although Latin words reached my ears, I understood each and every one, albeit without truly comprehending why. For I'd never learnt Latin, other than the rote responses given in church services. The discordance rippled through me, for a vague recollection of studying the language flitted across my mind. Then this faded under a flood of confusion. The bitter tang of bile filled my mouth.

I tucked my hands under my apron to hide their shaking. I had to learn as much as I could as soon as I could. The angel who'd rescued me from freezing to death had left me with these men telling them only to welcome me as a newcomer to the House of Memory.

My feet ached from walking about gardens, warm and filled with verdant growth.

"There, is this not a wonder? A sight such as this surely runs counter to any notion of Hell." The black-robed man stretched out his arms and spun in a circle, pointing at one flower then another.

Only beauty met my gaze, far more so than any place I'd seen before in my life, but his reference to Hell unnerved me.

He refused to call this Heaven, so if not Hell either then where was I? I'd expected the angel to bring me to my family, my baby, but instead they'd left me alone with strangers. Who'd provided ample food and drink, arranged a bath, found me clean clothes . . . and shown me wonders beyond imagining, all empty of people. "Where can I—"

"There are things in this world such as you have never dreamt. Many good, and many not. The key is always to push beyond and beneath and ask why this, why here." The black-robed monk slapped his hands together. Nearby bees darted away.

"I don't understand." I searched for sign of anyone else, man or woman. The quiet man glanced at me, but only in passing. "Have you brought me here to make confession?"

"No such purpose entered my thoughts, and indeed I am not suited to serve as your confessor," the talkative one gestured at his garments. "But Moneta has brought you to me for good reason and I will see you taught. You must learn to avoid the temptations and twisted ways of others. For you will need guidance, my sister, in this new realm to which we are called to bring the good word and help purge the last remnants of corruption, that we may bring about the return of Eden."

He stretched his arms wide and turned in a circle, face upward toward the sun.

"Eden?" The neatly delineated paths identified this as definitely a manmade garden, unless God preferred stepping stones in a myriad of different sizes. It lacked any sign of an apple tree!

"This isn't Eden." The gray-clad man shook his head, pressing his hands together in prayer and touching them to his lip.

"No, not this. But the lost Garden of Eden is secreted away here." The black-clad monk gave a sharp nod. He stopped circling and pointed at me, then the other. "Our task is find it, guard it, and keep the demons away. Follow in my footsteps, and you shall be one of those who earns a place within."

"Will I find my baby there?" Such longing and intensity throbbed in my blood.

Yet I, Bea, started separating from Madeline-Jeanne. The memory kept rolling, as though my own, personal, full-sense movie—but I turned observer.

All due to the disconnect between her experience of reality and mine.

For *I* recognized the two men escorting her around: Silvestre and Liam. The latter matched well enough with my memories of him, but not Silvestre.

Oh, he dressed the same and his face hadn't changed, but the Silvestre I'd met and worked with made sense. Mostly, apart from his periodic rants about women who didn't know their place. An advocate of equality of the sexes he wasn't and never pretended to be. But also hardly the first I'd run into in *my* life—not Madeline-Jeanne's. He readily worked with me, Yolanda, and other female interns, and seemed to save most of his sexist rhetoric for female Forgotten.

On the other hand, he never mentioned Eden or ideas about finding it somewhere in the museum. Or talked about demons and devils.

Granted, every single intern had at least one lost place or object or species they really *really* wanted to locate. Mine I'd probably fulfilled without knowing—to walk parts of America, particularly around Philadelphia, from the millennia before Europeans arrived. Unfortunately, lost places never came with identification of their modern equivalents.

But no one owned up to searching for anything on the scale of Eden. Lost temples, sure. Dinosaurs, absolutely. Origins of civilization according to any religion, whether Judeo-Christian-Islamic or other? Nope.

The dichotomy between the two versions of Silvestre proved enough to push me out of the memory and back into reality.

Upon which I lay flat on the carpet. Front-down, but head turned to the side and nearly puking from the stench of dirty feet wafting up from the carpet.

Yolanda and Tiy peered down from well out of arm's length. My arm muscles seemed to have the consistency of wet noodles. Several attempts at pushing up failed, as did a try at rolling over so I didn't have to smell bare feet up close and personal.

Tiy moved closer. Squatted and checked my temperature with the back of a hand. Shifting around, she tucked her hands under my arms and eased me over and up to a sitting posture. Dragged me backward enough to lean back against the desk.

Then she summoned a water bottle for me to drink. As I gulped down the first, she obtained two more.

"Twice in under an hour." Tiy remained squatting, one hand light on my wrist. Her fingers rested on my pulse and the base of my thumb, monitoring me medically or magically.

"This is worse. She managed to stay on her feet, before." Yolanda realigned for a better view of us. "Is there anything we can do to slow it down?"

"There are ways to manage or direct the memories, but others who've participated in remembrances will be the best source of advice, not I or any of the Forgotten." Tiy fixed her gaze on me, clearly shifting from addressing Yolanda to me. "Or you can memorialize her some way."

I shook my head hard enough to rattle my brains.

"Then the best thing is to locate Madeline's talisman."

"I texted all of the other interns. Everyone's got the description to keep an eye out." Yolanda pulled her phone back out, fingers flying. "But how many trillions of billions of things are out there. Assuming it isn't off where all the unmanifested things and places are when they aren't here."

"Talismans are always present and accessible somewhere in the museum, even when they're not physical. They stay at most a few hours' travel from where we are, and usually less." Tiy brushed off one of Yolanda's concerns with a wave of her hand.

I gulped down the second bottle of water, nice and cold, rather than worry about searching across great distances.

"Talismans aren't all physical?" Yolanda asked.

"I know of Forgotten whose talismans are songs, eternally playing in one part of the museum or another." Tiy drummed her fingers against the nearby desk. "And another Forgotten whose talisman is a very particular perfume. Taking a bottle of it out of the museum wouldn't be enough to remember them and end their existence here, it would have to be the recipe."

Finishing the second bottle, I squeezed it as flat until my

knuckles turned white. "That's all v-very well and g-good, b-but how the hell do we find Madeline-Jeanne's t-talisman?"

Tiy tilted her head sideways and gave me a level inspection. "You could help, if you're willing."

"Help how?" The water gave me strength enough to clamber up from the floor and back into the chair I'd been sitting in.

"A Forgotten and their talisman are linked and effectively magical parts of each other able to affect each other. It has to be so to give those Forgotten who do not wish to die a chance to keep their talisman within the museum, should some unwary bystander try to take them out." Her mouth narrowed into a grim line. "Perhaps, since you host Madeline's memories, you can link with the talisman and locate it."

"Sure." I nodded. "What should I d-do?"

"Feel for it." Tiy waved a hand.

"Feel how?"

"Hmm." Tiy's gaze grew distant, then her lips twitched. "For a more direct route, we might try hypnosis."

"Ooh, yeah. You can hypnotize her?" Yolanda bounced. "Excellent. Maybe we can infuse the magical link and set a tracker on it. Link it into our cell phones, or the map app, and run a quick retrieval to get Bea back to herself."

"How much we can do depends on Bea," Tiy cautioned, "but we should at least be able to get solid information about where the talisman is currently located."

Yolanda's enthusiasm infected me, though I didn't need much reinforcement. She dealt with the memories second hand—I had the first-hand view and reached my limit hours ago.

I refused to lie back down on the stinking carpet. Tiy smiled at my explanation. A moment later, a wave of energy rippled along the soles of my feet. The industrial carpet vanished, replaced by the thickest, most luxurious shag carpet ever seen. Pristine as if fresh from the factory, in shades of cream and gray. Bending down, I brushed my fingers across it to find a softer surface than any pillow.

"Will this do better?" Tiy gestured at the carpet. "Come, child, I'm sure you haven't slept much. Take a rest and rise refreshed."

Despite all the water I'd consumed, a sour taste lingered at the back of my mouth. My fingers and toes twitched. I slipped down onto the carpet. So soft, so easy to lie back on.

Smelled fresh and clean, rather like new-mown grass. As a kid, I loved to go out and lie in the yard as Dad or Mom moved the lawn. Rest on the lawn watching clouds blow across the sky.

"Lie down, and imagine you are somewhere safe and comfortable, warm, protected." Tiy's voice dropped to a soft, rhythmic whisper. "Remember the last time you went there. You don't have to try anything new. Rest and let yourself be wherever you wish."

My eyes fluttered closed. The soft carpet beneath me turned to grass. A lawn mower hummed in the distance, along with the tromp of Mom or Dad's feet. The luscious smell wreathed around me. Sunlight beamed down, turning the insides of my eyelids red.

Insects buzzed around. I waved hand to ward them off.

The insects changed to a soft voice whispering in my ear. "Part of you is misplaced, but this is not a problem because you can magically go to where your absent part is. All you have to do is want to be with your talisman—and wish."

Wish.

I didn't want to leave the lawn. Being a kid again, when my family remained whole before my parents started arguing and growing apart, when we all stayed together, brought a warm, fuzzy feeling to my heart and head.

Though a cold spot manifested between my hands. An

emptiness. Something I expected, but gone. Misplaced? The gap left me incomplete.

I wanted to be whole.

Wished it.

Nothing changed for a long moment.

Then the warmth turned to cool.

The lawn to hard, flat stone.

The smell of fresh-cut grass shifted to the scent of the sea, bright and fresh and almost creamy. Definitely not from anywhere along the Atlantic coast that I'd ever gone.

I curled into a fetal position.

Tiy whispered in my ear, voice light and soft. "Absorb where you are. Send up a beacon. Let us see and know."

I sat on a shelf in a dark, narrow room. Fresh air blew, but I couldn't see where it came from or where I sat. Or who or what else occupied the chamber, but something did.

I wasn't alone.

Other items sat on shelves alongside me. A cold ring set with several jewels. A long, narrow bowl emanating warmth. A twisted length of cloth. A sword in a worn leather sheath.

"Where are you? Tell me all you know," Tiy said, soft and low.

A loud bang made me jump. It echoed over and over. The reverie shattered into a thousand, a million pieces. Each shard pierced my head until I shrieked in pain.

Woke back in the admin suite, screaming my throat raw.

Chaos ruled. Yolanda moved next to me, hands bright with defensive spells. Tiy crouched on the other side, alternately yelling at the intruders to "wait their turn" and rubbing my head with soothing strokes.

Too many people, too much noise. I stopped screaming and curled back in on myself, eyes closed. Moaned as every stomp or whisper made my head hurt more.

A hand slipped around my shoulders and laid something cool at my lips.

"Drink."

A mint-grapefruit scent filled the air. Breathing it in gave me a little ease. I wrapped my fingers around a cool vial, and drained it a drop at a time. The sweet liquid flowed through me, easing my throat and then my head. I still ached all over, but managed to open my eyes and ears, and even sit up and pay attention.

Silvestre loomed large in his usual black robes. A snarl turned his face into a mask of anger and hate. Fists raised, he glared at Tiy. "This is your doing, witch. Satana. Your laxity and evil ambition has brought doom upon us all."

Three figures stood arrayed behind Silvestre.

"Silvestre and Liam, with Rumaisa and Ibrahim." Tiy's hand tightened around my shoulder, fingers digging in for an instant before she let go and rose to her feet. "An interesting quartet. You do not often venture about together."

Liam, as always, wore undyed robes. He stood with head bowed and hands folded over his heart. One sandal-clad foot tapped restlessly against the thick shag.

Ibrahim, whom I'd often seen in company with Jay Doe, stepped forward. In his mid-teens, he towered over six feet yet had a lankiness suggesting he'd not reached his full breadth despite the wispy mustache and beard slowly filling in over sepia-brown chin and cheeks to reach the deep brown-black hair he kept trimmed in a high-low fade. He wore an orange T-shirt and loose black sweatpants, paired with sneakers in black and neon green.

The last new arrival, Rumaisa, appeared no older, but Ibrahim's stance subtly deferred to her. A dupatta of blue and gold draped over her head and around her neck, covering most of her dark hair and framing a round face and lustrous golden-sand complexion. Large gold earrings glimmered at her ears, and a few bangles at her wrists. Gold embroidery dazzled from her long azure shirt, which fell to her knees though slit along the sides. She wore thin pants of a darker blue below, tailored to fit close to her legs, but bright turquoise-blue Crocs adorned with gilt sunflowers covered her feet.

Glaring at all of us impartially, she dropped unexpected news into the silence.

"Nimur is missing."

"And so," Ibrahim added in a bass voice, "is Jay Doe."

❧ 4 ❧

MISSING

Chaos. Words, words, words. Voices, voices, voices. Everybody talking at once, nobody listening, all shouting over each other.

Too many voices!

I scooted back against the desk. Wrapped my hands around strands of the soft carpet. Leaned against solid wood. All the same, my shoulders hunched. I curled inward in a vain attempt to become smaller, stay as unnoticeable as possible, and sneak out at the earliest opportunity.

Tiy and Silvestre faced off in Latin, plus Liam and Yolanda in English. Ibrahim and Rumaisa stood closer to me, exchanging comments filled with sibilant sounds and a lot of tonal variations. A few phrases registered, unfolding sensations of emptiness and shifting balance—not because *I* understood the words, but they meant something to Madeline-Jeanne.

Then in the blink of an eye, everyone swapped around.

Tiy wound up talking to Ibrahim in lyrical strings of vowels and consonants. Yolanda and Rumaisa used English, but their voices got buried under Silvestre and Liam's Latin phrases. The latter pair cut off each other's lines, each jumping in as soon as the other finished a thought.

Only for everyone to shift again. Arms waved and they became a blur of colors and voices. How did they hear each other? Or even hear themselves think?

Nimur missing—impossible and unreal. Inconceivable, even.

How would anyone even know? Nimur *was* the House of Memory, and vice versa. Surely their absence would trigger calamities and catastrophes—or at least changes—within the walls. But nothing had changed.

And Jay Doe . . . I'd seen her here yesterday afternoon. Why would she wander off? As a Forgotten she had to know her way around and ways to get back—or at least send word. Nab a lost burner cell phone with a couple minutes left on it and call back. She'd been hanging around in D.C. for weeks, with Ibrahim and Rumaisa all the times I'd seen her.

The last I'd seen her, she hosted Nimur. So if they both went missing together . . .

Though the problem of Nimur vanishing nagged at me. They might not have a body of their own, but they had no problem taking over their hosts and reshaping them to their liking. Flesh, if not clothes.

Wait.

Jay Doe's clothes.

All the noise made my brain fuzzy. I pressed my hands against the smooth wood, scanning for ways to slip out of the room.

The others had reorganized into groups of three, blocking the way. I'd have to force through them. Or explain when realization remained a hair out of reach . . . too much trouble either way. What if they didn't believe me and kept talking or making me explain?

Any delay risked whatever I'd seen, even if I didn't know

for sure I'd seen it, vanishing into the virtual storerooms of lost clothing. Clothes materialized in the exhibit, but they had to dematerialize too or it would get overrun. It never showed the same clothes twice, because with all the people in the world, pieces of attire got lost so regularly the display spouted new lost items without ever running dry.

Rising to my feet, I swayed and grabbed hold of the desk. Pins and needles prickled along my legs until I shook them hard. Earned a glance or two from Tiy and Yolanda, then Silvestre and Liam. The arguing or yelling or whatever it was they'd got to didn't stop. All the words turned to a blur.

I grit my teeth and surged away from the desk. Half-shoved, half-staggered through them. Caught an elbow in my side and nearly tripped on Silvestre's robes, or Liam's.

Nameless urgency fueled my unsteady steps. Blood pounded at my temples and ankles, rushing through arteries and veins.

My fingers slipped on the door handle. Second try, wrapped my hand around the warm metal and yanked.

The sudden inrush of air and noise—the distant clatter of the Sunday morning opener crew setting up—washed into the admin suite.

Silence reigned, sudden and so welcome if I weren't half out the door.

"Where are you going?" Yolanda called after me.

"Checking something," I said. Going on instinct made my stomach churn and a bitter tang fill my mouth.

I glanced at the elevator.

Too slow. I raced for the circular staircase winding around the foyer. Thank fortune this part of the museum almost never changed. Light streamed in from the glass windows lining the front and the varied chandeliers hanging at staggered intervals from the high ceiling. Below, the opening crew appeared as distant insects in green, cream, and copper.

Sliding my hand along the railing, I pelted down the stairs. Every footstep jarred the bones and aching muscles in my legs. My clenched teeth ached.

The foyer started to blur, the simple tiled floor turning to dirty cobbles marred by muddy potholes. The walls narrowed, becoming grimy. Many someones followed me, based on the clomp of boots and heavy breathing. A sewer stench filled my nose until I sneezed.

NOT NOW! This is important!

A sense of quiet fell on the back of my head, both connected to me and separate. Footstep after footstep on uneven earth or stair after stair, I kept going.

The memory flash retreated. My sight cleared, returning to the expected foyer and the various interns and employees waving at me as they went around their business. The thump of boots turned into the clatter of the others from the admin suite rushing to press against the balcony above and gaze down at me.

The sewer smell vanished beneath the warm, perfume of various dryer scent balls and sheets all mingling together into one god-awful dead flower pile. At least the museum hadn't opened yet. The outer doors remained closed, albeit with a few bodies lined up and faces peering in.

On reaching the ground floor, I lurched across the empty space to the lost clothes installation. The laundry baskets groaned and creaked as they circled the dryer. A hot pink man's swim suit popped out of the dryer door and landed half-on, half-off a white plastic laundry bin.

I focused on the clothes already there, not new arrivals. Dug my hands into the closest laundry hamper—an octagonal affair of mesh and wire. Static electricity ran through me, making me shiver while I stood arm-deep in clothes still warm from passing through the dryer.

Lost socks galore. Wool and cotton. Long and short.

Unmarked and stained or torn. But whatever I sought unquestionably did not involve socks.

I pushed them aside or tossed over my shoulder underwear in all sizes and more styles than I wanted to think about.

Same with the shirts, pants, dresses.

My nose itched from all the concentrated scents. My hands grew warm and dry. The edges of my fingernails caught on the finer fabrics.

Laundry basket after laundry basket, hamper after hamper, I went through them all.

Nothing grabbed me as being what I searched for, but the quest weighed heavy on me. I couldn't stop, had to see it to the end, check everything, leave no piece of clothing unturned.

No matter how people yelled at me to stop.

To cease making a mess and throwing clothes everywhere.

To explain myself.

But I needed to check more clothing first. Some always dropped through gaps between baskets and hampers. In addition, the hampers dumped their contents into the pit below periodically.

I had to find it.

Grasping hold of cool plastic handles, I yanked out a basket, sending it flying over my head. It hit someone else who'd come up behind me by the cry of pain.

I mumbled an apology as I scrambled over the edge and pitched down before the opening moved along.

Fell far. Hadn't realized how far to the bottom of the pit. Luckily, I landed on a thick pile of soft clothes though I still lay flat and stunned face down for a moment. My mouth and nose squashed against a linen shirt with too many buttons, making breathing tough.

I scrambled onto my hands and knees a good five feet or so down. The laundry hampers and baskets circling above me filled at least one to two feet. If I stood up straight, I'd hit my head.

Staying on all fours, I rummaged through the clothes and circled the central pillar supporting the dryer—inching forward and tossing clothes to the side or behind me as I went.

Voices yelled in the distance, far enough away the words fuzzed. They all talked over each other, too, making for a mix of high and mid-range shouts plus some sonorous bass sounds, probably Silvestre praying or cursing in Latin.

Flickers of light penetrated the darkness, as gaps between baskets passed overhead. A brief big whomp of illumination from the empty spot left when I'd yanked the plastic bin out.

The clothes retained warmth. This made the lingering smells of detergent and fabric softener stronger. My nose itched, but I refused to take time to scratch.

Cloth disintegrated or dematerialized beneath me layer by layer. Something circular whisked around beneath me, zipping by with a soft whir. Everything dropped a little.

I shoved clothes under me, careful to never allow my hands or legs to rest on the floor or touch whatever lay beneath the cloth.

The moving lights distorted my vision. Time after time, I accidentally slipped my hand through a bra strap or jock strap. Almost strangled on a pale white sheet with lavender flowers and green vines.

A grinding noise right near my head nearly deafened me. Overhead, the baskets stopped circling, bobbing with the suddenness.

"Out of there! This instant!" Silvestre's face appeared in the opening where I'd removed a basket.

"We can't stop the dematerialization." Tiy called from behind him. "Whatever you do, don't touch the bottom!"

"G-got it." A flash of neon pink and green caught my eye. "One more moment."

About a foot of pink-and-green fabric showed, next to a pair of blue jeans. On the bottom or close enough. Rather than crawl over, I stretched out and grabbed the corner of soft chiffon.

I yanked. The cloth stretched, but didn't move. The other end stayed stuck under the jeans. Wrapping the end I held around my left hand, I tugged again and again as I cleared off other clothes with my right hand.

Two feet, three. How long could one scarf be?

I shoved faster, but the cloth around my hand constrained my ability to free the rest of the length quick enough.

Even in the dim light, the far end sparkled as the cycle beneath continued—and the scarf started to dematerialize.

I'd done too good a job wrapping it around my hand. Scooted backwards, trying to get the fabric off my hand. Couldn't get clear in time.

Rainbow sparkles blinded me.

All of a sudden, I became cocooned in cloth. Bound tight around and around me, as though I'd been wrapped in a winding cloth like old time corpses.

Unable to move. Not even my toes. Lungs working hard, with little space. Only a little air passed through, barely enough to breathe and stay conscious. Odd taste, bright and clear.

Except I panicked. Panted. The taste of copper bloomed in my mouth. Blood thudded in my veins.

Shh. A soft whisper in my ears, or my head. Unfamiliar, and yet not. The sense of others near me. No movement, all in my head. But something kept me company. A fresh sea smell flooded through me, as though I'd fallen back into the hypnotic state, only to vanish an instant later.

Something tore me from the winding cloth. A force sent

me head over feet, tumbling up, down, and sideways as though sliding through a dark tunnel in an amusement park. Banging and ringing filled my ears.

My lungs expanded. I dragged in a humongous breath. Otherwise, I closed my eyes and pulled my arms in against my chest, lengths of fabric weighing on the left.

After a couple of minutes, I came to a lurching stop. My back and buttocks rest on a hard, hot, unyielding surface. A long piece of metal pressed against my left side. My legs canted up and over an equally unyielding surface, feet dangling.

I blinked. Brightness, but nothing else, not even scorching air.

Above me curved fitted pieces of bright chrome with a distinct ridge down the middle.

A similar ridge pushed against my side. Whatever contained me shoved, trying to rotate, but my weight prevented it from moving.

My ears took longer to settle. When the ringing stopped, a dozen or more voices clamored in the distance. A little more comprehensible than before, but not much because the metal surface distorted and echoed.

"Bea?"

"Those feet, are they . . .?"

"Beatrice?" Silvestre's usual pronunciation stretched to more than four syllables.

I lay inside the dryer, part of the lost clothes exhibit.

Though industrial-sized, the dryer had less space inside than the chamber below. I banged my head as I pushed up, enough to knock me off balance.

The dryer rotated a third or two-thirds around. Left me face down, which allowed me to wiggle out backwards.

Hands grabbed my feet and legs and helped lever me out. I emerged, dizzy-headed and swaying, onto the platform.

Next thing, I sat on the floor with a warm hand holding my head down between my legs. I shivered all over. Gasped for air a breath or two, then straightened up.

Tiy stood over me, arms crossed. Silvestre to her side, and all sorts of other people in an uneven semi-circle around us. Everyone from the opening shift, plus Yolanda, Ibrahim, and Rumaisa.

Paulo and Liam knelt and braced me, the former with a bemused air and the latter with a wry half smile as he gave a sardonic chuckle. Paulo's uniform shirt had a long wrinkle down the front, but otherwise he appeared neat and tidy from braided hair to jeans and matching jean-covered sneakers.

Quite the contrast to me, who'd turned into a mess. Hot, sweaty, and all mussed-up but still in possession of all my clothes if not my wits.

The dryer kicked back into gear behind us, tossing shirts and socks at our backs.

The chiffon still tangled around my hand, the loose end lying across my lap. I lifted it high, swooping up the trailing ends with my free hand.

"Wait a minute." A front desk staff member stepped forward and stooped to stare at the chiffon. Pale skinned and lean, he scratched a head covered in salt-and-pepper hair and blinked twice. "Is that the same scarf cycling through the dryer this last hour or so? I was fixing to call maintenance, 'cause nothing's supposed to repeat in the exhibit. All new lost clothes only, one-and-done."

A soft babble broke out from others of the opening squad, as they quibbled over the scarf. Evidently more than one had noticed repeated manifestations of neon pink and green.

"You mean I c-could've waited and it would've shown up again?" I sank back against the rim of the exhibit. All the fuss for nothing?

"What is special about this?" Tiy bent and began to tease the twisted folds from around my fingers.

"I think it's—" I broke off into a squeal.

Rumaisa had pushed her way through the crowd and grabbed the cloth. Gave a great big yank, trying to get it away from me. But it tangled too tightly around my hand to slip off in one go.

"This is Jay Doe's! How did you get it!" She glared as she wrenched the chiffon off bit by bit. Nearly twisted my fingers in the bargain. I screeched and tugged back.

"Go slower," Paulo grabbed the fabric, giving my fingers a bit of ease.

Rumaisa snarled, eyes flashing.

Paulo startled, dropping hold of the cloth.

Ibrahim, who'd been with her and Silvestre, sifted through the crowd to her side. Whispered in her ear, at which she slowed and took it a bit easier albeit with no less speed.

All the same, when she finally unwrapped the last of the cloth I barely breathed for sharp pains shooting up and down from the tips of my fingers to my wrist. I cradled my hand against my chest.

Rumaisa ran the cloth through her hands, then gave one end to Ibrahim. Between the two of them, they pulled it taut to show dust stains.

Jay Doe's scarf, with a few hairs still caught in the hem.

On second glance, several of the dust stains resolved into partial footprints. Indrawn breaths and whispers echoed throughout the large chamber.

"Rumaisa, is it Jay Doe's?" Tiy moved forward. Folks shifted to give her room, along with Silvestre in her wake.

"Yes." Her hands shook as she stroked the cloth.

"She wore it yesterday," Ibrahim said.

"She had it on when she summoned Nimur." Liam squinted at the cloth. "I believe it became part of Nimur at the subsumption, for I don't recall them wearing it. Do you?"

I shook my head as his gaze swung to me, still rubbing my sore hand.

"Where did you see them last?" Tiy asked.

"I left them in an old kitchen about a half-hour by back hallways from Lost Time. Meant to go back, in case Nimur forced Madeline to Sleep and needed help settling her body, until I caught Bea heading out to remember her." Liam jerked his head at me. "I've not seen them since—"

"I crossed paths with you as you brought the baby back." Silvestre broke in, waving a hand at Liam. "There seemed to be a disturbance shortly after, but that must've been Bea remembering Madeline."

"And Bea left the museum, not returning until this morning. Very well." Tiy glanced up at the immense clock installed on the wall above the entrance. Outside, faces pressed against the glass, staring in. She lifted an arm high to command attention. Lifted her voice, words coming through clear in the sudden silence. "Jay Doe is missing, possibly Nimur as well. We need to check all the halls and exhibit rooms closest to the entrance before we open. The farther reaches can wait until after, as time's short."

"We have to close the museum. Call it an emergency." Silvestre positioned himself in front of her, chin high.

"No. Remembering comes first. We don't shut for anything but safety reasons. Though visitors will only be allowed in checked areas." Tiy flapped a hand at him. Pivoting, she pointed to Yolanda. "You'll be fastest, check the main floor. Call the hotline if you find Jay Doe, Nimur, or anything suspicious."

"Got it." She sped off before Silvestre mustered any objection.

Tiy clapped her hands, drawing all attention. "Everyone

else: gather into three groups. Core staff to cover all necessary functions to the front desk. All Forgotten to my left. Any discretionary staff to my right, unless you don't have a cell phone, in which case swap with core or join the Forgotten."

I took two steps toward the discretionary group, then stopped in place. I might've been one of the last to see Nimur and Jay Doe—but not the last. Haru and Madeline remained when I ran away with Madeline's true name.

Turning in a circle didn't show me enough. I rose up on tiptoe but lacked the height to really scan the crowd.

"What're you doing?" Paulo had headed in the same direction, paralleling me.

"Noth—" I started to shake my head, then stretched my neck. Gritted my teeth and swallowed hard, before forcing out the request for help. "Do you see Haru anywhere?"

"Who?"

I drew a quick circle in the air and snapped my fingers to summon an image of her from yesterday—quilted robe and Rolex and all.

"Hmm." He did a turn of his own, then shook his head. "Nope, nowhere to be seen."

"Who?" Liam peered over my shoulder, breath over-warm on my ear. "Oh, Haru. Good call. I haven't seen her either since yesterday afternoon. I presume she stayed while you dealt with Madeline."

"She was there when I left."

"Someone else missing?" Tiy joined us, body vibrating with coiled energy.

Paulo summarized the situation, both of us still glancing around.

"Haru." Tiy's gaze fixed on the image floating in front of us, and she gave a half-laugh, half-sigh. "She'd come in handy."

Her eyes narrowed as she switched to examine me. "I didn't notice her amid all the . . . you saw her yesterday?"

"With Jay Doe and Nimur." I nodded.

"Can you find your way back?" Tiy asked.

"I think so." Certain landmarks I couldn't miss, but those first frantic parts when I'd run without direction . . . "maybe."

"Make sure. Wouldn't hurt to check for Haru, and also for clues as to Jay Doe and Nimur, since no one's seen them since." Tiy scanned the Forgotten.

"Finally, something practical." Silvestre stood to one side, twitching to the point his robes swung around his legs. Practically created his own little wind, or whirlwind, swirling out to graze anyone who came near. "I'll go with her."

"Or you can send me." Liam lifted a hand. "I followed Haru with Bea and Jay Doe, though I left before Nimur pronounced judgment on Madeline and didn't make it back." He pinched his nose, face twitching. "I returned the baby to his father, as you recall."

The remembered smell of baby poop floated in the air for a moment. Based on the expression on her face, Tiy caught it as well as I.

"At least the child took no harm. But no,"—Tiy waved at Liam and Silvestre—"you both will be needed to organize this lot. Rumaisa, will you or Ibrahim go with Bea?"

They'd been whispering, but stopped and glanced at each other.

Rumaisa inspected me from head to toe, then nodded and stepped forward.

"You've got your cell phone, right?" Tiy whirled back to me.

I fished it out of my pocket and held it up.

"Good." She rapped her fingertips together. "Report as soon as you reach the spot and be ready to describe everything. Don't touch anything unless you have to. It may be the last place they were seen, so I'll send a team to do a thorough analysis."

After a solid pat on the back, she moved off to start pairing up Forgotten with interns and employees to check the second and third floor halls and exhibits, and the cafeteria and store rooms below.

A sudden weight pushed my shoulders down. I'd only thought about finding Haru, figuring out if she'd gone missing too. But Tiy's reference to not touching and sending someone to analyze it . . . it might be the scene of a crime, of whatever had happened to Nimur and Jay Doe. Not to mention Madeline-Jeanne. Would we find her body lying there? Or had Jay Doe and Haru had a chance to do whatever they did with the remembered?

Over to the side, Rumaisa and Ibrahim had been discussing something, not in English. Ibrahim wasn't happy.

"Keep this safe." Rumaisa handed the scarf over to Ibrahim and headed my way. She stalked, with her arms crossed over her chest, chin low, and eyes narrowed as she fixed on me. "Let's go."

Another turn on the hot seat.

We could go to Lost Time and trace the path through the tunnels, but without Haru and Liam leading the way, I might miss the right turns. Perhaps Madeline's memories in my head would deign to share the route she'd taken when she ran away with the baby?

Silence.

Then again, reliving the memories and then replicating the route risked wasting additional time.

"I'll have to retrace my steps." A big no-no, though no one ever exactly explained the penalty. Only shuddered as they passed the warning on. Though Yolanda sniffed every time an intern mentioned it around her. She went over the same ground all the time, she'd said: whenever she ran into an unexpected stairway or ground unsuited to wheels, and experienced no great misfortune.

Rumaisa's lips twitched. "Physically retracing steps isn't the worst thing in the world. If it will ease your worries, this will the first time for me and the two of us together."

I'd focus on those firsts, and hope Yolanda's luck rubbed off on me.

But what if it didn't?

"Well?" Rumaisa tapped a foot against the floor. The gilded sunflowers on her Crocs seemed to whirl around in circles.

Rather mesmerizing . . . or unfamiliar memory inducing. The hall started to swirl. Bright sun shone down, so powerful even squinting left spots and lines dancing in front of my eyes. Sweat poured from my face and neck, left bare—

A sharp yank on my hand sent a burst of pain up my arm, but dropped me out of any unwanted memory.

Lurching forward, I slammed into Rumaisa. My nose mashed into her throat. Setting her hands on my shoulders, she helped me rebalance on my feet.

"Sorry." I rubbed my nose with my non-aching hand.

"Stay in the here-and-now." Her bracelets chimed as she adjusted the set of her tunic, mouth set in a thin line. "Jay Doe and Nimur take priority. Whatever's going on in your head, set it aside until later. We've enough troubles for the day. Let's get going."

"Right-o." Whirling around, I strode off to the stairs. Would've made a much more elegant statement if my shoes hadn't squeaked against the floor.

Hand over hand on the cool railing, I climbed back up a third as fast as I'd gone down. The slap of Crocs against tile indicated Rumaisa followed hard on my heels.

Right on my heels. Breathing down my neck, or at least

breath hot on my back. Silent otherwise, except for a faint whistle with every third or fourth inhale.

Once up and off the stairs, I led the way to the exhibit of lost books. The unmistakable scent of old paper filled the air as we passed through the entryway. The tables lay as before, in the same arrangement. No empty spots visible, though at least one of the display books had been swapped with another.

I stopped at the center-right table, with the illuminated manuscripts. Here lay a large book with blue and purple sea serpents stretched across two pages. The smallest of the books had the most color, a green, gold, and purple basilisk twining among a stand of oddly-shaped palm trees. A mid-sized volume nearby featured a bold red-and-gold beast with hooves and a fish tail forming the initial letter of a word in Latin.

A faint whiff of salt water set my nose twitching. Here and gone, in the time it took me to realize what I smelled. An olfactory phantasm, perhaps, or a forgotten scent wandering through the building. Always so hard to tell, and no time to wonder. Not with Rumaisa standing next to me, arms crossed and foot tapping restlessly against the thin carpet lining the floor.

"We want the back way into a fun house." The lost books room had far too many entrances or exits. Double doors at either end, plus three wide archways on each side. Tall book-cases between, of course, filled with treasures I'd love to take the time to peruse.

I'd run past the table with open bestiaries, so I disre-garded the openings closer to the main entry. Started towards the nearest of the others.

A sudden chill enveloped my neck and back.

"What's a fun house?" Rumaisa followed, peering around me at the door.

"You d-don't know?" I had only vague memories of having been in one when I as a child myself—but surely she'd watched movies or television shows, or even children's cartoons. Or not. She appeared in her early twenties, but could be much older. "They've been around for decades in the U.S., at least."

"I never went to one in the world." She stood straighter, exuding brittle patience. "Enlighten me."

"It's a . . . something you'd find at an amusement park or a state fair." Lousy comparisons unless she'd been to one of them either, outside or inside. "It has weird things, fun stuff to play with. Slides and spinning disks and floors that move up and down like waves as you walk on them." I moved on from arch to arch, stretching my neck to catch sight of what lay on the other side.

"Ah." A rueful chuckle escaped her. "Disneyland. Coney Island. King's Dominion. I've seen portions here in the decades since I became Forgotten."

"Basically. In our case, we want one with a bunch of mirrors showing us differently—taller than we are, or shorter. Thinner or fatter."

At which I caught a glimpse of a mirror through the farthest arch. A regular one, albeit in an extremely ornate gilt frame. More hung from the walls beside it as I moved in. A display of mirrors all as decorated and beautiful as the bestiaries next door.

Familiar. I'd been there recently. It must lead to the squiggly mirrors, someway or how.

"Follow me and you'll get to see some of a fun house soon enough." I poked my head back into the room of illuminated manuscripts.

Eyes narrowed and jaw set, she unlimbered enough to scuff across the carpet, gaining steam with every step.

"This is it?" She wheeled around, eyebrows raised high, as she entered the room of mirrors.

"No." I took a diagonal route over the gray-and-green industrial carpet to the archway catty-corner. Light shone through the rest of the entrances. Only this appeared dark, or shadowed, as the fun house had been. "Here."

The small of my back itched. Gritting my teeth, I managed to drag myself to the very edge of the shadows. My feet seemed planted on the floor. Coldness enveloped me, causing me to shiver uncontrollably.

Rumaisa arrived at my side, a beacon of warmth. She peered into the darkness, then turned and offered a hand. "We'd best hold hands, so we don't lose each other. No knowing where we'll end."

"Good idea." I laid shaking fingers against her palm, and sighed at the warmth. "Okay, here we go."

I nearly stumbled right off the mark. Pale, faint light glowed overhead, no stronger than a brace of stars scattered across the ceiling. Below lay a black-and-white tile floor. The first tile undulated beneath me.

Rumaisa didn't let go, but giggled as she followed me. Tripped and fell forward into my back. I fumbled into a wall. Hit my cheek hard as she followed right after. My free hand didn't meet solid wall, instead it continued forward into open air.

"This way." I inched sideways over the shifting tiles, into the doorway.

Another giggle from Rumaisa as she followed. A moment later, she slammed into my back a second time.

My fault, in this case, for I stopped in my tracks after only a few steps.

A bank of mirrors faced me. One stretched me taller and thinner than a giraffe's neck. Another turned me squat and formed of concentric tires. A third reformed my body into a zigzag.

All three returned a double reflection—triple once Rumaisa's head appeared above my shoulder.

They showed Madeline-Jeanne as well as me. Together with me. Her image overlapped me, but where we both appeared her image manifested with more strength and color. In comparison, I seemed washed out.

Her clothes had changed from the outfit she'd worn when I'd seen her in life. Or what passed for life for the Forgotten. A lace-edged cap covered most of her hair, leaving only sleek bits exposed around her face. A matching lace ruffle—narrow, but delicate and intricately formed—decorated the edge of her square neckline. Her dress, of a sober dark blue, nipped in at the waist before falling to an inch above the floor. The tips of brown shoes peeped out from below. A thin apron of white tied around her waist, the end reaching to her knees.

Her stance mirrored mine, or mimicked, or whatever. Blank, sad eyes of brown stared out. Tall or squat or zig-zagged, her face had a mournful cast. Crusted lines from the ends of her eyes showed she'd been crying, though her face appeared dry.

I hadn't seen her before, the other time I rushed through the fun house.

My fingers wrapped tighter around Rumaisa's hand. A soft grunt escaped her. She wiggled free, then wove her fingers between mine again.

"Let's move along." Curving around me, she turned her head and took in the whole scene, tongue clicking.

"D-don't you see her?"

"See what?" Rumaisa leaned in closer to the mirror, then nodded. "Ah, of course. You remembered Madeline yesterday, did you not? You're shadowed. It will pass, when you no longer hold her memories so fresh and close."

"Shadowed." An awful description. Madeline-Jeanne had far more reflected solidity than a shadow.

I snuck a step or two closer. Madeline-Jeanne moved with me, every movement exactly replicated. A bitter tang flooded my mouth. Shivering, I swallowed.

"You're the instrument of her death, so you'll see her until your work is done." Rumaisa patted my hand, voice soft and encouraging. "No, I haven't seen her talisman. Yes, I've watched for it. Maybe some aren't, those who have given up. But it is not for us to decide who should be remembered or, at the last, truly forgotten and cast into darkness."

The second half of Rumaisa's words registered first, giving me hope Madeline's talisman would show up. Then the first words and their implications dawned.

"What d-did you c-call me?"

"I beg your pardon?" Rumaisa eased her posture long enough to wave at the distant glow of sunlight through the entrance around the corner. "Is this the right direction?"

My feet obeyed, shuffling along the level floor. I twisted, watching Madeline-Jeanne doing the same.

"You said I was the instrument of her d-death."

"True." Rumaisa fell in behind me, ensuring I didn't stop. "You said her name outside. That killed her. Executed her, as Nimur ordered it. You were the blade, not the hand that wielded it."

Not news, really, for Diego had said as much the day before. But it sounded a lot nicer the way he said I'd brought Madeline-Jeanne out into the world to be remembered versus killed her. Executed her. Was the instrument of her death. The blade.

Though Madeline agreed to be remembered.

A faint, distant whine tickled my ears. I shook my head and glanced around the gray and growing light as we approached the door—searching for a mosquito or some other pesky insect.

Then, as we stepped into full sunlight, the whine shifted into a baby's cry broken with the occasional sob.

"Ssh," a man's low voice hummed. "My brave, good boy. I know it smells and itches, but I'll have you clean in no time."

Something about the voice seemed familiar, though I couldn't put a name to speaker. It wasn't Rumaisa, for sure.

I turned in a circle, searching for the source . . .

Then flattened myself against a hard wall. Sunlight shifted to florescent lighting. The dusty midway of some forgotten amusement park faded into gray-washed walls and immense flat screen televisions with split displays. One side of each showed the activity in the center of the room: a man kneeling on the floor and changing a baby's diaper. An older child, nose wrinkled in disgust, scuffed a sneaker against the floor.

The man and the child barely registered.

The baby held my attention. So small and precious, with those little fists waving. Legs pumping. Body seeking to wriggle free.

My baby. At last, as promised, my baby. I'd missed him so much.

Hold on, little one. I'll save you. I'll have you back in my arms and never let go again.

A stinging rap on my cheek broke the vision. My head snapped back as Madeline-Jeanne's memory of watching Cindy and Jose with their father shattered.

Rumaisa stood in a wide-legged stance before me. Clouds of dust floated around her feet.

"Ouch." I rubbed my aching cheek.

"I am sorry"—she turned her hands out—"but pain is one of the few ways to break into such a reverie."

"Thanks for breaking me out of the memory, but . . . how did you know?"

"I have lived in the House as a host for nearly fifty years.

You're not the first to face the perils of remembering. This is no time for wallowing in the past. You suggested searching for Haru—so let us move on. Better to take action than do nothing." She moved backwards, extending her arms wide and making a circle. "Where next?"

Her head jerked suggestively at the set of footsteps marring the dusty midway. They led out in an incomplete circle only to turn back to the burger shack next door to the fun house.

What an eyesore. Not someplace I'd ever eat in the outside world, no matter how much of a bribe anyone offered. Once upon a time, a big sign had hung over the window boasting a burger, what appeared to have been a mug of beer or soda, and a cup of fries. The paint had faded somewhat, but worse, it had started peeling so the food had the appearance of having chicken pox or the measles. Whoever had nailed boards across the serving window had done a poor job, leaving gaping holes some graffiti artist turned into a pornographic representation of an orgy involving at least seven whole or partial headless bodies.

Plus it stank worse than a gallon of soured milk or bad eggs.

"Brace yourself." I drew in a deep breath and covered my mouth and nose with one hand. Then darted through the door next to the window. Fortunately still ajar from my previous trip, and thus requiring no touching of the greasy handle.

Storming through the dim environs, we followed my footsteps to the back door. Which I also didn't remember running through, but must have done so—and somehow closed and latched behind me. I fumbled for the tarnished brass knob as I ran out of air and had to take another breath. Worse than the first. Sent me into a fit of coughing.

Rumaisa pushed me to the side and gave the door a

kick. Nothing fancy, merely a good old slam of a foot against rotting wood. Her Croc left an imprint on the wood planks.

The door opened inward, based on the rusty hinges fastening it to the wall, but instead the door creaked and swung open outward. Then it slammed to the floor with a mighty crash.

"After you." The rush of cleaner air made breathing easier. I waved a hand and stood back long enough to let Rumaisa precede me. "We're almost there."

She sailed through, chin high, then stopped and moved aside.

"Now where?"

"Through one of the doors. I'll recognize it when I see it." I followed her, staying a good foot away.

"Then get started." Rumaisa waved a hand at the immense space. Her mouth moved as her eyes trailed over the walls, possibly counting the doorways for her fingers turned inward to her hands one by one.

A long room lay before us. The compilation of at least three hotel ballrooms, maybe more.

All the wall segments boasted doors and archways between displays of kitchenware. I focused on the carpet. My first pause in running the day before, I'd stood on an over-done pattern of red, blue, and gold. Today my shoes made only the softest shuffling sound as I strode across a section of black-and-gold carpet, then blue-and-white.

My belly roiled as I walked, because the shuffling of my shoes kept almost turning into the swish of skirts. As though Madeline-Jeanne walked with me, invisible to all eyes but not to fun house mirrors.

To distract myself, I tried making conversation with Rumaisa—by asking the first question to pop into my head.

"How did you realize Nimur and Jay Doe were missing?"

"You tell me." Rumaisa gave a choked laugh as she followed in my wake.

"If I knew, I wouldn't've asked." I angled over to start peering through doors at the far end of the red, blue, and gold carpet. A fourth former hotel ballroom—this in a simpler but eye-blazing light green and pale gold color scheme—loomed before us. Since I didn't remember it, I figured the old kitchen we opened somewhere off this chamber. Maybe.

"Think it through. I'm a host, you surely remember that." Rumaisa kicked at the wall, leaving a second dusty footprint behind.

I froze for a moment, but she'd put no magic into her movement so nothing happened. My breath burst out of my lungs with a squeak.

She laughed.

"I asked a simple question, trying to start a conversation." Think it through indeed. Good advice only if I didn't already have finding my way back filling my brain, apart from Madeline-Jeanne's memories ready to spill.

Turning my back on her, I grabbed hold of the painted wood trim framing a door. Ajar, so I only had to give it a nudge to open more and peer through.

Walls of soft peach and the blaze of well-polished chrome met my eyes. New appliances took pride of place: a gleaming double-door refrigerator, six-burner stove.

Not the room we wanted by a long shot.

I pulled back and stalked on to an archway nearby.

Also not right, although very different. Wooden planks formed the walls, with cracks between them. A chill wind whistled through, raising goosebumps along my skin where it reached me. Plain old dirt served as the floor, with a big hole dug in the center and laid with wood for a fire. An empty iron pot sat on a rickety tripod.

Shaking my head, I drew back and started off to the next in line—this one several lengths down.

Rumaisa hadn't followed me to the first doors, both close by, but she fell into step as I moved further. Warmth emanating from her body helped dispel the residual chill of the wind.

"Jay Doe's still new, not even here five years yet."

I almost didn't recognize Rumaisa's voice this time, so quiet and heavy with fear. Other than a glance at her from the corner of my eyes, I pretended not to notice, in case she'd stop.

"When she didn't come find me or Ibrahim after . . . It's her first remembrance. After all the other firsts, she's always wanted to come and talk." Rumaisa'd wrapped her hands tight together, wringing her fingers. "When I realized what she'd been part of, I searched for her. Alone, then with Ibrahim. She wasn't anywhere and no one had seen her. Worried, I sought out Nimur to ask after her—I'm the senior host since Yong stepped down, and age has some privileges."

"How c-can you ask when they t-take you over?" I stumbled to a stop near the next door. Clapped a hand over my mouth, but too late. The question escaped, because it didn't make sense.

"I write down my questions on a piece of paper and leave it with a pen nearby when I call them. The answers appear by the time they leave me." A huff escaped Rumaisa. "No, there's no need for such lengths. We can speak, heart-to-heart, when we share the same space." Her shoulder slumped. "But they didn't answer when either of us summoned them. They always do, even if only for a brief moment, only long enough to indicate they'll be back. This time I sensed nothing."

Different urges set me swaying in place. To go and comfort Rumaisa, or at least pat her on the back and remind her Jay Doe surely lived, Forgotten couldn't be killed, and other things she undoubtedly appreciated. To ponder all the new information she'd shared—and the problem of Nimur not responding. And, of course, continue to contribute by locating the room where I'd last seen Jay Doe and Nimur.

I might've stayed there, trapped, but a faint whistling sound made my nerves jangle.

As I turned to check for the source, whitewashed walls caught my eyes. An immense fireplace with baking ovens and a kettle hanging over blackened bits of wood, but no fire. A long wooden trestle table. A rocking chair. Candles burning without shrinking.

Haru sprawled across the floor. One leg extended straight out, foot twisted probably due to the weight of her platform sandals. The other leg curved beneath it. Her torso curled to one side. Her arms had fallen outward to either side, palms open and Rolex band glinting in the light. The cloth binding her hair had slipped downward, so the dark strands pooled around her.

But her chest rose and fell rhythmically. A light, whistling snore escaped her parted lips.

She slept.

"Weird, am I right?" I asked. "I know Forgotten rest overnight same as normal folk, or t-take naps, or Sleep, b-but not like this."

"It's all wrong." Rumaisa brushed past me to kneel next to Haru. She stretched out her hands, fingers fanned and thumbs and forefingers touching so as form a triangle. Kept a good four inches between her body and Haru's as she swept her hands back and forth. "Most of us seek familiar places to Sleep. Comfortable. Either the place we most loved in the outside world, if it lost there and findable here, or the closest equivalent."

Sitting back on her haunches, she shot me a fierce glare. "Does this strike you as a place she would want to be?"

"No, though . . . how would I know?" I squatted on the other side, staying farther away from Haru's still form. A leg muscle cramped, and I dropped down to sit with my legs crossed.

"I met her when I first became a host but have not seen her for decades." Rumaisa lowered to lie on her side, examining Haru's face. "What do you know of her?"

"I met her in a forest in her homelands. D-don't ask me where or which. I think Liam said something yesterday about her Sleeping and she said she had a while. B-but . . ." I circled my hand, finger pointing at the walls. "This is the room where we found Madeline-Jeanne and the baby. Where Jay Doe summoned Nimur. I d-don't think Haru p-planned to Sleep here."

"Then she won't mind being woken up."

"Wait, you mean to wake her?" I jumped to my feet and shuffled backward, nearly banging my head on the fireplace mantel. "What about the whole never rouse a Sleeping Forgotten?"

"We need information. She's likely the last to have seen Jay Doe and Nimur." Rumaisa's eyes narrowed as she surveyed me, then she waved a hand for me to back up further. "You're more breakable than I am. Go as far away as you can get. Don't watch me, or you might mess things up. Call Tiy and let her know what we've discovered."

I scooted over to the far end of the room where an immense set of wooden cabinets took up almost half the wall. A banged-up trestle table with hundreds of knife marks across the top filled in the other half, with various bins and things beneath.

A narrow door lay between, shut tight. Despite the uneven bottom of the door resting an inch to a half-inch above the stone floor, no light or sound or anything filtered through.

Bits of dust marked the floor here and there, but most had been kicked clean by all the feet tromping around. No mystery there, since I'd arrived at the end of the scuffle nabbing Madeline-Jeanne.

Not a peep out of her memories at my thought.

The air had a distant aftertaste, sickly sweet, causing my eyes to tingle.

I pulled out my phone and called the admin office. One ring, two, my fingers inched toward the rough metal latch holding the door shut.

"Museum of All Things Lost and Forgotten, can you hold please?" Yolanda managed to squeeze the whole phrase into a single run-on word.

"I—"

"Thank you for your patience, we'll return in a moment."

No chance for me to do anything but stand and wait. Granted, the museum provided pleasant music to listen to while on hold; in this case, jazz jam sessions or performances never recorded or whose tracks had gone astray.

The a-syncopated beat and driving clarinet line set my body jiggling. I took turns letting one leg shake and quiver, then the other.

Better to the music than the sounds from the far end of the room. Soft thuds. Slaps or claps. Rumaisa spoke phrases in languages. I recognized none, but some triggered shards of Madeline-Jeanne within me. Splintered awareness bled into me, and some of Rumaisa's phrases registered as pleas for Haru to wake. *We need your help.*

All the while, the latched door called me to open it.

Opening doors risked danger. One might guess what lurked on the other side but never be sure, especially around here.

But what if it led to Jay Doe or Nimur?

The phone stayed on hold, jazz kept playing . . . and I

stopped resisting. Yanked the door open and leapt back in the same moment.

Darkness, but a shadowy darkness.

I summoned light but anticipated what I'd find before I stuck my head through: the tunnel through which we'd tracked Madeline down in the first place.

As before, it stretched out in either direction. Scuffed dust marked where we'd passed, or maybe where others had since additional footmarks stood out against the stone on both sides. The sickly sweet smell hung in the air, strong enough to set my eyes watering.

A large and bulky object had rolled up against the wall near the door, mostly oblong with a gadget of some kind at the head. It resembled a fire extinguisher, except it wasn't red and had odd characters imprinted on the canister part— nothing recognizable as any alphabet or logograms I'd seen before. Definitely not Roman or Cyrillic or Greek or . . . so much easier to say what they weren't.

"We appreciate your patience. How may I direct your call?" Yolanda's voice rang in my ears a bare second after the music cut out.

I banged my neck on the doorway as I jumped sideways.

Grunted in pain.

"Hello?"

"This is Bea, reporting in." I rubbed my neck with my free hand.

"Oh, Bea! We've been waiting to hear from you. I don't know why your call didn't register as internal."

"Where are you and what have you found?" Tiy cut in without any crackle or sound to indicate I'd been transferred. Whispers underneath her voice suggested Yolanda had handed over the receiver.

"We found Haru, but she's Sleeping. D-doesn't seem to be natural. Rumaisa's t-trying to wake her, but—"

"Done." Rumaisa called from across the room.

Whirling around, I switched to the phone to speaker. Haru sat on the floor, curled over and retching. Her face had a greenish cast. Her hands clutched her head, massaging her temples. Rumaisa knelt at her side and rubbed her back. With her other hand, she slapped the floor. Took three tries, but a first aid kit finally lurched out to rest next to her.

"She's awake, but off color, pretty sick." I said. "We're in one of the lost kitchens, off an immense room displaying pots and pans and stuff. It's where Jay Doe and Nimur confronted Madeline."

"Got it. I've flagged your location and a team of Forgotten are on the way to examine everything. Any sign of Nimur or Jay Doe?" Tiy's voice easily carried over the distance, despite the background noise increasing around her.

"No, but they should be sure and check the t-tunnel opposite the fireplace." I stuck my head through a second time, pain in my neck having subsided to a dull ache. The strange, sickly smell definitely originated there, likely from the odd object. "There's a weird object there smelling something awful—maybe some kind of knockout gas?"

"Will do." More background noise on Tiy's end.

Quick footprints rapped behind me, then Rumaisa poked her head through to check out the tunnel. Chimes and soft thumps came from the first aid kit. Haru, now sitting on the ground and looking much less green, rummaged through it.

"Stay there, the team's tracking you, not the room." Tiy said. "As soon as they show up, all three of you are to expedite back triple speed. There's been an unexpected development."

Rumaisa pulled back to scowl at the phone in my hand.

"What next?" she asked.

"Jay Doe's voice is coming from her shawl. Very quiet, but unmistakable. She's saying your name and Ibrahim's over and over, and doesn't seem to hear anyone else."

VANISHED

We returned to change and organized chaos.

The admin suite had quintupled in size. Half of the added space contained computer workstations with all manner of different computers, the new alongside obsolete behemoths churning and whirring to the point people raised their voices to be heard over the clacking. One of the big, tan monstrosities featured wheels of tape or something turning circles. At the other extreme, a high-tech bank of monitors surrounded Yolanda.

All the comfy chairs had vanished, along with the thick carpet. A new layer of burgundy and navy blue industrial carpet covered the floor beneath dozens of thick, semi-transparent rubber mats. A dozen or more office chairs on rollers, none matching each other or the carpet, filled the void, along with several creaky stools. A third had people sitting in or on them, working away at the various computers, tablets, and phones—except for Liam in one corner fussing with a rickety children's abacus whose rainbow-colored beads rattled as he shot them up and down the rods.

At the center of the room sat a pale gray oversized box

with red rubber lining the corners, and high enough to serve as a table. Layered maps and papers covered the top, a few printed but most manuscript and in at least four alphabets or syllabaries.

The density of old and new technology in one place generated heat, magnified by all the bodies. Someone had cranked the air conditioning high fan and intense cold, given the blast from a nearby vent in high in the wall, but with lousy results. My feet turned pink and my legs oozed drops to the point my sweatpants stuck to my skin. Higher up, my arms gained a faint blue tinge and burst out in goose bumps while my teeth chattered. Even when I rose on tippy-toe and stretched a hand up, the air got only cooler the higher I went. An indoor inversion.

Nearly everyone in sight had an extra layer or two for their top halves. Grabbed from the array of lost clothes at random, given the miscellany. A puffy down coat in white with notable stains at elbows and hem nearly swallowed Liam. Silvestre had squeezed himself into a red cable-knit sweater. Tiy had donned a winter holiday sweater of glittery silver-white snowflakes against a dark blue background.

Smug in a warm, olive-green army jacket, Paulo gave me a hoodie sporting a helmeted duck running with a football. It worked, and I stopped shivering. Leaned against the wall, then nabbed a water bottle from Liam, who swung around in a circle handing them out. Strawberry-flavored, alas, but I drank half anyway.

Rumaisa slipped away from me over to the side of the doorway. Ibrahim had arrived a moment or two before us, and handed her a coat which she donned. Sibilant whispers drifted from them, but no words registered with me.

Haru settled into a chair. The quilting in her coat evidently kept her warm, but her skin retained a faint greenish cast.

"A healing draught, Silvestre, if you'd be so kind." Tiy waggled her fingers at him.

"A couple of drops only, no more. We don't know how much we have left, and there may be other needs before Nimur is found and freed." Silvestre shifted to fill the space between Tiy and the big first aid box. His hands fiddled with the latch as he raised his chin.

Tiy breathed deep, shoulders and chest lifting. Eyes blazed and mouth opened, but before she let loose Silvestre stepped around her and extended a hand bearing a small vial of green liquid. He bowed and smiled at Haru, sending a sharp glance in Tiy's direction.

"I see the two of you haven't changed." Haru accepted the vial with a smile and sigh. "I'm surprised one or both of you hasn't left and returned to the places you used to live in. I may wander, but I always go home."

"These are my pastures, by choice." Tiy tapped the carpet with the tip of one foot.

"And my sheep to guard." Silvestre crossed his arms and perched on the top of the first aid kit.

Rumaisa gave a polite cough. "You said Jay Doe's calling for me or Ibrahim?"

"You or Ibrahim, though she said your name more often." Tiy nodded. "Her voice came from the scarf, so soft we almost didn't hear it until Yolanda noticed—but it seems to have stopped."

"Here it is." Yolanda rolled out from behind her worksta-tions. Turned, and held out the folded length of fabric.

Rumaisa slipped her hands under Yolanda's and lifted it. The soft folds of pink and green rested gently atop her palms. "Jay Doe? Jay Doe? Are you there?"

Everyone packed close around. No matter how I pulled myself inward—hunching shoulders, wrapping arms over chest, pressing legs together—a hand or arm or leg brushed me any-which-way.

The mumble of conversation dulled to a few sibilant whispers.

"Hush." Rumaisa bent, pressing an ear to the fabric.

In the distance, a tiny, tinny voice spoke. It grew louder, as though merely resting on Rumaisa's hands turned the dials on the speaker up a notch with every syllable.

"Rumaisa? Are you there? Answer. Please?"

"We're here." Rumaisa lifted the cloth close to her mouth.

"Me as well." Ibrahim positioned himself behind Rumaisa and spoke over her shoulder. "Can you hear us?"

"Yes. Finally!"

Jay Doe's voice had a strange quality above and beyond the odd way it sounded. Her words came from the cloth, but at the same time they reverberated through the walls, ceiling, and up from the floor into me and probably the others too. Rather like a car going over a rough dirt road.

"Where are you?" Rumaisa's hands trembled.

"I don't . . . it's nowhere I've been before."

"Is Nimur with you?" Tiy leaned in, careful not to touch the cloth. "Can you even hear me?"

"Yes, I heard," Jay Doe said. "Nimur's here. We're trapped together. They're holding onto my body while I speak with you. They managed to get my scarf to swing through the lost clothing display in hopes you'd notice. I've been trying for ages to reach you."

"Where are you? Are you okay?" Rumaisa shifted, turning a cold shoulder to Tiy and curving in toward Ibrahim. He moved back, but only a half-step. The two of them formed a V, with the folds of cloth guarded between them.

"We're wrapped up, rolled up, in a long length of cloth. Air comes through, but the cloth is strapped around us and we can't get out."

"Even Heka? Nimur?" Tiy hadn't moved, but she had the height to look and speak over Rumaisa's shoulder.

"I think . . ." A heavy sigh carried through the scarf, fluttering the folds of cloth. "It's my talisman around us. A quilt my mother made . . . Whoever trapped us wrapped it so tight it completely encloses us. It's become a sack of some sort. So close Nimur can't even find enough space to slip through the fastenings."

A dozen or more whistles and groans filled the room, Forgotten nodding in every direction. Almost in time with each other, although their faces showed different emotions: puzzlement for Haru, anger Silvestre and Rumaisa and Ibrahim, weariness Liam, and grim determination Tiy.

"Can't Nimur dissolve and get out and get help?" Yolanda asked. Surely a being who manifested anywhere had the power to pass through Jay Doe's talisman.

A minute or more passed, with the Forgotten shaking their heads although no one said anything.

"No, they cannot. Talismans are sacred. Infused with Nimur's power." Jay Doe broke the silence.

My hands formed a cradle, as though I held Madeline-Jeanne's talisman. Sacred. Special. Part of Nimur. Yet hardly something capable of being turned into a sack and wrapped around a person. How many talismans fit the description?

"But Nimur can draw power through it. If they summon enough, they may be able to tear it open—but it will require a lot of magic." Jay Doe said. "Find us. I'll help you as I can. Find us and free us, before Nimur has to destroy everything to be free."

"We will do all we can." Tiy slammed a fist against the wall. Other Forgotten and sorcerers followed suit.

But the cacophony made the admin suite melt away. The world changed.

An immense store room filled with infant clothes

surrounded me. Shirts, hats, onesies in every color and fabric imaginable rested in uneven piles on rough shelves hanging from the plank walls around the room's perimeter. A wide door bisected the far wall. Hung on wheels, it rolled open or shut with squeaks and groans. Maybe the original served as a barn once upon a time, but no more.

It had become a warehouse for clothes. Above and beyond those placed on the shelves. In the center of the concrete floor stood a mound of clothes at least five feet tall at the center and twice as wide.

No signs of ice or snow in sight, but the room had the chill of an overactive refrigerator. A thick shawl of red and blue wool wrapped around my shoulders, the hem falling to mid-calf. Tassels dangled from the corners, bobbing against my plain blue skirt. Oversized sheepskin slippers shifted around my feet and made soft shuffling sounds with every step.

Only one point emanated warmth in the big expanse. Located somewhere on the other side of the pile, it radiated a trickle and made my fingers ache to get closer.

Pacing around the pile, I stopped a third of the way and shoved my hand in, about a foot up from the floor. My hand and wrist became as nimble as a serpent, shifting and pushing ever farther until my cheek pressed against a soft, pink, linen baby dress big enough only for a newborn.

My fingers closed over the source of the warmth and extracted it with care and delicacy. Merely holding it drove the chill from me.

My talisman—and promise I'd find my child again someday.

"The cap's not safe here, not anymore." A soft voice whispered in my ear, careful not to press against me. At least an inch of air remained between us. "Nimur is changing things, moving them around."

"He'll need it when I find him, to keep warm." I pressed it against my chest, arms folding over to protect the fragile cloth. Closed my eyes and rocked the closest substitute to holding my babe.

"Let me hide it for you, to make sure it's safe."

Currents moved around. Something—someone—took hold of the edge of the cap and whisked it out of my arms.

I opened my eyes and lurched forward, but the room had gone dark. All light quenched. My talisman's warmth dissipated. Went far away.

Around and around I whirled, trying to summon it back.

Until firm hands fastened on my shoulders and held me still. Hot breath blew by my ear.

"Where's the baby? Find your baby!"

"Stop it." The hands on my shoulders turned into Paulo's. He whispered too, but so different than the voice in Madeline-Jeanne's memory.

Dizziness made my head spin, rolling around on my neck. The world around me formed a single, immense blur of colors bleeding into each other. I blinked several times before my sight resolved into the previous scene of Forgotten and a few interns and employees clustered around Rumaisa and Ibrahim. All of which I watched from a slightly different angle. Evidently I'd started turning in midst of the memory, and stopped part-way around—only with Paulo's intervention.

The Forgotten shouted a dozen or more questions for Jay Doe and Nimur, all sorts of queries about what the captives saw or heard or smelled. Was the air dry or moist? High altitude or low? Hot or cold. Or whatever whatever whatever because the more they talked the more they talked over each other.

They had enough years and experience to carefully gather information so as to ascertain figure out where Nimur and Jay

Doe were and what to do next. At the rate they nattered on, they'd easily go over the same pieces of information a dozen times or more.

A distant warmth impinged on me. The same as in the memory. I might not have noticed, if it not for the mixed up cold-hot, the recent memory flash. The impression carried no physical warmth but . . . Emotional? Spiritual? Metaphysical?

Madeline-Jeanne's talisman.

Much more interesting than trying to parse out the voices babbling around me.

Why hadn't she known where to find it, back when Nimur asked? She hadn't said she didn't know its location. Rather that it wasn't in the room, though it had been near once.

A vague warmth indicated its proximity in relation to me, but in a very general way. Which way—sort of up and over and not near at all but . . . somewhere. If I went in the right direction long enough I might stumble across it.

"What?" Haru shouted from the far side, overwhelming all other voices. Body stiff and head tilted to one side, she waved a hand at Rumaisa, then Ibrahim. "You're both hosts and spend most of your time together in this corner of the House? Along with Jay Doe, the third host? All three in the same location?"

"Yes." Tiy nodded, with a note of resignation. "It's the new custom, for hosts to linger in company whenever a new one joins. They help each other adjust to life—"

"Are you asking for trouble?" Haru's tones stayed even, but she slowed and enunciated each word with great care. "Don't you remember when Sandoval burned Eriselda and nearly destroyed Marco? Or Bilgin attacked Fedor, Tjandero, and Upatissa, nearly killing them?"

Tiy leapt in to defend herself, and for once Silvestre entered the lists on her side, but Haru kept recounting words and names with meaning for the Forgotten. Ibrahim had a puzzled expression, but Rumaisa and nodded and frowned at some of the strings as did Liam.

My stomach growled. The crowd hardly needed me. Might as well sneak off to nab lunch.

I slipped backward through the crowd toward the door.

Paulo frowned down at me as I passed behind him. "Where are you going?"

"For lunch. I'm hungry, okay?"

With bad luck, my words fell in a pool of silence.

Everybody heard me and many faces turned my way. The quiet extended, apart from a small chuckle from Liam's corner.

"That's a good idea. No an excellent one. Food will improve our tempers." Tiy nodded, not glancing Haru's way. "And help sharpen our brains. Bring some back for all of us."

For all of them? But I wasn't about to argue. I'd make sure I got something to eat first.

A sigh of relief escaped as I slipped out the admin suite door. Outside, in the museum proper, the air no longer bobbled back and forth between too cold and too hot. The only voices resounding in the distance held happy notes: visitors exploring, laughing, enjoying.

None of them had ventured to this far corner. I had space to turn around, to breathe, to hear myself think.

Space and food beat curiosity every time.

Slow steps helped keep my muscles loose. Indulging in a few stretches eased some of the aches from yesterday's run. The admin suite had moved from the second to the third floor, and shifted backwards in the mundane building. A few turns, led me to the balcony overlooking the foyer and the grand staircase that led up to the rooftop restaurant. Special spells piped in arctic air from some of the colder lost places preserved within the building to keep the glass-enclosed space a decent temperature despite the heat of summer.

My growling stomach wouldn't let me stay still there for long.

Lines stretched in front of the entry to the cafe proper. More people wandered around within, almost a crowd.

Rather than face them, I slipped around the side and through the door to the kitchen.

A hand wrapped around my wrist as soon as the door clicked shut behind me. The narrow hall offered no room to maneuver. Solid wood paneling lined one side, but the other had an open door leading to the cafe manager's office.

"And just what're you here for?" A white-haired, white man, a good foot-and-a-half taller than me but only three-quarters as wide, stopped me in my tracks. Let go of my wrist once I remained still, then rapped my head with his knuckles. "Answer promptly when asked."

"Lunch. For the admin suite." My stomach rumbled.

"You, too, I take it." The cafe manager patted his own belly. "I've been expecting someone from there all morning, with all the coming and going and toing and froing."

He nabbed a fruit-and-nut bar out of the air—almond, mango, and blueberry—and stuffed it in my hand, then led me around the edges of the organized chaos of the kitchen. All off-white with chrome fixtures and florescent lights overhead. Bangs and chimes, thuds and calls for more of this ingredient or dish on the double.

A sizable bin sat on a table in the far corner, the clear sides revealing an array of wrapped sandwiches and savory pastries. A porcelain platter atop held at least three times as many cookies as people in the admin suite.

He gave me a once over, tsking and shaking his head. "You'll need to make two trips. I don't care how strong you think you are, you're not taking both at one go and dropping them halfway. And don't bother magicking them down, because it fusses with the taste."

"Got it. I'll take the sandwiches first—"

"No, take the cookies and I'll handle the sandwiches." The noisy surrounds had concealed the sound of Paulo's approach.

"Or the other way around." I lifted the cookie platter off the top to set on the side, but Paulo swept in and nabbed the heavier sandwich bin.

"If you insist." Hefting the cookie platter, I headed for the exit.

Except the manager stood in the way with a puzzled air. "Where are you going?"

"The stairs down." I jerked my head in the general direction.

"Let's take the elevator." Paulo nudged me with an elbow and nodded at the nearby door.

The staff elevator door, a nondescript steel gray, stood out from the otherwise white-and-chrome environs.

With a ding and a whoosh, the door opened though I hadn't seen either Paulo or the manager press the button.

The version of the elevator Yolanda and I rode earlier, the fancy box with paneling and wallpaper, had vanished. Instead, a thoroughly modern chrome-edged glass box loomed in view. The change sent an uneasy ripple through my limbs.

"It's only one flight of stairs." I stayed put as Paulo shifted to block the door from closing.

"Will the platter survive?"

Lips tight, to the edge of pain, I stomped into the elevator and shivered. I planted my feet in the middle of the smoky marble floor rather than lean against the glass walls, in case they decided to break.

Originally the glass no doubt allowed riders to enjoy some beautiful vista. Confined within the museum, the clear expanse offered views of dirty, dusty walls and gears surrounding us.

My breath started to come a bit faster. My toes twitched in my shoes. The floor vibrated as Paulo entered.

"It'll be all right, Bea." Paulo pressed the button for the third floor with an elbow, then moved to stand next to me, my shoulder to his arm.

Too close. I inched away to allow air between us. The space started to heat up, faster than it should. At least Paulo didn't follow. He only lowered his chin to rest on his chest and swallowed. Loudly.

The doors closed and the cage started to descend. Smooth, although in the distance gears creaked and moaned. Inch by inch we moved down and came to a stop. Then nothing. No settling to match the exterior door. No movement of the interior door.

Nothing opening.

Stuck.

The air grew hotter. Staler. Harder to breathe.

The glass and walls blurred. The platter's weight on my hands reduced to nothingness.

My pants turned to skirts, shirt to a loose blouse, and hair turned long enough to braid and fasten atop my head, a heavier weight than sunglasses or even double sunglasses.

Fog or steam or smoke or something surrounded me, carrying the tang of sea salt. Sudden chills flowed over my body, turning my fingers as cold as icicles.

The thick air hid everything. I couldn't even see my hands or the wall opposite.

The ground shifted, as though I stood on sand. Even a small tentative step resulted in nearly losing my balance and falling. I froze instead. Dropped, curled into a ball, and waited.

The air turned cool, but the ground remained several degrees warmer.

Whispers sounded and echoed from every direction.

"Where's your baby? Find your baby!"

The memory shattered when Silvestre took the platter from me. Sweat beaded his forehead, but otherwise he appeared calm and cool.

One minute cold to the bone, the next hot. Alone, then with in a small space with Paulo and Silvestre, the latter manifesting out of nowhere. First empty-handed, then holding a heavy platter, then hands light and empty again. The sharp contrasts threw me.

Reeling back, I hit the glass wall.

The elevator door sat half-open, half-closed. The elevator floor rested an inch above the actual floor.

Paulo hopped down. Set the bin of sandwiches on the floor, then offered me a hand.

I ignored it and got out on my own, then wrapped my arms across my chest and rubbed at the goosebumps lining my skin.

Silvestre followed out of the elevator, also needing no assistance. The skirt of his robe swirled around his legs as he inspected—and tutted—over the still half-open door.

"Bea, if you'd be so kind as to have out-of-order signs placed on all the floors?" He nodded at the door as it slowly squeaked closed. "This elevator and all others except the public elevator and freight elevator."

Realization dawned slowly. The two elevators he'd specified existed in the actual building. Unlike the others, they didn't swap in and out drawing on Nimur's power.

Rubbing my shaky hands together, I drew an out of order sign in the air. Red lines manifested where my finger passed, then resolved into an actual sign plastered over the door nice and big with letters and tall as my hand. Took only a moment to make replicas appear in other elevators.

"What about translations," Paulo asked, in a low deep growl.

"How many languages?" A snap of my fingers made the words on the sign multiply. Spanish, Russian, Chinese, and Arabic equivalents appeared, along with a place-holder set to display any other language as needed.

"Nice work." Silvestre shook his head, as though a wet dog trying to dry. A strange expression crossed his face as he gazed at the elevator.

"How long will it be needed?" I ran a finger across the top, then snatched my hand at the flash of pain from a paper cut.

"Until Nimur is found, at least." Silvestre adjusted his hold on the cookie platter. His expression resolved into weariness. "It's a sign of how much trouble they're in, needing to retract their power. There will be less for the rest of us to use to find them, until they are free."

He trotted off down the corridor. Paulo followed, clomping under his heavier load.

I carried nothing at all except worries. Planted there, on purpose or accident, by Silvestre. The museum had started to malfunction due to Nimur's imprisonment, but Silvestre hadn't really shown surprise. He'd expected something like this.

How often did Nimur go astray, or get captured?

Then there was the problem of Madeline-Jeanne's two memory fragments in less than an hour, both involving someone whispering to her about her baby. Coincidence? Yesterday's had had only a tangential relationship to what was going on in my life. Yet several of today's seemed more connected, albeit without any clue as to why.

<<Does making friends with Madeline's memories mean she's still alive?>> I texted Diego.

Within moments, my phone dinged an answer.

<<No. Yes. Maybe.>>

<<???>>

<<Short answer: no one knows.>>

Some help. <<What's a longer answer?>>

He typed for a long time. I rapped my fingers against the phone case, gritted my teeth, and waited.

<<Something may survive in us. Making friends means memory shards are less random. Painful memories less likely to flash through us when we're already down. Possibly some intelligence—theirs or ours—behind it.>>

So Madeline-Jeanne might pick what memories of hers I experienced. Nimur and Jay Doe had vanished right around when I said Madeline-Jeanne's name, and from the same room. Maybe she'd been a pawn in a bigger plot.

Though, what help this offered to figuring anything else out, beat me.

Unless she held secrets still to unfold.

<<Thanks.>> I sent back.

By the time I reached the admin suite, the air conditioning had given up. A faint, intermittent whine, not painful but most definitely annoying, pulsed from the ducts. The air lay mostly still and over-warm, despite the door being propped open with a spell of concealment. A strong one, too, with Yolanda's casting written all over it.

Not a single sound or stray word escaped the spell. My ears popped as I passed through, and a half-dozen conversations suddenly manifested.

Despite my delay in the hall, I arrived as Paulo removed the cover of the bin. Giving into hunger, I snatched two savory pastries. Then retreated through the ravening hordes falling upon the food to a free corner over by Yolanda. She had three monitors showing maps of different parts of the museum, real and virtual, flashing. Several of them I'd walked within the past week. The fourth monitor showed a list of search results scrolling down. The last display, closest to me, held nothing more than static notes.

I dropped into a mauve-and-black standard office chair with no arms. The seat squeaked as it sank a few inches beneath me.

At the sound, Yolanda rolled her shoulders and gave me an abstracted smile. Next moment, she stared at the pastries and licked her lips.

After a quick glance at the pastries' filling, I asked "chicken or veggie?"

Then handed over the veggie at her request, and contented myself with the chicken. The flaky crust practically melted in my mouth, while the chicken and pesto filling half-satisfied my stomach.

Yolanda nibbled on her pastry, still studying the monitors.

"What're you doing?" I asked.

"Trying to match up the description of where Nimur and Jay Doe are being held. Working on the assumption they haven't been taken too far from here." Yolanda tapped our location at the center.

"Any luck?"

"Too many possibilities so far. Jay Doe described the temperature as temperate albeit vaguely damp, which isn't much help." She paused the scroll search results, then shook her head and started it back up. "They're in a stone building of some kind, but haven't been able to determine what kind of stone except it's definitely human-made. No sounds of people or animals anywhere, but the distant crash of waves from a sea with a bright, fresh, and almost creamy smell."

"How many millions of places does that describe?" The maps showed several locations fitting the general criteria. Something about the description nagged at me.

"Tell me about it." Yolanda moved the mouse to swap out one of the maps for another.

"Mind going over the description again?"

"Sure." Yolanda tilted her head and her eyes narrowed as she gazed at me, then she glanced down at the notes and read off the items.

Warm but not hot.

Damp.

Human-made building of stone, type unknown.

No people or animals near.

Close to sea smelling bright, fresh, and almost creamy.

Exactly like the sea I'd smelled earlier, when Tiy hypnotized me.

A wave of dizziness crashed over me, and I slipped under again to lie on a hard surface. Walls of stone surrounded me, without any particular chill. The air held moisture, and a fresh, bright sea smell.

My eyes didn't work, or my mouth or ears. Nonetheless, grunts and moans from something nearby impinged on my awareness, along with the crash of waves on shore.

"Nimur? Jay Doe?" Magic made the words sound tinny and not like me.

Sudden silence. Stillness. The form stopped moving.

"Bea?"

I bounced back to myself, my body, and the admin suite—now at the center of a tight circle of faces. My shoulders hunched up to my ears.

No one spoke. The stillness weighed on me, especially with all eyes fixed me.

"Bea?" A thin voice broke the silence, and the eyes and faces whirled away. Letting slip a sigh of relief, I, too, shifted around to face Rumaisa and Ibrahim.

Ibrahim held the folds of cloth, Rumaisa's hands around his.

"Nimur heard Bea calling for us." Jay Doe said.

"Excellent." Tiy pushed her way through to stand next to me and clap a hand on my shoulder. "Then we'll send out two teams to hunt down your location, Jay Doe. One with Rumaisa and Ibrahim and your scarf, and one with Bea."

Wait, what?

❧ 6 ☙

OVERLOOKED

I was absolutely, positively, and completely lost, standing atop an unknown cliff on an undetermined shore, watching waves roll across an unidentifiable sea.

My shirt and sweatpants no longer smelled very nice. Neither did I. My hair hung limp and clumpy with sweat. Every muscle in my body ached.

Yet the glorious sea drove all of that from mind. Dark blue depths swirled around the base of the cliff, marked with ample white caps. Surge after surge and wave after wave crashed against the stone slabs below. Scrabbly grass with a scent reminiscent of sage covered most of the surface, save for barren spots where the earth baked hard until it cracked. No trees or buildings as far as the horizon, so not for miles. Few clouds marred the intense blue sky. Birds flapped in the distance, out over the waves, pale gray against the bright sky.

A lovely wind passed around me, drying my skin and hair except along the center of my back, under my faded red-and-black backpack. It whipped up some of the sea spray, complete with a scent reminiscent of sour milk.

Definitely not the shore we were looking for.

The cliff rose at least forty feet above sea level. Liam stood ten feet to my left, after which the cliff face curved inward in a shallow harbor and an equal distance on his other side, Silvestre. Both wore worn, scratched boots instead of sandals, but their robes, undyed beige and black respectively, as always, fluttered in the breeze.

Tiy had sent out three groups. Haru, Rumaisa, and Ibrahim intended to track the undefinable connection between Jay Doe's scarf and her. They'd thrown around various words, of which I only recognized dowsing and couldn't picture what they intended. Another group worked on retracing the path the villain or villains had taken when removing Jay Doe and Nimur from the kitchen where Rumaisa and I had found Haru.

We searched for a place with the right smell, feel, and with a stone structure.

A high-pitched call broke the silence. Strange and piercing, it blasted at the upper end of my hearing range for several seconds before descending several octaves and falling away. It repeated two or three times.

Two birds out over the waves darted at each other. Batted, beat with their wings. An instant later, one hot-winged it for shore while the other blared the call again.

Except . . . the form approaching land appeared less bird-like with every downstroke of its wings. From a respectable distance, it might be an albino or pale gray vulture. Once it drew closer, the sharp-angled wings tipped in black, long neck, and rounded head with big eyes added up to a decidedly non-bird appearance.

We'd crossed into pterosaur territory.

Our numbers evidently convinced it to stay away, as it banked and swooped along the shore. Given the distance between us, it lacked the size to carry off a human.

Might the flick of a tail in the sea indicate the presence of a sea monster of some kind?

We'd spent at least a half-hour of traipsing through museum displays and assorted pastoral scenes. Silvestre, who'd chosen the route, insisted they'd serve as a palate cleanser for me. The landscapes featured increasingly subtle appearances—rolling hills in winter, hard-baked desert flats, and more all lacking in much in the way of olfactory stimulation so as to allow me time to internalize the fresh, clean scent we sought.

Finally, we'd reached a shore—but one in no way resembling where we needed to be.

"Are we there yet?" as I gestured at the sea.

Silvestre and Liam both bore puzzled expressions.

"You tell us." Silvestre padded over the grass to align himself next to me, shoulder to shoulder. "Does it smell right?"

"No." Caught out, I closed my eyes. "There's a b-bitter under-taste. Like eating salad and suddenly finding a piece of k-kale in the middle of the lettuce."

"So we're seeking a sea that smells sweeter?" He pressed his hands together in front of his black robe, very priestly.

"Yeah. Or, c-cleaner at least." I shrugged and stuffed my hands in my pockets. The soft fabric of my pants clung, slightly damp with sweat. The physical opposite of the scent we sought. "Fresher."

"Good to know." Silvestre rested his chin on steepled fingers, directing a cool glance at Liam. "You have the baseline?"

He nodded.

"Of course this isn't the place." I turned around, arms outstretched as I pointed at the open vista. "There're no buildings anywhere."

"Perhaps Nimur and Jay Doe are in a cave." Liam said.

"No, it was a room, not a cave."

Liam tilted his head in acknowledgment.

"Not even a manmade cave?" Silvestre stooped dug his fingers into the earth, scraping to show the rock only a few inches below.

"No." I frowned, dredging up the memory but trying not to slip back into the hypnotized state again. "The walls are stone on stone. There's a window, not much of one. More of a slit."

Liam lay down and headed for the cliff's edge. He resembled an inchworm: stretched out flat, pulled his legs up and hunched his belly, then stretched out his front. All the way to the edge, where he peered down and around, then returned in reverse.

Rising, he dusted himself off.

"There are a few caves. In particular one down there." He pointed diagonally to where the cliff curved inward. "I couldn't see all the way in from where we are."

"It's a moot point." Silvestre lowered his gray backpack long enough to roll his shoulders. "As Beatrice notes, this is not the sea we're looking for. Let's move on."

He led the way, robe swaying against his long legs. I fell in behind, and Liam after me. A trio of ducklings, we waddled along with me always in the middle as the two men took turns leading.

Each shift from seaside to seaside involved me traipsing along behind a pair of boots with a black or beige hem twitching in front of me. The skin between my shoulder blades itched whenever Liam or Silvestre trod too close on my heels.

We walked about ten paces along the cliff. Grass crunched underfoot with each step. The wind gusted around, blowing bits of torn greenery at me. I covered my nose and mouth with one hand.

An instant later, my breath caught in my throat. No oxygen to breathe, no air, *nothing* except a creepy-crawly sensation as though inch worms covered my body and I couldn't throw them off.

I stumbled forward a step into a different world. Still a seaside cliff rising above deep blue waters, but set lower than the last one—maybe fifteen feet high tops. My sneakers skidded a foot on smooth, hard-baked rock before I came to a stop. Only a few scraggly weeds bowed and swayed in a heavy, chilly wind, their roots digging deep into cracks.

White-capped waves frothed in the sea, crashing against jagged spires as high as the land on which the three of us stood. Birds called again, but a species of prehistoric pelicans rather than pterosaurs. One landed on a rocky outcropping only a few feet off the cliff and stared at us, its narrow pouch swaying in the wind—or rippling with the escape attempts of a captive fish.

A heavy brine smell wafted up from the base of the cliff, likely tainted with fish carcasses. Shivering, I wrinkled my nose as I rubbed my hands along my goose-bump-covered arms. The sun, high overhead, offered little warmth to penetrate the cold of the wind.

"Still wrong."

"Are we any closer?" Silvestre pulled a long, thin, pewter water bottle and unscrewed the top. After taking a swig, he produced a handkerchief and dampened it to wipe sweat from his forehead.

"No, there's t-too much brine." My teeth chattered. "Can we move on? I d-don't remember it b-being this cold."

"Warmer and less briny." Silvestre tucked his water bottle away. "Onward we go."

Once again we swapped directions and leader. Following Liam made little difference from following Silvestre.

Except for speed. Within two steps this time, the air

thinned to nothingness and creepy-crawlies oozed along my skin.

We bopped to another sea.

A beach this time, rather than a cliff, although sadly not much improvement in warmth or smell or anything. My feet sank into the soft sand, which instantly started seeping into my shoes. No birds wheeled or called nearby. A layer of gray clouds hid the sun, though the almost-still air held only a residual chill. The sea barely moved, with no waves in evidence. Only wavelets.

"Not this one either." Liam had succeeded in getting us somewhere warmer and less briny, but this sea had no smell whatsoever.

Plus, my head still spun from the quick turnarounds.

Within a couple of minutes, they bounced us to two more places. First a lake of some kind, glass-smooth and smelling only of the pond lilies growing along the shore. Silvestre asserted it would cleanse my olfactory senses, as if he would know, though I went along with it. Then back to a cool beach, but near a sea so sulfury I clapped both hands over my mouth and nose. Silvestre winced and coughed. Liam, who'd guided us there, stuck it out although a muscle twitched in his cheek.

"This is g-getting us nowhere." I turned my back to the turgid waters and trudged up the hard-packed beach toward a dune. "Worse and worse."

"Truth." Silvestre fell in step with me, Liam on my other side.

Again the world turned to nothingness and creeping pressure on my skin. Longer this time, or maybe it only seemed so during the moments where I lacked the ability to move or breathe.

We emerged onto a cliff similar to where we'd seen the pterosaurs—except without any beings in the sky, or the bitter hint to the sea odor. The waters at the base seethed in a slightly pale blue under a warm sun, with scattered clouds in the sky and almost no wind. Waist-high grasses of sage green bloomed about us, save near a rocky rise where an oddly smooth cliff thrust a dozen feet above.

"Still wrong." I scratched my head. "We're not even c-close. Words aren't enough. They're not . . ."

"We're trying this wrong." Liam bowed in my direction. "You lead, this time."

"What?" I blinked.

"You're the one who knows best what we're searching for, and what we're not." Liam waved a hand at the sea, a half smile playing on his lips as he turned to Silvestre. "If we put Bea in the lead, we should be able to narrow down which sea much faster. We'll still have the whole of the shore to investigate, so why not cut matters shorter?"

"That's an idea." Silvestre turned and gave me the once-over. "Are you willing to try?"

"Sure." A lump formed in my throat. "But . . . how?"

"What do you mean?" Silvestre asked.

"You and Liam both flipped us to new places so fast." I flapped a hand at the surging waters. "I've never managed it without a lot more effort, and usually by conjuring up a doorway."

"Doorways are an excellent mode to shift between places, but less useful when traversing the out-of-doors." Silvestre folded his hands together and leaned the bottom of his jaw atop them, a contemplative and highly irritating stance.

"Fine, but how do you go from one unknown landscape to another?" I mirrored him. "Unless you've seen all these before?"

"Focus on the connections." He grunted, but let his hands drop away.

"Say what?" I stretched my arms over my head and

stamped. Trampled a couple dozen stalks of grass in the process, only to stop as something slithered between my feet.

"Whenever you move from one place to another, there's always a connection. A common element. Something similar or related between them, whether or not you recognize it." Silvestre jerked his head at the sea.

"Focus on where you want to go. Imagine the most important feature in your head and let your desire shape where we go," Liam said. "Don't try for too much. Even the oldest among us rarely manages to manifest more than three desired elements."

He grabbed my hand and Silvestre's with infectious enthusiasm.

They asked something simple of me: remember the smell. Concentrate on the cleanness and freshness as I walked forward, on finding a matching place.

Five steps. Six.

I focused on the smell, the grass-topped cliff became no more than waving tips against growing cloud-cover in the sky.

Ten. Eleven

We lurched closer to the sheer rock face rising to one side. The smooth stone had a reflective cast, showing blurry versions of our faces.

The world shifted, but nothingness surrounded me long enough my lungs started to ache. Creepy-crawlies skittered along my skin.

In a burst, things returned to normal. I yanked my sweaty hand from Liam's grasp, then braced both palms against a stainless-steel table, gasping for breath.

We'd gone way off-course, away from the sea entirely.

An empty, abandoned laboratory surrounded us, all white walls and cabinets gone dingy with dust. Covered jars and glass flasks lined the countertop at the far end of the room, their varied contents adding flecks of color. A dash of dark brown, orange, and a large container with a miscellany of browns and beiges. A door hung ajar at the far end, but shadows hid whatever lay outside.

Everything mismatched where we'd been, except for the smell. Closer than any of the seascapes, a light, clean, and *almost* fresh aroma filled the air—depending on where I stood. To the left, all smelled fine, but to the right a faint sour aftertaste tainted the odor, resembling nothing so much as milk going bad.

"Now this is interesting." Liam's boots clattered against the black-and-white tile floor as he prowled around the table to inspect the array of jars. "I'd expected something a bit less . . ."

"Indoors?" Silvestre laughed, a huff of a sound followed by a gusty sigh with enough force to ruffle my bangs. "Different enough for a painful transition, even under better circumstances."

"Say what?" Nose twitching, I turned around and around in search of the source of the smell.

"The more in common two places have, the less it hurts to pass between them. Though, in truth, the hurt this time likely came as much from Nimur being imprisoned."

"That's why?" It wasn't me? My hand rested on the cool porcelain rim of a deep sink.

Silvestre showed no shock or alarm at what he'd revealed. Nor surprise. Likewise Liam, on the far side of the table, grunted and continued to stare at the jars.

They held so many secrets. Jagged phrases and insults that roared through my brain. Why not let more spill out, in such a time of need? A cold seeped into my fingers and toes, and formed a mass in my belly.

I breathed deep, inviting calm.

Instead, I got a nose full of the almost-right sea smell. Something rested at the bottom of the sink, a small white dish no bigger than my palm—covered with the residue of a gooey, creamy substance.

"This is the smell we need to source." Pointing to the dish, I whirled around to check that Silvestre and Liam listened to me. "At least, it's close. The real thing is fresher—no sourness."

"Interesting." Liam remained on the far side of the room, though he straightened and tilted his head to one side. A distant expression crossed his face. "Vaguely familiar, don't you think? Though I can't quite place it."

"I prefer land to sea, but this does have an appealing edge." Silvestre reached in and retrieved the dish. Dipped a finger and stirred, which unfortunately made the sourness increase. A fleck of green turned up. Hopefully not mold, but he returned the dish to the sink and tried the faucets. The cold water still worked, so he washed his hands.

For some reason, this made the laboratory fade away. Instead, I walked through a hospital with the same kind of white-white walls and tiled floors. My skirt swished around my ankles. Long strips of lace likewise fluttered at my wrists, attached to the crisp blouse I wore. Boots a hair too tight constrained my feet, the heels clicking against the tile.

Grime and ashes stained the walls. Mold boomed in the cracks between tiles, and crept up in dark gray and green swathes.

A long window interrupted the wall, or once had. Pieces of glass remained, jagged and sharp. Some of the missing glass had fallen into the hall, but most covered the floor in the room on the other side. Empty, save for faded ribbons of blue and pink dripping from the moldy ceiling—and a few bassinets abandoned on the floor.

The same voice as before whispered. "Where's the baby? Who took the baby?"

"Aha!"

Jerked back to my surroundings, I rose a half-inch off the floor and dropped back with a jarring thud. The constant repetitions of whispered queries echoed in my ears.

No more. I willed the message to register with whatever remnant of Madeline-Jeanne resided in my brain. *Unless you have anything clearer to share.*

Nothing but silence in response, save for a sudden shiver along the front of my body.

Silvestre thumped me on the back. "Are you all right?"

"Yeah, just surprised." I fumbled for my water bottle. Cool as the laboratory. After drinking, I pressed the glass against my heated cheeks and forehead.

"Good." He patted me again, then headed around to Liam's side. "What did you find?"

"I saw shells such as these on the beach we last visited. They may be the common link." The jar scraped against the counter as Liam pulled it out and popped the lid, spilling the array of brown and beige shells across the steel table in the center.

Clam shells, scallop shells, and some lovely swirled cones bearing flashes of green and red stood out against the dust and plain steel gray.

I picked up one at random, a dainty light-brown scallop shell with edges tinged in a pale peach. A small label pasted to the inside bore a handwritten note, blurred and illegible thanks to time or water. The shell held no scent of the sea, neither where we'd been nor the sea we sought.

"Something like this brought us here?" I asked. "It's so small!"

"The connection of the smell, the shell, and you being so new. Sometimes, when one focuses hard on one detail, chance comes into play." Silvestre waved a hand over the shells. "Let's try this again."

"What should I think about this time? The smell again?" I shrank away from the sink and moldy dish.

"Perhaps focus on being by the sea, first, to get us back to a shore," Liam said. "Then we can try the smell again."

"Okay." I turned around and headed for the doorway.

"Where are you going?" Silvestre caught my sleeve, stopping me.

"We're in a room, we have to get out through a door unless you want to break down a wall."

He quirked an eyebrow. "We got in without going through the door."

I opened my mouth, then snapped it shut. Given the angle at which I'd run into the table, we'd manifested one-third of the way around the room.

"Transitions to and from places and within houses are restricted to doors-only close to the public access points, the museums proper, to reduce the odds of panic should visitors stray through the wrong way." He patted my shoulder. "Using doors is traditional for people familiar with large buildings, but hardly required in most of the House of Memory."

"Here's another trick." Liam circled the table. Picking up the biggest of the shells, he laid it on the floor at the far end before joining us at the near. "Use a landmark of some kind to trigger the transition from place to place. Tell yourself you'll be somewhere else when you pass a specific tree, or rock or other landmark."

"Or, if you're alone and cannot find a good landmark, turn around believing you'll find a new landscape." Silvestre added.

Neither appeared too comfortable, Silvestre gripping his robes tight enough for his knuckles to whiten. A tic leapt in Liam's jaw.

We'd have to face the same pain and lack of air going back.

"This time, we'll use the shell—think about the sea, and a beach . . ."

With joined hands, we walked together. They hung back and let me take lead. Focusing on the shell, I willed us to go back to the seaside. Preferably one with the right smell, but first and foremost a sea somewhere.

Every skin cell quivered as though slimy bugs crawled all over me. Air vanished and I couldn't breathe. Shouldn't be able to hear, either, yet the void held an almost-perceptible scream at either end of my registers—too high-pitched and too-low—as though transmitting Nimur's agony and anger.

We hit a short beach running. I stumbled and lost hold of them, falling to my knees. Braced my hands against solid earth this time, instead of steel. Between my splayed fingers lay a shell similar to the one Liam had dropped on the floor.

Drawing in a deep breath, I sagged closer to the narrow spit of sand. My exhalations disturbed motes, starting a miniature avalanche.

Although still not right, we'd made progress. This sea approximated the scent so closely but remained wrong. Maybe there was something added, a hint of . . . Gas? Kerosene?

We were in the middle of a short beach—assuming it deserved the title—the brief stretches of sand interspersed with sizable boulders of gray and brown. A cliff rose high above, and even higher the white beacon of a tall lighthouse. The sun hadn't set, but gone from sight. Streaks of color lined the horizon far out over the sea, and the chill of evening wrought a shudder from me.

"It's so close."

Silvestre knelt at my side, tucking his hands under my arms and helping me to my feet. I swayed, but stayed up without him keeping hold.

"Well done. You got us back to the sea, and the smell . . ." Silvestre's nostrils flared as he breathed deep.

"It's not right yet."

"And you're worn out. Nor am I much better." Liam scowled at the encroaching sea, each wave eating up more of the narrow spit of sand. "Let's find a place to rest, not here, and everything may become clearer in the morning."

They took hold of me, clasping my hands in theirs, and led me through one last transition. This passed much easier than the previous two—with no primal scream.

They settled on a camping spot far enough inland to be away from the high tide. Although not the same shore as we'd come from, this also smelled close. Still not quite right.

The mix of sand and grasses offered a reasonable place to sleep. Some of the grasses grew in tall clumps, but others proved short, stubby, and soft to the touch. They had a sweet smell more than capable of washing away the last whiffs of soured milk.

Nearby a creek cut through the earth as it wound down to empty into the sea. The banks started out steep and a foot or two high, reducing down to nothing at the edge of the beach. Despite the low water level, the burble of the creek reached our camp site and it might aid me falling asleep.

As the sun sank in the distance, a gorgeous sky unfolded overhead with full colors. Streaks of gold, orange, red, purple, and blue rippled as they shifted from one side of the sky to the other while the deep, unrelenting dark of night slowly swallowed them all.

Pulling out my phone, my head drooped over the shiny surface. So much to report and so little progress. Rather than risk a long conversation, I texted Yolanda.

<<Stopping for the night. We've made progress, but too tired. We'll start again first thing in the morning.>>

<<Got it.>> she sent back. <<If you need me, call or text.

I'm heading home but will have direct access to Tiy and the others. Sleep well.>>

A few instants later, one of the other hunting parties called and I handed the phone over to Silvestre.

Although tempted to remain and listen in, I turned and traipsed to an open spot amidst the swaying fronds of grass. With no delight whatsoever, I pulled out the pup tent Paulo assured me I'd have no trouble putting up.

He lied.

A loose pile of blue and green nylon fell on the grass, a loose lump topped with a mass of chrome rods and hints of rope.

What would men who predated modern camping by centuries know about putting up pup tents? Not much. Neither even planned to use a tent, instead intending to wrap themselves in blankets.

They tried nevertheless. Pulled and prodded, while I sat on a nearby grass clump regretting everything since I'd set foot on the Ambassador's Stair.

In the meantime, Madeline-Jeanne's memories sunk further into my bones. She, too, had never indulged in modern camping. Nevertheless, she'd lived with far fewer physical comforts than I. Bit by bit, various physical knowledge or experience embedded within me. How to sleep on a hard pallet, or the floor. Eat whatever I had at hand, no matter how old or disgusting. Conduct certain essential bodily functions in the outdoors.

In the end, magic prevailed and provided me with a narrow tent, complete with three layers of doors fastened and unfastened by separate zippers.

Comfy, no. Cozy, no. Even after unrolling a mattress pad as thick as my thumb, and laying out the sleeping bag on top.

Rather than stare and suffer in advance, I left camp and clambered down the bank of the creek. A thin, squiggly column of water trickled to the sea. With every wave of the incoming tide some water rushed backward up the channel, but stopped well short of where we camped.

Squatting on a flat of semi-dry mud, I checked for unpleasant bacteria in the water. The spell flashed green and good-to-go. Bending over, I washed my face and hands. My hair still felt stringy and limp, so I dipped the top of my head in. Shook it clean and dry, and instantly felt better enough to listen when my stomach growled a demand for dinner.

I stood and stretched, not yet ready to scramble back up out of the creek bed. The same general landscape continued there: grasses and dunes all the way to the horizon—especially with the growing dark.

A crackle broke the general silence. Jerking around, I blew out a breath at the sight of lurid red and orange flames shooting up from the campsite. They settled down to a soft glow accompanied by additional crackles. Wisps of smoke reached me, making my nose itch.

"Need a hand up?" Liam towered above me atop the raised bank.

"Sure."

He stumbled backward as I scrabbled up the side . We both tumbled onto the nearby dune. The impact drove half the wind from my lungs. I panted as I clambered to my feet.

Liam beat me, rising first with chest heaving as he dragged in air.

Once on our feet, he discreetly pointed out a section of long grasses for me to use for necessary purposes. He and Silvestre would go in a different direction, which he also indicated.

"Thanks." The clumps of grasses lay equidistant to the camp.

"Be wary of the creek in the night." He squatted a foot back from the edge of the bank, peering down.

"I wasn't planning on going anywhere near it. Especially not in the dark." Talk about a good way to trip and fall and break my neck.

"Good. But take care in the light as well." Bracing his hands against the earth, he inspected the sloping dirt. Then rose and dusted himself off. "There's something off there. Might be no more than the weather, for you can see a big storm passed through not too long ago. Yet it brings back other memories. With Nimur captive, the various parts of the House of Memory will start to unravel and disconnect. Voids may manifest anywhere, but in particular those markers people use for navigation or to shift from one landscape to another, such as the creek."

Hunger and an actively growling stomach distracted me from his words. I got half-way through eating a cold chicken on rye sandwich before the implications of Liam's words dawned.

"You mean, Nimur's been captured before?"

"Yes and no." Silvestre paused between bites of his own chicken sandwich.

"Or no and yes." Liam opted for a pita stuffed with a fried egg and pickled onions with a fierce sting capable of making my eyes water even at a distance.

"Really? Then why haven't I heard anything before?" I washed the last of my sandwich down with a swig of cran-apple juice. Readjusted my seat so my bare feet rested close enough to the fire to stay warm, without risking burns from sparks.

Each immediately took a bite and chewed with great thoroughness.

The fire crackled and cackled. The sky grew dark overhead, the last of the sunlight vanishing along the horizon. The shift turned Liam and Silvestre's faces into mixed pools of light and darkness—no longer so familiar and friendly.

"They're not comfortable memories." Liam swallowed and coughed.

"You can say that twice." Silvestre unscrewed the top of a small, brass-covered flask. The metal glittered in the firelight as a sharp, alcoholic tang tinged the air. He offered it to Liam, who declined.

"Disasters, major and minor, happen because something goes wrong." Liam rubbed his temples. "Someone says something wrong. Or confides in the wrong person. In all . . . everything's wrong."

"It's been a while, too, hasn't it? How long since the last major catastrophe, fifty years? Sixty?" Silvestre popped back a swig from the flask. Capped it, then started counting on his fingers.

"Which are you thinking of? The invasion?" Liam asked.

"Invasion?" The air grew ever cooler, save close by the fire.

Liam glanced my way but didn't answer. Snapping a wrist, he summoned a dark cloak from somewhere and wrapped the cloth around his shoulders as he hunched near the fire.

Following Liam's lead, I fussed located a shawl to cover my still-drying hair. The darkness and shadows loomed ever more menacingly in the distance.

The silence grew, until finally Silvestre broke it. "A hundred or so soldiers armed with machine guns and sorcery stormed in through the Berlin-based museum."

"They did a lot of damage before we cleared them out." Liam picked up a stick and drew lines in the earth. Stick-men carrying guns. A tank.

"Remember the pirate crew—what was their ship, the *Jolly Nancy?* They showed up searching for buried treasure, shortly after I accepted Nimur's offer." Silvestre resorted to another swig of alcohol. "They left holes everywhere. I nearly wrenched my ankles a dozen times."

"You should've been here for the conquistadors searching

for the fountain of youth or cities of gold, I forget which." Still holding the stick, Liam shifted around and began drawing more stick men, waving swords. "They stumbled into one of the dinosaur habitats. All left, eventually, a little less whole than before."

"Less whole . ." I squinted to make out the bigger scribble Liam dug near the swordsmen. An allosaur? "Did the dinosaurs eat them?"

"One tried. One of the smaller, or fewer would've escaped. Turned out the dinosaur didn't appreciate the taste of boiled leather."

Silvestre might've counted years on his fingers; I counted the anecdotes.

Conquistadors, date unknown. Probably Spanish.

Pirates, date also unknown but probably sometime in the seventeenth century and, given the ship name, likely English.

Berlin invasion during one of the world wars?

Either way, surprise surprise, the most memorable attempts to take over the museum—at least to Silvestre and Liam—originated among European peoples. Asking Tiy or Rumaisa the same question might offer differ results.

"They meld together to some degree." Silvestre rose, dusted himself off, and picked up the rolled blanket he'd been leaning against. Pummeled it into a squarish shape, then put it back down and retook his place. This time he sat at more of an angle.

"There've been that many?" I asked.

"About one every generation or so." Liam waved his hand in a half-and-half gesture.

"In truth, the pirates and soldiers were more laughable than anything else, even with all the destruction they wrought. They came from outside, and did not know enough about Nimur and the House do much lasting damage." For his third swig, Silvestre must've downed a quarter of the flask, expression turning sour. "Those who work or live here wreak the worst disasters."

A dozen memory fragments jousted in my head, half mine and half from Madeline-Jeanne. Haru had mentioned hunting destroyers and flung a long list of names at Tiy and Silvestre.

"What happened?" If only I lay snug and tucked up under heavy blankets in my bed in the Quarters reading all this in a book or watching it stream across a computer screen.

"Nearly destroyed the House ten times over." Silvestre tapped his fingers against the side of the flask. Still half-full based on the sloshing.

"Ten times ten, or more." Liam kept drawing in the earth, shifting from figures to lines. Xs or crosses. "Failed every time."

"Haru mentioned some of them. Sandoval? Bilgin? Aapo?"

"Bilgin," Silvestre's eyes flashed in the firelight. "Power drove him. None of the hosts offered him a chance to join their ranks, so he tried to take a place on his own. Captured two of the hosts, nailing their—"

Liam grunted, a loud intrusive sound, and stopped Silvestre in his tracks. He flushed, deep and dark, and turned away from me.

"We freed them," Liam said. "But the damage lingered for long after he'd been remembered and ceased to walk among us."

I grimaced and wriggled. Nails and skin, ick. "What about Aapo?"

"That predated my arrival." Silvestre's flush slowly decreased.

"Aapo never left the world as much as most of us, no matter how much time passed since his arrival. He sought out every story, every tidbit of news about his people and home. When the Spanish conquerors arrived," Liam grunted again, teeth briefly showing white in the darkness, "those same who invaded here but more of them, he wished to leave the House. To lead any who would follow to defend those he loved. Nimur refused, for the Forgotten may not leave alive. Aapo took hostages to force their hand. It ended badly on all sides."

"Sandoval also wrought havoc before my arrival, but only by a decade or two." Silvestre turned to Liam. "You faced him along with Haru and Tiy and others, didn't you?"

"By the end." Liam laid the stick aside and wove his fingers together, pressing them against his chest. "Sandoval came from Navarre as I recall. An attractive man in many respects. Well-read, thoughtful, persuasive, though he never became a host. He quickly gained followers. Adherents. Believers, who did not care he'd spent his time in the mundane world as a witch hunter."

Witch hunter. The words alone sent shivers down my spine. I huddled closer to the fire, the better to stay warm—and to catch every one of Liam's words.

"Then he spotted witches among us, or so he claimed. His first choice landed upon a young woman recently brought in. Eriselda. A Forgotten for less than five years, who became a host." He stopped and turned sideways, gazing out into the dark and presenting only his profile.

"Like Jay Doe?" I asked, when the silence grew too long and heavy.

"In appearance not at all, but in other respects yes. Some say Sandoval took against Eriselda because Nimur made her a host so fast and not him. The truth will never be known, but he claimed she had bewitched Nimur."

The fire crackled, leaping higher although no one had tossed any more fuel upon it.

"What happened?" Night loomed around us, offering concealment for any force interested in lurking amid the dune grasses. Each question brought answers inviting more queries, and increased the odds of me lying awake for hours rather than falling straight asleep. Still, better to ask and learn.

"He snatched her. Tortured her. Burnt her at the stake, while several other Forgotten watched." Each word fell hard and sharp into the cool air.

"Burnt . . . she died?"

"Oh yes." Liam nodded not only with his head but his whole torso.

"But the Forgotten, you . . . don't . . . not here."

"She was the youngest, and so still the most mortal." Liam jerked up from his seat. "The second Forgotten Sandoval burnt had more years here and survived. We stopped Sandoval, but arrived too late for Eriselda. *I* came too late."

He stalked off into the night. In the direction of the grass set aside for him and Silvestre to use, but no doubt he kept walking. Regardless, he rushed out of sight within moments and became one more shadow in the dark.

"I should have let the name lie." Silvestre laid a hand on the fire, dousing the flames down to coals.

"Did you know?" My voice trailed off.

"Less before than now." He pulled the blanket from behind and wrapped it around his shoulders. "I suggest you rest. He'll be back, and better for a night's sleep."

Would I, though, with no one to share it with and hash out meaning? I couldn't call my friends, or even try texting other interns. This information seemed ill suited to share except in person, and with care and caution.

And fear.

The Forgotten could die, the youngest at least. One had once burned. Liam had tried to save her and failed. Danger threatened another, no wonder he'd stalked off.

Tent in the wilderness, check. Fire, check. Scary stories, check. Only marshmallows to cook over the fire remained missing for a full camping experience. After the stories, I really wanted something sweet.

They'd frightened me enough I might not get any sleep.

Silvestre turned away from me, kneeling and praying in quiet, sonorous Latin phrases over his clasped palms.

I slipped into my tent and set up protective spells against insects . . . and things bumped about in the night.

Without the flicker and crackle of the fire, the night turned silent. Quieter than the Quarters—where some measure of noise always snuck through. Traffic and car alarms. The other interns banging around. Water rushing through aging pipes.

Also more hushed than my mother's home. No wind rustling leaves in the trees or making the branches scratch against the side of the house. No cats arguing in the back yard. Or my mother or sisters bumbling their way to the bathroom in the middle of the night.

Not even any sound from Silvestre or Liam—neither snored or rolled over or made any sound whatsoever.

Only the burble of the creek, a rush of waves, and whistle of the wind broke the stillness.

And my own breathing.

Stuffing my clothes into my backpack, I turned it into a pillow. Pulled on an oversized purple nightshirt and crawled into the sleeping bag. Magicked my finger into a toothbrush and cleaned my teeth.

Then lay awake wondering.

Better to not go over the day's events. Too many things had happened. I remained stuck in the middle of them. Time enough to review later.

Simpler things, more distant, preoccupied me.

What happened to Sandoval and the other Forgotten who'd watched? No doubt forced remembrances, but I pitied whoever had had to carry their names out. Hoped the interns or employees or whoever had slipped the talismans out too, so they didn't have to live through any of those Forgotten's memories.

More importantly, what about Eriselda? Surely Tiy and Liam and others located her talisman and arranged for it to be taken out and remembered.

Pulling out my phone, I texted a quick query to the remembrance hotline. The slow connectivity delayed things so much my head started nodding before I received a response back: they'd check on it and get back to me.

Took me another half-hour or more to fall asleep . . . into horrible dreams.

A tight-packed crowd surrounded me, people to every side and all of us penned in so close we couldn't sneeze without hitting someone's face. If one of us fell, we all would. Hot, onion-and-garlic-flavored breath warmed my neck and made me dizzy.

Before and above stood a podium. Darkness covered the land, and crowd. Only a single greasy, orange-and-red torch flared, in the hand of a wild-eyed man in a dark robe. His pale skin glowed in the torchlight, showing an unkempt mess of black hair atop his head but a carefully oiled and trimmed beard and pair of curling mustaches on his face.

"Suffer not a witch to live!" he cried, and every throat echoed his words.

"God has given us many gifts, of which this is far from the least." He raised the torch high. "Fire with which to cleanse ourselves and our world."

The crowd pulled back. Torches flared into existence in an oval around a central, unlit stake. A woman, bound and gagged and dressed in rags, writhed as she sought to escape.

She had Jay Doe's face.

Log by log and stick by stick, the base of a massive bonfire manifested around her. Distant voices called, their words blurring, but the flashing light revealed Tiy and Haru, Rumaisa and Ibrahim, Liam and Silvestre, fighting their way through the crowd to the stake.

Too late, for with a "For God's sake!" echoed by a hundred, a thousand voices around me, the man lowered his torch to the bonfire. Flames burst into existence, consuming the dream, the nightmare.

When they receded, I huddled against a wall once again part of a crowd. Others pressed close, pinning me, as mobs yelled in the distance. Again torches flared. Flickers of light and shadow danced across elegant walls. A rock sailed through the air, crashing into a window and sending flickers of glass everywhere. More rocks followed, hitting me but I couldn't hear my own shriek of pain.

The dream changed again. Glass reformed into thick panes. Wreathed in shadows, I knelt against hard tiles and pressed my cheek against the protective panels lining the museum's third floor balcony. Below crowded hundreds of adults and children dressed in all manner of outlandish attire. Dinosaurs, witches and wizards, princesses and superheroes. The museum's annual Halloween trick-or-treat bonanza. No one realized I hid in the shadows to watch, save another lurker whose whispers assured me demons had stolen my son and I had to save him from them.

Such a relief to wake, even nearly bashing my head against the poles across the top of the tent. Panting. Sweating. Losing moisture at such a rate, I fumbled in the dark for my water bottle and wound up snapping my fingers and using a flicker of magic to summon it. Removed the cap with trembling fingers, nearly spilling precious drops. Drained it dry in a couple of seconds.

Only to sag back against my makeshift pillow. Nearby, my phone glowed with the message app. The top text, from the hotline, mentioned a *Ballad of Eriselda*.

Instead of opening it, my finger slid and highlighted another: the one word my future self had sent, which never vanished no matter how many times I deleted it.

Run.

When did my future self mean? Surely I'd run enough already.

The reappearance of the message prompted me to rise to my knees and unzip the very top of the tent doors.

A strange, cool-but-not-cold fog filled the air, glowing palest silver as though lit by starlight. A spiraling trickle seeped into the tent, bringing the smell and taste of not seawater but mist and rain.

The sane, sensible thing to do would be zip the tent closed and crawl back into my sleeping bag for what remained of the night. No more than a few hours, after all.

Unfortunately, I'd consumed a lot of water. Grabbing my phone for a flashlight, I slipped my feet into my sneakers and ventured out.

No more than two steps out and the tent vanished. No matter how I turned around, stretched out my arms, flipped my fingers, I couldn't find it. Turned the phone up to full flashlight app power. The light reflected off the roiling fog, nearly blinding me. Turning it off helped, but left me in the dark.

Pulse pounding, I shook from head to toe. Swallowed a bitter bite of spit in a mouth gone suddenly dry.

"Silvestre? Liam?" The names emerged as little more than a croak.

The fog had stolen my voice and the world around me. Left me in a strange beach-like nothingness. No tent. No fire pit. No Forgotten rolled up in blankets. Sand and grass underfoot, but nothing else.

Every attempt at sitting down and finding a place to stay in it until morning came—if it did—failed. The earth heaved beneath my feet, sending me walking into the unknown.

Clumps of grass scratched my legs. Sand got into my shoes, caking my feet. Goosebumps lined every exposed inch of skin.

Then I missed the bank and fell into the creek. Landed on my hands and knees, phone still clenched in one hand, in lukewarm water halfway up my thighs.

Staying on all fours, I clambered out. Lost my breath for a long moment, during which every cell in my body twitched spasmodically, but I made it onto dry land.

Very, very sandy dry land still covered with heavy, glowing fog.

I stopped there, and sat.

The bank of the creek seemed wrong. Slipping into it without registering the slide down the short, steep side I might accept. Yet I'd crawled up a much gentler incline of no more than half a foot. Either I'd wandered along the creek toward the sea, or I'd come out somewhere other than where I'd entered.

Liam hadn't liked something about the creek, worrying about Nimur's power draining away there and leaving cracks behind.

Perhaps I'd stumbled through one such gap onto a beach, given the sand on which I sat.

Or I'd moved to *another* beach, from somewhere else in the world and time.

The fog began to shift, lifting and thinning but in uneven patches. It rose an inch or two from the warm earth, and let me see my own hand a foot or two away from my face. Not details, or even the uneven roundels of my fingernails, but the outline of my hand at least.

I blew out a huff of air. The fog thinned more, but only enough for a few more feet of vision.

Another hand appeared nearby.

Not mine, but a human hand connected to a very human arm.

"Liam? Silvestre?" The fog hadn't returned my voice. I croaked, softer than any frog. Practically a whisper. Indeed, my attempt resembled the whisper in Madeline-Jeanne's memories.

I should run away. Or at least move further from the hand and arm. Yet what if they belonged to Silvestre or Liam? And they needed my help?

Rising onto my knees, I bent over to get a closer view. Reached out and touched the skin, dark against the fog. Still warm.

Then two strong hands fastened around my neck. Fingers pressed tight.

My breath caught. Lungs seized.

A solid form pressed against my back, pinning me in place.

My hands rose automatically to grab hold. I scrabbled at the constricting grasp. Scraped. Scratched.

Pain everywhere. Blossom of blood in my mouth, sore lip. Ache along my throat, where fingers dug and palms pressed close.

Lurched forward, nightgown hem fluttering around my thighs. Sockless feet growing cold. Legs cold. Only head and hands warm.

Dizzy. Nothing visible but spots of light dancing in the fog. The world darkened.

Had to fight.

No energy.

"Ibrahim?" A voice in the distance. Rumaisa—but where had she come from? "Ibrahim?"

The hands throttling me loosened, flinging me forward. I landed across a warm body. The impact further drove air from my gasping lungs. Panting and desperate, my throat ached with each drag of air. Sharp bursts of pain flared around my neck.

The body beneath me retained heat, though it was akin to lying atop an oddly shaped bolster or sofa. The chest rose and fell but slower than mine.

I lay limp, imitating a fish and gasping for air.

Fog lifted, inch-by-inch, revealing a familiar face and length below.

Ibrahim.

We should be far apart, but I'd tripped into wherever he was, or vice versa, or we both wound up in a third place or . . . Too complicated. Brain refused to process. Tried to hold on. Scared of letting go.

Wrapped shaking fingers around one of his arms, savoring the warmth.

Damp. Shivering.

Dawn light slipped through the fog, breaking it further and faster. Turned the world into stark contrasts between light and dark, showing the clear imprint of fingers around Ibrahim's neck.

Yet he breathed still.

I tried to whisper his name. Managed only "buh."

A moment later, a whirlwind parted the fog. Rumaisa arrived, towering over the both of us, fully dressed though with mis-aligned buttons at the top of her long shirt and the scarf over her hair so precariously perched it slipped halfway off.

The last remnants of the fog formed a nimbus of light around her, then the world went dark.

7

ASTRAY

I woke to warmth and a soft blanket. My body sprawled on a firm surface, arms to either side and legs loose. Someone had cleaned my feet of sand and grit, and like-wise restored my nightgown to a fresh state. A damp cloth rested across my aching neck, drops of water oozing from the corners. Breezes wafted over me. A minty taste filled my mouth, as though I'd brushed my teeth before lying down.

The mint smell mixed with the fresh, clean scent of the sea—almost but not *quite* right for where Nimur and Jay Doe remained captive.

Nimur and Jay Doe.

Hands around my neck, strangling me.

Returning memories sent shivers through me.

"Easy, Bea." Rumaisa stroked my forehead. "Open your mouth and take a little more of this."

Her hand slipped under my head and raised it off the flat surface. My jaw dropped and mouth gaped. Something cool and minty dropped onto my tongue. I swallowed reflexively.

OW! Pain flared around my throat. Once again, hands seemed to fasten there, fingers to dig deep.

Then a flood of energy raced through me, blasting most of the pain out of the way.

"Thanks." My throat still stung from speaking, but only a shadow of the earlier pain.

The world whirled in a blur of reds and oranges. Blinking several times dispelled the blur, and everything sharpened into focus. I lay on a sandy beach, similar to the one where I'd camped the night before. The red and orange proved to be the sky filled with gorgeous streaks of color. In the distance, the sun rose over waters reflecting back every iota of red, orange, purple, and pink.

"Morning?"

"Yes."

The old adage about red sky at morning, sailors take warning ran through my brain. Did the saying apply in the House?

Beside me knelt Rumaisa—with a still form on her far side. Grass-covered dunes and the glorious sky provided a heart-breaking backdrop for Ibrahim. He lay on a thin pallet atop sandy ground. His chest rose and fell slightly, but nothing else suggested life. Worse, his arms lay folded across his body in a classic funeral arrangement.

Rumaisa wore the same clothes as the day before, though she'd doffed her jewelry at some point and swapped the Crocs for hiking boots. Unlike my vague memory of the night before, she'd properly buttoned her shirt and wrapped her head with her blue dupatta, then tied Jay Doe's pink-and-green scarf around her neck. Both ends of the latter cascaded across her front.

Though no tears dewed her eyes, red outlined them and tracks of tears remained along her cheeks. Nevertheless, she managed a weak smile as she tucked an almost-empty bottle of water of life into a plain blue backpack.

"How do you feel?"

"Okh—." I winced at a light spasm of pain, and the sound of my harsh croak. One hacking cough later, and my throat seemed better enough to try again. "Thanks for t-t-aking c-c-care of me. How's Ib-b-b—."

"He will live, but needs healing." Rumaisa grimaced. "He is no longer a host."

"So he'll recover?"

"Someday, though likely not in time to host Nimur again." Again, her head lowered and her eyes bored into me, a heavy emphasis on the last words that I couldn't parse.

"B-but you said he'll need healing. He's not d-dying?" How old was he? Liam had said the youngest Forgotten remained mostly mortal. Jay Doe only had five years, so he had to be older but how much . . . He'd remained warm when I fell across him, and still breathed. "He's old enough, not mortal?"

"He's been in the House twenty years. I still remember the day he arrived. I hosted Nimur when they offered him a place here, where his family might live on through him." Every word came through clear, though her voice dropped to scarce above a whisper. "His skin hung on his bones, left more dead than alive as he bled into the dust. I've seen many people in their last minutes. Most, when Nimur shows, ask questions or stare open-mouthed. So many who might become Forgotten lose their chance from moving too slow. Ibrahim took only a moment's thought to accept."

She gazed off at the glowing sea, still reflecting the sky but in more pastel colors. Her posture stiffened, shoulders growing rigid.

But her hands, folded in her lap, shook.

My pulse beat hard at the base of my throat.

With her fine-honed control cracking, she reminded me of my oldest sister. I reached out and took Rumaisa's hand.

Rumaisa startled and nearly pulled free. At the last

moment, she slipped and her fingers grabbed and held, firm and hard but not to the point of pain.

"Given his quick thought and determination, I expected him to become a host." Her body eased slightly, shoulders and back turning more flexible. "As he did, no more than a couple months later. Faster than I had. The instant a vacancy became available. One of the best of us. No wonder whoever imprisoned Nimur and Jay Doe went for him before me."

"Maybe chance, finding him first." Talking still hurt my throat, but my hand ached more as it went all pins-and-needles. I wiggled my fingers. Her grip eased, enough to let blood circulate.

"No. Haru took the first watch and Ibrahim the second." She jerked her head, jaw brushing the pink-and-green scarf. "He should've woken me, to keep an eye out and reinforce the protective spells, but he didn't."

They'd set guard spells and taken turns watching over each other in the night. Neither Silvestre nor Liam so much as mentioned us doing the same. Or anything defensive. Perhaps they settled it between themselves and neglected to mention it to me as men-taking-care-of-the-weak-woman, a more appealing notion than either or both assuming we'd be safe.

Then again, I hadn't mentioned the matter either. I'd thrown up a quick spell on my tent, which only protected me —and only in the tent, or I wouldn't have a bruised throat.

But I didn't missed the contradiction between Rumaisa's description of hosting and Jay Doe's.

"You remember Nimur making the offer to Ibrahim." The pain in my throat made me stop and swallow, but I pressed on after. "Yet Jay D-doe d-didn't expect to recall anything when Nimur t-took her over the other d-day." Our hands pressed tight, our sweat mingling and pooling in the gap between our palms.

"Age," Rumaisa answered, with a bitter chuckle. "The longer I host Nimur, the more I remain aware of my surroundings. It's a sign I don't have much longer to go as a host."

"Makes sense."

"Everything makes sense here or no sense at all. No in-between." Rumaisa let go of me and wiped her palm against her pants. Faster than lightning, she grabbed hold again.

"I've heard fifty is the usual span for a host."

"Yes. A year or two more, and the role will pass from me to someone newer to the house." Her head tilted back, eyes half-closed and expression distant. "Seems like yesterday."

"What?"

"When Nimur came for me."

I breathed as quiet as a mouse. Her grasp eased as she spoke, as though confiding helped.

"I had never heard of Nimur before they appeared, after a landslide destroyed my village. My home. My family. I survived, but under earth. Unable to see. Feeling the air around me grow staler with each breath." Her hand slipped from mine, and she entwined her fingers over her heart. "Then *they* came and said it was not my time to die. I might live and render service, caring for those things lost or forgotten to the world, though known to God, if I would but take their hand."

She sat still and quiet for a moment, then whispered something to herself. Bent over almost doubled before the rising sun. Light glittered around her and warmth rolled off into the air as breezes danced and tugged at the ends of Jay Doe's scarf.

"And here I am." She gave an oblique gesture at the surrounding landscape.

"And a host." I sat up, keeping the blanket over my lap and legs.

"One of two hosts." Rumaisa touched Ibrahim's arm again.

Again the emphasis on two versus three. "Why should it matter?"

"Did you meet up with Ibrahim in the night and fight him?" She lifted a brow as she nodded at my neck. "Strangle him and he fought you off?"

"No!" My hands flew to my neck, an unthinking gesture that only served to reawaken the dull ache in the muscles and skin.

"I didn't think so." Her kind smile held a hint of indulgence.

My stomach grumbled. Her smile broadened as she dug in her bag for an apple, which she polished and handed to me.

"That means someone else did." Her expression turned solemn, every hint of a smile vanishing. "We stopped for the night in a place removed from all other people, completely unconnected to any other landscape. Yet you somehow stumbled here from wherever you camped—in the midst of a fog, a very convenient fog. Haru has gone to find Silvestre and Liam, but she will take her time about bringing them back. For the odds of anyone beyond the six of us being near are long."

I bit into the apple, sweet flesh and juices filling my mouth. My appetite vanished, but I forced myself to finish the fruit all the same. "You think one of them attacked us?"

Rumaisa held up both hands, three fingers raised on each. "It was not you, or I, or Ibrahim," she turned down two fingers on the right and one on the left, "and I swear Haru is clear as well, for she and I searched the fog together." Another finger went down on the right. "Only two possibilities remain, acting in concert, or one of them alone."

"Why?"

"I don't know. But Ibrahim's injury changes everything."

She stood, dusting off the few grains of sand clinging to her trousers.

"You said he isn't a host anymore. Does it matter? Do you need a third soon, or Nimur and the House will fall over like when a tripod loses one of its legs?" I struggled to my feet, grappling with the blanket. Bad enough to be inadequately dressed compared to her, but worse to also be seated and craning my neck to see her face.

"Nimur is hardly a tripod." Her lips twitched as she watched me fumble to wrap the blanket around my waist. "Hosting is not . . . It ebbs and flows between us. Three or four is the best number for sharing the burden. Five is too many; two too few. And there are now only two."

For all her smiles and sharp glances, strain showed clear on her face. New lines fanned out from her eyes. A small tic fluttered along one side of her jaw, and moisture oozed from her forehead despite the mild temperature and even though she hadn't done much more than sit next to me for several minutes.

A memory flash whipped through me, not Madeline's but my own although it took me the same way as hers. Hands fastened around my throat. Rumaisa and Haru called for Ibrahim. Then a muttered curse resounded in my ears, as the strangling grasp released.

Because the attacker had heard them coming? Or realized I wasn't Rumaisa?

"What happens if you go down to only one host?" I gave up on the blanket and let it pool around my ankles. Goosebumps flared along my legs, but subsided quickly.

"Dangerous   instability.   Discordance.   Destruction." Rumaisa tilted her head to one side. "Why?"

"What if whoever strangled me was after you? I mean there's no reason to attack *me*." I shrugged and threw out my hands to either side—only to have Rumaisa shake her head.

"On the contrary, people from the outside world are at the greatest disadvantage and danger the farther into the House they venture. Too many of the oldest Forgotten fear sorcerers, convinced the living seek to carry their true names outside and remember them. Why else would Tiy send so few sorcerers in search of Nimur? Only you and the other, accompanying the team tracking the path from the place Nimur and Jay Doe vanished." Yet even as she explained the danger I faced—something no one else had got around to mentioning—her gaze grew distant. Then furrows appeared in her brow and her lips parted in a snarl. "Yet if the attacker meant to injure me and Ibrahim, to the point neither of us sufficed to serve as host, only Jay Doe whom they already have captive . . ."

Her head whipped around at the sound of voices in the distance.

Rumaisa's hand fastened around my wrist and she pressed a finger against my lips. "Keep this to yourself and let no sign show. If Liam or Silvestre is indeed intending to take the House through Jay Doe, you are the greatest threat. There is no one else nearby to take the load. Be ready."

Silvestre or Liam, Liam or Silvestre. Why would either—but I couldn't disagree with her logic. I wrapped the blanket around me, keeping my head down, as Haru, Liam, and Silvestre arrived bearing backpacks and solemn faces. All dressed as before, and none with any sign of injury or mark to indicate they'd spent part of the night walking around in the fog.

One and all showed horror and shock at Ibrahim's condition and mine.

Haru asked me to tilt my head around and inspected the damage remaining. Her gentle hands traced a line or two.

Silvestre prayed over me, inscribing crosses in the air, then turned to Liam and held out a hand palm up.

Liam dug into his bag and pulled out a bottle with a few drops of water of life.

"Better to save it." Rumaisa flashed her own bottle at them, equally low. "We may need the remaining drops later, as there won't be more until Nimur is free."

Neither Silvestre nor Liam accepted Rumaisa's assessment of Ibrahim's condition without checking him—which did not include news his hostship had passed. They touched him with care as they inspected his bruises.

No one managed to explain how the beach we'd camped on became aligned with where Haru, Rumaisa, and Ibrahim slept. They shared lots of guesses and talk, only a tenth of which I understood in no small part because they slipped from language to language without missing a beat or remembering I might not follow along.

After only a few minutes of this, Rumaisa clapped her hands. "Enough. We need to take Ibrahim to safety, and find Nimur and Jay Doe."

Haru gestured along the beach. "I can lead us to a retreat with only one change of landscape required. We'll need to bring Ibrahim."

She cast meaningful glances at Liam and Silvestre, who promptly volunteered. But it turned out not to mean them carrying his body. They floated him through the air.

The preparations gave me time to steal away with my backpack, complete with everything I'd packed. I dressed in suitable clothes—uniform shirt, jeans, and sneakers. Sweat soaked my nightgown, and I fumbled more than I should in changing.

By the time I returned, everyone was ready to set off. Haru and Rumaisa went first, then Ibrahim's body floated along between Silvestre and Liam.

I followed.

The grass-covered dunes on our land-side shifted between

one step and the next. The ground diverged. Hard-packed earth formed a thin beach along a rise of deep red-brown rock. The stones gleamed in the morning sun. In the distance, the difference between shore and cliff-top increased dramatically within a matter of feet.

Instead of rising with the cliff, Haru led us along the shore. White-capped waves crashed and sent ripples of water racing toward us. Each fell short, as the tide ebbed. The mass of rock loomed over us, higher with every step. Ten, twenty, thirty feet and more. Easier to deal with from the bottom staring up—but only as long as the tide kept going out.

Several lengths ahead, a second cliff, or a track up to the top, rose from the beach. Same deep red-brown rock as before. Baby-sized compared to the other high above, and only three or four feet wide. The top proved smooth enough to walk on, and Haru led the way along it.

Silvestre and Liam paused to catch their breath and trade places, fore and aft, as they kept Ibrahim's body floating along between them.

I waited to go last, so as not to be in Silvestre and Liam's way. To catch my breath. To brace myself for climbing up a narrow track with a cliff face on one side and no barrier guarding dropping off the other.

To give myself enough space to cast spells checking for danger all around me. Rumaisa's suspicion the villain accompanied us ensured my skin prickled every time Silvestre or Liam glanced my way. If she guessed right, did either of them consider me a danger?

Though she hadn't offered any reason why they'd turn attacker.

My steps slowed and I fell farther behind.

An all-too familiar burst of nothingness and cold whipped through me, then the cliff changed and the sun altered its place in the sky from dawning to late afternoon or vice versa.

Shadows swallowed the whole of the path, which narrowed to only two feet wide. Below, the beach vanished. White-capped waves crashed against sharp, dark rocks sticking up from the seabed. The air held the sting of brine; this sea smelled the opposite of the one we searched for.

I forced my lungs to take in deep breaths after two or three shallow, sobbing ones. My left hand scrabbled for purchase against the stony wall still rising twenty or more feet above. I grabbed hold of an outcropping: dull, sandy-brown rocks instead of ones gleaming with red highlights.

Rough to the touch, the cliff face had a pitted appearance. Cave mouths marked the wide expanse, in all sizes and depths.

I caught up with the others as Liam guided Ibrahim's feet through an opening not much wider than the path.

The wind hadn't blown hard until I reached the narrow, arched opening. A sudden gust wrapped around me.

"Turn back." The chill rush of air moaned. *"Abandon hope. Only those who are Forgotten may enter here."*

As soon as Liam's heel passed through, the opening vanished. Rock filled the air before me. I ran my hands across it three times, four, to check and double check. Tried closing my eyes and walking ahead, but took a layer of skin off my nose and palms as a result.

"Hey! D-don't leave me."

Wrapping my arms over my chest, I turned around with care. Knocked a pebble off the path and leapt back against the cliff face as it skittered down. The wind died down enough to let me absorb every ping as the small stone hit the immense wall—and even the plop as it dropped into the roiling waters.

"Hold tight."

Haru's voice, or I'd have fought when she grabbed my shoulders and yanked me backward. A wave of relief flooded through me, relaxing my muscles for a few moments. Yellow and orange light flashed as something zapped me. The stench of burnt hair made me choke. Bits of ash covered my shoulders, light gray against the shirt.

I sagged against a stone wall, patting my hair to be sure I still had most of it. A small antechamber surrounded us, large enough for five people to stand in and with a single seat carved out of the wall for someone to sit on. The stone here held layers of luminescent rock providing light to see, but softening all colors—the grayish light of twilight or dawn.

At the far end, far being no more than a few paces away, lay stairs carved through the stone. Chiseled, given the marks, and no doubt by hand, but long, long ago.

"I didn't forget you." Haru patted my shoulder, glancing over at the stair. "I wouldn't have, even if we didn't need you."

Thumps and cries to "watch out" and "easy now" indicated Silvestre and Liam took Ibrahim wherever the stair led.

A broad-chested man no taller than Haru or I appeared at the base of the stairway, blocking the way. His blue-black skin gleamed as though recently rubbed with lotion or oil. A necklace of opalescent shells hung around his neck, falling to midchest. He wore a knee-length skirt or kilt of gray fabric and no shoes. He ran a hand over his close-shaven head as he squinted at me.

"I had to give her visitor rights." He clicked his tongue. "Won't be a way of keeping her out again."

"I doubt she'll ever find her way back." Haru acknowledged his words, but turned a skeptical gaze my way. "Will you?"

"Not hardly," I croaked. Coughed, swallowing a mouthful of dust, then pulled a bottle of water from my backpack and drank until the dryness went away. The stranger hadn't taken his eyes from me, so I raised the bottle in his direction. "I lost track of where we went yesterday. If I ever get back to D.C., I'm not sure I'll *ever* venture this way again."

"There's truth enough." His lips turned up at the corners, though it didn't count as a smile. "You may speak of what you see here, I won't withhold it from you, but only with those who already know."

"Okay." I pushed away from the wall, straightening to my full height, all of a half-inch taller than him. "How will *I* know?"

The words escaped me, but low enough he shouldn't have heard. Haru yes, but him no. Except the room's acoustics evidently carried. He smiled as he turned away and headed up the stairs.

"You'll know." Haru gave my shoulder a last squeeze before following in his wake. "Come, see where those who did not choose to Sleep are taken to rest and heal."

Again I took last place and trailed behind others. The benefits included no one nipping at my heels or breathing down my neck, plus the sure knowledge everyone ahead of me had found somewhere to go since no one turned back. At most, I occasionally caught a glimpse of Haru's heels and the hem of her coat.

The stairs switched back-and-forth, going deeper and deeper into the cliff. Assuming we still walked inside a cliff. At this point, we might have moved into a mountain or a windowless castle tower.

My world shrank into a series of narrow passages smelling variously of brine, dust, and a mix of mint and jasmine. All with stairs and low-hanging ceilings that regularly required stooping to avoid banging my brains.

Every single section stretched wide enough for only one person. The guardian, for lack of anything better to call him, might be short, but he must've worked some spell to pass

Rumaisa going up as he came down—much less Silvestre and Liam with Ibrahim.

To keep focused, I counted steps. Much as I wanted to tote up the switchbacks, too, I gave up after the second because each passage had a different number of steps. Ten the first, then eleven, then seventeen.

Despite rising higher, I had no trouble breathing. My legs ached from the climb, and I pulled over to stop and lean against the walls a couple of times, but in the end I made it.

Two hundred and twenty-six steps.

The last five widened enough for three or four people to pass abreast. An arch rose overhead, all gray stone except the key at the center, which had a ruddy cast reminiscent of the red-brown cliffs.

On the other side lay an immense circular cave or chamber, probably cave given the lack of windows. The walls of gray stone had a soft cast as though they might be soft or nonexistent to the touch. Rather reminiscent of the fog I'd sloughed through earlier, though brushing my fingers left thin scrapes across the tips. They existed without ornamentation, as did the matching floor.

Light filtered down from the roof high overhead—at least two stories, maybe three. As with the stairway and antechamber below, it had a grayish cast as though I stood in a place of twilight and dawn, never day or night. The temperature fluctuated between cold and hot without rhyme or rhythm. I shivered or sweated or sighed in relief, but in reflex because it didn't matter anywhere near as much as what faced me.

Beds.

Lots and lots of beds of so many different kinds. Futons, piles of fur, a round bag of sweet grasses.

Farther to the left, a big four-poster capable of sleeping three or four adults easy, complete with tapestry curtains of red and green. Beyond hung a hammock woven out of bark, fastened to two solid, healthy palm trees, each stretching nearly to the ceiling. To the right sat a wooden frame. Ropes tied long-ways and width-ways formed a net.

Each and every bed contained or supported an unmoving body, representing a mélange of races, ages, and appearances.

At the center of the room, Silvestre and Liam kept Ibrahim suspended in the air. A tall Forgotten with almost-white skin and pale yellow hair stood beside them. She wore a floor-length gown of gray wool, with thick bands of gold and purple embroidery at the neck and hem. Their low tones echoed throughout the chamber yet I couldn't make out a single word.

A third Forgotten with skin of burnished gold and thick black hair paced a wide circle around the others. His modern green scrubs and white sneakers made for a stark contrast with the others.

Rumaisa kept him company, also speaking in soft voices. Apart from the echoes, none of their words registered.

I remained near the door with Haru and the other Forgotten, who hadn't introduced himself, by my side.

"Where are we?"

"This has many names, but you may call me Chiron," the Forgotten tilted his head, one corner of his mouth twitching into a hint of a smile, "and this Chiron's retreat."

Given he'd claimed the name of a famous centaur, I snuck a glance at his very human legs.

"Most who Sleep do so by choice, which means they also choose where. This is one of the places reserved for those Forgotten who didn't consciously decide to Sleep. Their bodies insisted, to allow time for them to heal." Haru nodded at the different beds, and the unmoving figures within them.

"You mean Ibrahim won't wake up?" My gaze snapped to Ibrahim's body still floating at the center of the room—as unmoving as any of the others who Slept. "I thought you said he'd recover."

"He will, but we who live long lives on the cusp of death do not heal with speed." Chiron gestured for Haru and me to follow as he turned away from those at the center. "He may rest here for months, years, or decades. Some require centuries before healing enough to wake."

A metallic taste blossomed in my mouth. I pressed a hand hard against my belly, swallowing hard. Not only had Ibrahim lost being a host, whoever attacked him had stolen a chunk of his life—and the guilty party was likely one of the men helping ease Ibrahim's body into a place of rest.

Chiron took a circular route around the perimeter of the chamber, away from where the others headed. The other new Forgotten joined Silvestre and Liam in ushering Ibrahim's form away. Rumaisa followed, turning once. Her eyes met mine, dark and intent despite the distance between us, and she gave a sharp nod.

As we walked, a blurriness stole over the bodies. Invisible veils divided resting place from resting place, and the beds from casual passersby. A nice touch, protecting the vulnerable from being seen unconscious.

Even among the wide variety of sleeping arrangements, one in particular stood out. Blue-green water filled a thick, rectangular stone enclosure. Despite the blurriness, the body suspended in the water showed evidence of gross burns.

The crackle of wood burning filled my ears. Smoke poured into my mouth and nose, making me cough.

The movement dislodged the memories, not from Madeline but my recent nightmare.

Perhaps this Sleeper had suffered from Sandoval's attack, the other victim burned before Forgotten intervened.

My pace slowed, feet sliding across the stone rather than striding.

Chiron grimaced as he gestured for me to catch up. "Everyone here has injuries only time can cure," he said when I drew close again. "Those there are whose talismans I'd find and see carried outside, if I did but know where to locate them."

"We search, as we can." A similarly grim expression passed over Haru's face. "I'll pledge another try, once this task is done. One day they'll heal and wake—or we'll see them remembered."

The farther we walked, the more our arrangement shifted. Instead of Chiron leading Haru and me, we became a line of three across.

"Are you a doctor or healer?" I asked.

Chiron paused before answering. "I work here at this time. Always some do, to keep the Sleepers safe and welcome back those who wake. Four now, the three of us here and the last who prepares your way back to the rest of the House."

At which he escorted us to a section of the chamber with no beds, only piles of thin, flat cushions in all colors surrounding a low table. The nearby wall stood as a rare straight section in an otherwise circular chamber. It had three entryways. To the right lay an elaborate affair of gilded columns and an arch over a pair of doors heavy with gold and brass, on the left a plain single door of weathered gray wood, and in the center a set of louvered batwing doors in ebony.

A sudden quake rattled through the chamber. The vibrations passed from one side to another, trackable as bed after bed shook or swayed in turn. Overhead, the light flickered and a gust of heat wrapped around me, followed by chill. I had my feet planted firm, but still swayed and nearly fell.

"The third time this day." Chiron wiped sweat from his forehead with the back of a hand.

"Nimur's trying to escape. We aim to find them." Haru

settled down among the cushions. "Either way, so long as they're freed."

"May you both succeed." He walked over to one side, and pulled from the wall a series of multi-paneled painted screens. Some gilded and others plain white, but all bore images. Cranes in water here. A tree in spring blossom there. A winter branch against a ruddy sun over tempestuous waves.

"He's keeping watch, to ensure the others do not approach without warning. Rumaisa will keep Silvestre and Liam occupied for as long as she can. She promised to fuss over settling Ibrahim in to rest and heal." She nodded for me to take a seat.

I settled on a pile of cushions, sinking down. Overhead, the faint gleam of a cone of silence rose along the edges of the screens to enfold us in quiet.

Nothing from outside broke it.

Nerves suddenly all a-jangle, my hand rose automatically to touch the healing bruises at my throat. I forced it down into my lap, twining my fingers.

"Do you trust me?" She sat straight and poised, yet tension vibrated from her.

"Some."

"What of Tiy, do you trust her?"

"Yeah." I nodded.

"Call her."

I glanced at the cone of silence surrounding us. Still, this wasn't the mundane world but the House. Different rules prevailed. Pulling out my phone, I called the admin suite and set it to speaker.

"Museum of All Things Lost and Forgotten, how may I help you?"

The sound of Yolanda's voice eased me. I huffed as I set the phone on the table between Haru and myself.

"This is Haru, is Tiy there?"

"Have you located them?" Barely a breath passed between Haru's words and Tiy's. She must've been right there.

"No, though we're close." Haru bent forward, resting her hands against the table's edge. "It's complicated."

"Go ahead."

"My group and Silvestre's somehow crossed paths. In the night—and not by chance." Haru clasped her hands together, knuckles whitening. "A thick fog arose. Someone used this as cover to strangle Ibrahim. They also tried for Rumaisa, or so we suspect, but got Bea instead. She's sore, but all right."

"Bea?" Yolanda asked, distant but audible.

"I'm okay. Mostly." I swallowed, wincing as residual quivers of pain sparked around my neck.

"Good. You take care," Yolanda said.

"How is Ibrahim?" Tiy asked.

"He lives, but Sleeps and is no longer a host." Haru lifted her clenched hands to press against her chin, a low growl escaping. "I didn't arrange the overlap, nor Ibrahim nor Bea, nor Rumaisa to my knowledge for I choose our resting place. The odds are against an unknown stranger having found and tied us all together. That leaves Silvestre and Liam. One or the other is in league with whomever reft Nimur away—or is the villain."

A thump came through from the other end. The phone shook and rattled atop the table, skittering sideways.

I grabbed my pants and twisted the fabric between my fingers—better than touching, again, the bruises around my neck.

"Silvestre has made no bones of his interest in power, but this is a tortured way to obtain it. Liam has shown no desire to rule, but he's also never fully recovered from failing to save Eriselda." A heavy sigh escaped Tiy, residual flurries of air somehow transmitting across the distance to flutter my and Haru's hair. "I would not have guessed this of either, but I agree all indications are one is involved or responsible."

"More, this may be the work of only one person or a very small group. Rumaisa has been as much in communication with Jay Doe as is possible—and since they were left tied up no one has been near them. We suspect the objective is to reduce Nimur to only one host and then . . ." Haru's mouth opened and closed several times. Loosening her hands, she wrapped them around the edge of the table, leaning closer to the phone.

But her eyes fixed on me. A trickle of cold ran up my spine.

"I propose a test, to bring us closer to Nimur and Jay Doe, and confirm or deny who is our villain. When we know . . . I hunted their names and I have both. I will share the villain's with Bea, and send her outside for remembrance."

Blood rushed from my head, leaving me dizzy. The world wavered around me as my torso inscribed minute circles in the air. I already had one set of memories atop my own to deal with, though at least the sense of Madeline's presence had started to ease.

She wanted me to take another?

The villain?

Bad enough to consider taking bad memories. Remembering kidnapping Nimur. Assaulting Ibrahim. Strangling myself.

Worse if I witnessed from the other side the life of someone who'd worked with me.

"Hmm." Tiy grunted, then sighed. "As well you do know their names."

"This is all well and good, but Bea hasn't recovered from remembering Madeline yet." Yolanda said, jumping into a brief silence. "She'll have to get all the way from . . . wherever you are, to out of the museum." A deep breath and then she went on. "I'm closer to the door and can move fast. I volunteer. You-could-call-me-and-share-the-name."

A sudden warmth bloomed in me, driving out all the tremors. Everything seemed brighter, until Haru shook her head.

"I wish I might." Haru ran a hand through her hair, dislodging strands as she cupped the phone. "It is not possible. Anyone who picks up a talisman may take it outside, but names . . . Unless Nimur is involved, true names must be spoken by the sharer and heard by the rememberer *while in the presence* of the person who will be remembered."

"As a precaution to prevent enemies from learning a name and passing it along while safely far away." Tiy huffed again. "I am sorry, Bea, but if it is of any comfort, you won't be the first to face more than one remembrance in a short span of time."

"It also means the person being remembered has a chance to resist." Once again Haru stared at me, eyes dark and warning.

"So when Haru tells you, run!" Yolanda said.

Haru moved around the table to sit next to me. She didn't touch me in any way, or even glance my way anymore. Nevertheless, the heat from her body slowly thawed my outer shell. "Trust us."

"We need your help." Tiy echoed, voice turning thick and almost tinny.

"You're sure you'll know who?" I ducked my head, watching the dark screen of the phone instead. "That it's one of them?"

"This only worked because Jay Doe's talisman is large and can be wrapped around her and Nimur." Haru breathed, waited, then continued. "I'm sure. If you think about it, you know too."

I shook my head, refusing to agree, but my mouth opened.

For Nimur.

For Jay Doe.

For Ibrahim.

My voice shrank to a mere croak. "Okay. I'll do it."

A solid thump vibrated through the stone floor to set my bones rattling for a moment. Another earthquake? Haru leapt to her feet and gestured for me to rise.

"They're coming. We'll check in as we can."

"Go and do well," Tiy said, echoed by Yolanda.

Haru snatched the phone and ended the call, then passed it over to me. The cone of silence dissolved. Moments later, Rumaisa, Silvestre, and Liam rounded the far corner of the screens.

Before either said anything, the weathered wooden door behind us opened with a creak. A new Forgotten appeared out of gray, misty shadows. An actual elder, with thinning white curls topping a pale brown head. A royal purple toga draped over their long, tall body, with narrow toes peeping under the hem. A single survey of the lot of us, and they nodded to Haru and Rumaisa.

"The passage is ready."

"Well?" Haru extended a hand toward Rumaisa.

Her shoulders rounded as she lifted Jay Doe's scarf from around her neck. She passed the length over her lips; the cloth caught her whispers, without letting them spread more widely.

Another quake shook the room. Lights wobbled, and the temperature rose precipitously for a moment. My face flushed as I grabbed hold of the wall; small comfort everyone else's did as well. As soon as the shock ended, Rumaisa let go of the doorknob she'd clung to and paced around behind me.

"May I bind this over your eyes?"

"What?" A glance back showed her holding the scarf, doubled or tripled over.

"One may enter places such as this from nearly anywhere—and likewise exit wherever we choose." Haru gestured at the open door. "You will make the choice, you and Jay Doe."

"Okay."

I drew in a sharp breath as Rumaisa came up behind me. Her body pressed close against my back, in the same manner as the person who'd strangled me. A set of tremors racked me, and I bit my lip. Grabbed my pants with my hands to keep from knocking hers away as they rose to either side of my head. She didn't touch my neck, which ached anew as she laid the folded pink-and-green cloth over my eyes.

My eyes closed and the world went dark. Someone, Haru by brief pressure of a watch against my cheek, adjusted the folds. Her deft fingers tied the scarf tight around my head.

No sound of Jay Doe or Nimur. The fresh, clean sea scent burst anew within my nose with every shaky breath.

Rumaisa set her hands on my shoulders and Haru took my hands. The two of them led me to the doorway. The flow of air altered, slipping past me and rising up.

"Focus on what you remember of where the talisman is. Smell, touch, taste, sounds, everything but sight." Rumaisa patted my back as she stepped back.

Protests danced on the tip of my tongue, but I'd agreed to go along with the plan. To trust Rumaisa, Haru, and Tiy.

"The stairway is similar to the one you walked to get here, with walls on both sides. This, however, has railings on both sides for you to hold onto." Her hands tapped mine. I let go of my pants begrudgingly, and she lifted my hands to rest on the railings.

As promised, they existed left and right, except they weren't really railings. More protruding ledges of stone about even with my hips.

"Lead us as close as you can to Nimur," Haru said.

"And Jay Doe," Rumaisa added.

The smell of the sea filled my nose. I remembered back to when I'd touched Madeline-Jeanne's talisman: the feel of the narrow chamber, crash of waves in the distance.

An intangible barrier lay between me and the first step. Cold damp air mixed and rippled across my skin raising pins and needles everywhere. But it let me through, to start climbing narrow, uneven stairs chiseled from the rock. I hunched my shoulders against the closed-in feel as the stairway allowed only one person to pass at a time.

I started counting.

At fifteen steps, we made the first switch-back.

Fifty, and the stone ledges vanished. Wooden railings took their place. I rested my hands on those lightly because the wood seemed half-rotten and at risk of giving me splinters.

Eighty-nine, and the wood shifted to metal, slick but firmly fastened to the stone walls.

One hundred and thirty-two, and my fingers ran over pits and evidence of rust on the metal. A sea roared in the distance in my ears. The fresh, clean scent grew stronger, but the air grew dense and hard to breathe. Prickles of pain sparkled all over my body, in an unpredictable pattern.

Eleven more steps and the stairs and rails vanished. No walls either. I stumbled through a doorway onto rocks. Nearly fell, but caught my balance in time.

A breeze twisted around me, carrying the familiar scent. At last, utterly and entirely right.

I yanked the scarf off, losing a few hairs. A wide vista stretched out to either side: gray-blue waters rolling up against a wide swathe of sand dune grasses.

The shell of an upturned ship loomed over me. An old one, given gray wooden slats formed the hull. Holes where the wood rotted away revealed a lovely blue sky above, with wisps of white clouds. Apart from an occasional wind, the air lay still and slightly chilly.

A mound of sand started to give way as I moved forward. Rumaisa slipped Jay Doe's scarf from my hand as she passed. Buried her head in the folds briefly, then raised it to gaze down the beach.

At the far end a great mound of earth rose high into the sky topped with a castle, gray and picturesque against the blue, blue sky.

Silvestre and Liam followed, Haru last of all.

She stopped next to me, arm brushing mine.

Bent and scooped up a handful of sand.

"Where are we?"

I didn't hear an answer, but she nodded and let the grains trickle between opened fingers. Her shoulders rounded and head hung low. Swaying to the side, she leaned against me. Cupped a hand against my ear and whispered a name. As with Madeline's true name, the syllables didn't register. Yet this time, the name didn't become a heavy weight in my head. It sat lighter, but sharper, as though I balanced a knife point against my brain.

Liam or Silvestre, Silvestre or Liam. I glanced back-and-forth between them for a long moment.

Then, for the second time in nearly as many days, someone ordered me to run.

❧ 8 ❧

UNREMEMBERED

I ran.

Thick, humid air nearly choked me until I switched to breathing in through my nose and out through my mouth. My sweatpants fit loose enough to allow for a full range of movement, but I yanked my shirt tail out so it fell over my pants, rather than bunching up at my waist.

The uneven beach proved a beast to cross. Though the sand appeared smooth to the eye, every step required adjusting and adapting. First my toes ended up enough lower than my heel to pitch me forward. Fortunately, I moved fast enough and managed to land on my other foot, albeit harder than expected. My ankle wavered, but I pressed on—and nearly tripped into a hole.

Moving closer to the water helped even things out, but not enough. Every step still differed from the others, unpredictably. Grains of sand clung to my pants, some sifting down into my shoes and socks.

My phone shifted about in my pocket. Magic kept it from falling out, but it moved with every lurching step. Almost as though keeping time, or marking my progress or lack thereof.

Because I ran across a beach! With no trees or shelter anywhere in sight, and the Forgotten could see where I went no matter where.

I didn't hear any thuds behind, but would I with the wind blowing into me?

Better to assume someone chased me and be proven wrong than the other way around.

Regardless, I needed to get out of sight.

Move indoors.

Find my way back to the museum exhibit halls.

Then exit into the outside world.

No biggie.

First things first: escape the beach. Any part of the House connected to any other part as long as they had something in common. Focusing on the commonality forced the connection. Therefore, I needed a landscape that shared something with this. Preferably to speed my way toward the outside, not back at whomever might chase me.

The best option involved knocking off two items on the list and shifting to a landscape with a building big enough to have an interior door. Maintain a good pace and get inside, then start navigating my way to the museum proper.

Small problem: the shore stretched out as level ground for miles. Well, mostly level ground since anyone pelting across it wouldn't call it flat. A mucking big castle loomed, but much further away than I wanted to run.

What if I turned around? And moved to a new landscape also flat as far as the eye could see, to make it similar enough, but with a closer building—such as a house. Anything larger than a hut, so long as it had an interior door.

On the count of three.

One. Two.

I pivoted. The world stopped for a moment. Everything went black. Nothing to breathe. Instead of creepy-crawlies, my skin prickled as though a million pins-and-needles tapped away.

Then I jerked back. Whirled around and came to an abrupt halt.

No one behind me. No ocean only feet away. Air still humid, but a little warmer. Sun farther in the sky, though no way of saying whether it shone in the east or west or whatever direction.

The beach had changed into overgrown fields. I slogged through grasses grown waist high. Half proved stiff and dry, the rest still green and flexible. My pants protected my skin from scrapes, except for my ankles where the blades of some short, scrubby grasses amidst the tall lashed across the skin at the edge between socks and pant hem. Bits of chaff or seeds floated in the air, but nothing that made me sneeze.

A building did indeed loom before me. I only had to wade through the neglected lawn to reach it . . . and figure out which way to enter.

A palace rose at least three stories high, each story at least ten feet based on the tall windows. A red, tiled roof soared above, along with a tower over the central wing. Painted plaster overlaid brick walls, chipped here and there but still showing intricate geometric designs in shades of red and gold.

The main front door opened into an entryway two stories high: the second and third stories. Two curved stone staircases led from the drive up to the door. Or I might pass between them and enter on the lower level.

Every window on the first floor had metal grills over the glass panes. Didn't seem friendly or approachable. Even from a distance, the front door appeared left ajar.

What I knew about grand houses came from mostly from watching films, reading books, and working in the museum. The first floor might be for family, with servants' quarters and kitchens and stuff in other wings and the family quarters above.

Since I'd manifested a big house, I wanted to find the library. There had to be one, surely, with direct or close access to the book display in the museum. Or if not this house, then another such.

I aimed for the front door, to work my way through this house or whatever other country houses or palaces it led to—and find a book room somewhere.

Easier said than done.

My legs ached and feet slid around in my sneakers by the time I reached the right-hand stairway.

No sign of any pursuit, so I stopped and sat on the stone to retie my shoelaces. Clouds skittered across the sky, but the sun shone on the far side of the house. The west side, since the stone railing held residual warmth suggesting direct sunlight heated it earlier. In the shadow, the sweat drying along my spine chilled me.

The house would likely be worse, cooler and maybe damp.

Stone made for an uncomfortable seat. Pushing up, I grabbed hold of the stone railing and half-climbed, half-pulled myself up step after step.

Blood pounded in my face. I wiped sweat from my forehead with the back of a shaky hand. Rather than letting my momentum slow, I forged forward.

The door lay ajar, but only wide enough for a slender cat to slip through. The decorative wood bore faded paint to match the external design, but with the colors reversed. The hinges had stuck, or the floor warped, until I threw my whole weight against it. It swung inward so fast I nearly face-planted on the floor.

Pain bloomed at every point of contact, from hands and knees up my arms and legs. The slate floor didn't give, although the tiles had buckled in places.

Clouds of dust rose to either side. I coughed, covering my mouth and nose. Fumbled to check my pockets, but I'd neglected to bring a water bottle with me.

I clapped my hands together. Snapped my fingers. A minute later, a water bottle slammed into my chest. My breast hurt, but I grabbed it before it fell and rolled off. Plastic and lukewarm, but full and unopened. I nearly tore off the top and downed it in gulps. Had to force myself to stop and breathe between rounds, to ensure I didn't swallow too fast. Another snap of my fingers sent it to a recycling bin in the museum.

Clambering to my feet, I stamped. The slap of shoe sole against the stone echoed in the high ceiling above, but no groaning or creaking to suggest the floor might give way below me.

Once-elaborate wallpaper of green vines and pink flowers covered the walls, save where interrupted by doors. Squares and rectangles appeared brighter where works of art once hung. In a few places, strips of wallpaper started to curl away from the plaster walls behind.

The foyer stretched through the whole of the building. A bank of windows and glass doors at the far end appeared to lead onto a patio.

But not a library.

No furniture remained in any of the rooms leading off the foyer. The one to the right had light yellow wallpaper painted with pseudo-Chinese scenes seemed suitable for a parlor. More importantly, at the far end lay a closed door of dark wood which *might* lead to a library.

Or to a book room.

Even to the book display room.

Holding onto the thought, I strode across the wood floor. Ignored the squeaks and creaks as wood planks shifted beneath my feet.

The door stuck. Of course it did. Thankfully, it wasn't locked. As with the front door, a good heave made it lurch and open.

I stumbled through the doorway and staggered to a stop. Braced my hands against a display table, nearly knocking open books from the table. Familiar displays surrounded me with hundreds of beautiful, colorful books and the soothing smells of leather and parchment and ink.

I'd made it. Leapt from an abandoned house to the museum proper, faster than I'd have dreamed only days before.

Much as I wanted to stay, to rest and recover, I pushed back. Straightened. Braced my hands on either hip and arched my back, spine giving a full series of snaps, crackles, and pops. Dragged in a deep breath, lungs swelling and aching.

Movement at the far end of the room made me start. My elbows pressed tight against my sides, forearms up and hands forming fists.

The hem of a light brown robe swayed over sandaled feet. Long sleeves covered hands. A length of hemp wrapped around a narrow waist.

Though I already realized who I'd see, I waited to the last to lift my eyes to Liam's face.

He didn't even have the grace to huff and or sweat or show anything to suggest he'd chased after me. His complexion remained pale and demeanor calm, a stark contrast to my no doubt flushed face and heaving chest.

Him or Silvestre.

"Why?"

"No need to fear me. I mean you no harm." He stopped a dozen feet away, stretching his arms out to either side. Opened his hands to show he had nothing hidden away.

He still posed a danger. If he'd chased me here, or

somehow leapt ahead, then he'd also attacked me back in the fog. I jerked at the touch of my own cold fingers, having reflexively risen to touch the bruises at my throat. My breathing quickened, drawing and expelling air in an attempt to dispel memories of pressure on my airway.

"I'm sorry." Liam's face crumpled, eyes bright and shoulders slumping.

His clear regret helped ease the remembered tension in my neck and throat. I swallowed and managed to shift to slower, deeper breaths.

Maybe it wasn't him?

"I mistook you for Rumaisa—hadn't realized you'd stumbled across the divide behind me. It won't happen again."

His soft voice, barely above a whisper, set every hair on my arms and legs on end.

A different memory triggered this time, not mine but one I'd lived through second-hand. More than once, or perhaps different times that melded together. His quiet delivery matched exactly the almost innocuous way someone had stood behind Madeline and whispered *"Where's the baby?"*

Then a second recollection—from recent past, of him choosing Jay Doe to come on the hunt for Madeline.

"How d-did you make it here b-before me?" The question slipped out despite the residual ache remaining in my throat. Damage taken at his hands; I touched my neck and winced. Asking might distract him. A classic technique: getting a villain talking until I figured out a way to escape—get out. And then . . .

He smiled, mouth twisting at the ends and gaze going distant.

"I've lived in Memory's House for over a thousand years, long enough to learn many shortcuts beyond those I've shown you. As well, time enough to see through the facade to what lies below." He rested his left hand on a square table supporting a single object: an immense Chinese scroll partly unrolled to show a delicate drawing of fish. "It's of that I would speak with you."

He braced himself so casually, but in a posture from which he might leap into action on a moment's notice. He'd left space between us, but blocked the way to the doors at the end, the straightest way down into the museum foyer. The other doors might let me go sideways and then out, or send me further away.

I wasn't trapped, but I couldn't go back either. My leg muscles had started to quiver from all the exertion. My best option involved moving forward and out as fast as possible.

In other words, through him.

He might be thinking the same about me. But he died only if I escaped and spoke his name outside. I had a lot more vulnerabilities.

I needed something to defend myself, if he chose to attack. Snatching up the closest book, I slammed the covers together and held it in front of me. Simple, smooth leather barely touched with gold leaf warmed to my touch. Despite the centuries since its creation, the binding smelled as though fresh from the tanner; the leather carried a residual urine stench.

"No, please. Do not fear me." Liam remained in place save for raising his right hand, palm out. "I swear upon everything I hold sacred, I will not hurt you nor so much as touch a hair on your head. All I ask is a little time, to share and show what is wrong, and what I seek to fix."

"Swear? On what?" My arms shook, the book proving much heavier than I'd expected.

"Upon the word of the Gospels you hold in your arms, and I hold dear to my heart." He traced three crosses, over forehead, mouth, and heart. "Put down the book, stay where you are, and listen. That's all I ask. I will not move any closer."

Stay or go, listen or not, hold onto book or set it down . . .

I lowered the book, since I couldn't keep it upraised much longer. Instead of replacing it on the table, I clutched it against my chest—ready to raise in my defense as needed.

Liam shuffled his feet, he approached no closer. His face never turned away from me, gaze fixed.

"I do not seek power or treasure, or even control of the House. I'm trying to free Ge-mimor, Nimur." Again he stretched his arms wide as though desirous of grabbing everything in the room—in the museum—into a single embrace. "Free us all."

"I d-don't g-get it." I hugged the book closer, its corners digging into my arms and belly. Swallowed hard, the ache in my throat a reminder he'd attacked me—and been wrong even by his lights.

"We're trapped here. It took so long to realize it. Sandoval was wrong about witches cursing us, but right to peel away the gilt glossing and examine the rot beneath. A hard endeavor, to realize how thoroughly we all have fooled ourselves. I understand why others haven't yet seen it, at least those who are awake. Perhaps the Sleepers understand, but have given up."

He shivered, body folding in on itself. Hands raised in front of his face, fingers clawing at the empty air.

I didn't move.

"Nothing truly changes, do you understand? Oh, more lost and forgotten—things, places, people—are added all the time, but nothing ever goes away. We're stuck, unable to move forward or back. Neither alive nor dead, but suspended between." His head tilted back, neck muscles pulling taut and agony clear on his face. "We continue to exist, but separated from all that is good in the world. Worse, from God."

My feet remained in place, as though glued to the carpet.

"It's not Ge-mimor's fault. They're caught too. Turned inside out into Mis-gemynd. Evil memory. Unable to do anything but the same thing over and over, ever inviting more Forgotten to join our ranks. You saw the Sleepers who didn't choose to rest. There are many more who chose to Sleep because they cannot face this life nor are they willing to commit suicide to leave it." He made a wide circle with his arm. In the space outlined, image after image flashed of the Forgotten in all different numbers and resting places, from castle bedrooms to quiet clearings to desert sands, each and every one lying huddled in Sleep. "There are hundreds, thousands more elsewhere. All trapped. Captured and unable to make amends, repent, and seek God's forgiveness. We are all imprisoned here."

My torso swayed, shoulders inscribing minute ovals in the air.

"Give me time, a little is all I ask. Only so long as a day, no more, to explain to Haru." The images of Sleeping Forgotten continued to manifest in the air, never once repeating. Liam ignored the colors and somnolent faces as he turned to match me head-on—without coming any closer. "She's nearly as old as I, and surely aware of the ever-narrowing confines of our lives here. Our living deaths."

He stretched out a hand. "Hold my name within you for a little longer. Then ask Haru before setting it free in the world. I do not mind being remembered for myself, but let me finish the work of freeing the others first. That I not have to face God's judgment with the sin of seeing them struggle in captivity and having done nothing to free them."

Liam's earnestness washed over me. He'd found me more than once when I strayed off the way. He'd walked me back, patiently offering advice on how not to get lost too often. Told me, even then, sometimes the better course involved turning around and retracing one's steps rather than go further and farther into the unknown.

I met him my first day at the museum, when he slipped into the orientation room in Silvestre's wake. By any count, I'd known him for months, versus a few days for Haru, who considered he needed to be stopped.

Until then, I'd have said up, down, and sideways I trusted Liam.

But this talk of being trapped . . .

I trapped myself. Unable to move or do anything but watch his illusion. Face after face of Sleeping Forgotten melted from one to another. So many.

Ibrahim among them. According to Chiron, it might take decades for him to heal enough to wake. Others in the chamber had Slept even longer, centuries or millennia. A fate worse than death? Would any of them have knowingly chosen it instead?

But what of Tiy and Haru and Rumaisa? They'd decided to trust me to free Nimur.

My head ached. Nothing made sense or broke into easily digestible pieces. What to do? Who to believe, trust, follow? Stay or return or go on?

Worst case scenarios lay before me, with no good options.

If I let him go and helped him destroy the House and Nimur and all the other Forgotten—only for him to prove wrong—I might never realize.

But if he guessed right, and I ran away and said his name outside—then, when I gained his memories, I'd live the rest of my life unable to escape the horror of prolonging the Sleeping Forgottens' torment.

Tremors rippled through me, head to feet. Every part of my body shook, even my phone tucked safe in my pocket. My phone—where a single message from the future refused to allow me to delete it.

Maybe I made the problem more complicated than it had to be.

Did I trust myself? My future self had sent me a single piece of advice.

Run.

I bent over the table, head down as though pondering his request all the while gauging angles and obstacles. Inching the book down against the table and stroking the soft binding, I pretended to be lost in thought.

Without warning, I broke. Pushed my aching body back into motion. Pelted headlong along a diagonal curve out of Liam's reach, and aimed for the doors leading to other displays and hallways—and the main entrance to the outside world.

"No! Bea, please!"

I'd gone this way before, only a few days ago. Alone, then, not knowing what lay before me or behind, or what would come. Bearing the weight of a name whose owner wanted to be remembered.

This time the name in my head failed to push me on. Nimur hadn't given it to me. The bearer didn't want it spoken, at least not yet, given the rattle and slap of his sandals on the floor as he raced behind me.

His breath hot on my heels—on my neck.

Refusing to glance behind, to waste time checking how close he came, I took a winding path through corridors growing ever more choked with visitors. True visitors interested in seeing the displays or those trying to beat the heat. Didn't matter. They made for obstacles for me, but more for Liam.

"Hey, what're you doing?" A solidly built young Black man in shorts and a DC United T-shirt asked as I bolted past him and his friends—and glared at Liam. "Leave her alone."

A bunch of feet stamped on the floor, and the air on my neck turned cooler.

No matter how my muscles ached, lungs gasped for air, I drove forward through the pain. Picked my chances. Took angles through the corridors and squeezed through any gaps to trace the straightest line outward.

Every labored step brought me closer.

"Please, Bea, stop!" Liam called, voice farther behind. "Don't kill me yet. Give me a last chance."

The crowds turned into a blur. Nothing existed except the door gleaming in the distance.

Almost there.

I threw my weight against the metal handle, and it moved. Slow. Too much so, as the air behind me grew warmer. Hotter. Squeals and squeaks of rubber on tile and grunts as Liam caught up.

Too late. He grabbed only air as I slipped through the gap between door and frame.

Unable to leave the museum, he filled the frame as the door swung shut. Pressed himself against the glass. Eyes and voice pleading still for me to give him time to set everyone free.

"I'm not ready to die. Let me free them first!"

Who did I believe? My future self told me to run without saying anything about whether or not I should remember him. I had a hard enough time living with Madeline-Jeanne in my head, but Liam too? So much older, and steeped in determination to destroy Nimur?

Except if I didn't speak he'd try again. Someone else would have to carry his name outside and speak it.

And Madeline-Jeanne deserved some recompense.

I drew in a deep breath. Syllables manifested in my mouth without problem. Pain arced through my throat.

"Alhred of Lindisfarne, I will remember you."

Liam jerked. An expression of surprise flashed over his face. Then he disintegrated into glittering motes of dust. A wind blew, and they vanished.

The weight of his memories hit me, harder than Madeline-Jeanne. As though a thousand shards of broken glass whipped through me, making my body arc and jaw clench shut. The world turned to nothingness.

⚜

SOFTNESS SURROUNDED ME. A PILLOW CUSHIONED MY HEAD, smooth sheets stretched over the mattress beneath me, and another sheet covered me. Hints of perfume clung to the fabric, but not enough to do anything more than tickle my nose.

I lay in my own bedroom in the Quarters. It *felt* the same as always even though for the first blinking moments everything *looked* strange and unfamiliar.

Someone had undressed me and put me in my nightshirt, a super-size blue T-shirt, plus made the bed with clean sheets, white with sprays of yellow flowers. Very nice of them.

My legs wobbled beneath me as I lurched from the bed. I grabbed hold of the back of the desk chair. Although my arm muscles likewise seemed to have the consistency of wet noodles, I stayed upright. Took one shaky step then another, calves and thighs firming up.

Luckily the bathroom lay nearby. My throat ached much less, no worse than a sore throat. The mirror showed my tousled hair, but only the faintest of fingermarks around my neck. The minty taste of my toothpaste made everything brighter and taste better.

Things smelled better too, of eggs and toast. Wobbling back to my room, I nearly ran into Paulo setting a tray on the desk. Orange juice filled a tall glass, while two pieces of buttered toast framed a mound of scrambled eggs topped with a hint of cheese.

He wore black from head to ankles, feet bare and toes long and knobby against the carpet. His dark eyes glittered in the light, and he moved faster than I did. Got out of the way as I tottered back into bed.

"We heard you getting up. How're you feeling?" He pulled the desk chair back toward the foot of the bed and toppled into it with a smack.

I counted to ten before answering, making sure I spoke in English. "Okay. Weak. How about you?"

"Fine. I wasn't the one who slept for two days." Mouth straight, he glared at me.

"Two days!"

A tight nod.

"Not my idea." The tray held only enough food for one person. I wolfed down the orange juice, sugar coating my tongue.

"Hey, wait for me before you start spilling info." Yolanda's voice carried down the hall. She whisked into the room, filling it to the brim. As with Paulo, she didn't wear a uniform shirt but casual shorts and a green-and-white Arden College T-shirt.

"Hi." I waved at her. "Sorry you're having to wait on me again."

"This better be the last time." She said, her eyes as bright as his. "I didn't drag you back here, you can thank Paulo and others for that, but I magicked you clean and into your nightgown. So I'm owed answers first, before anyone else."

"Thanks." Three bodies in the small space generated more heat, but the air conditioning kept up. I drew the sheet over my legs and dug into the eggs. "I promise to write up everything for you and the website as soon as I can. But I need a couple of answers first. Did they find Jay Doe and Nimur? Are they okay?"

"Rumaisa led Haru right to Jay Doe and Nimur, bare moments before they would've broken out of the trap they'd been snatched into." Yolanda ticked off updates about the key players on her fingers. "Everyone's okay, except Liam. Silvestre might be a bit quieter than usual without his shadow, for he's taken the news hard, but otherwise all's well."

"And we're under orders to bring you over to the museum as soon as you're hale enough to make the trip." Paulo added. "For thanks and more questions and answers."

"Nimur and Jay Doe free and safe makes everything else worthwhile." I said.

"I hope you keep thinking it." Yolanda shook her head, the beads on the ends of her braids clacking. "You stayed unconscious a long time."

"Liam was a lot older than Madeline. More memories to digest." But his didn't press on me as hard as hers. Perhaps because I had spent those two days sleeping—and living a compressed version of his life, albeit in mixed-up order.

"Speaking of which, we've been in contact with Diego. Two remembrances in a short time is a lot." She jerked her chin at my sheet-covered legs. "You're going to have to take it easy."

"Yeah."

"But we've got one more piece of good news for you." Paulo twisted around and lifted something from the bureau.

Before catching even a quick glimpse, I knew what he held.

The fork clattered as I dropped it on the plate and pushed the tray away.

My hands curved to cradle a small baby's cap, formed of rolled linen carefully stitched together to keep him safe from bumping his head. A ripple of cold ran through me, but Madeline-Jeanne's memories lay calm.

Not so Liam's. A white-washed chamber bare of furniture save a rickety table replaced my bedroom. A thin slice of a window lay open, with no screen or glass. In the distance, waves crashed against land. A light spring breeze tugged at the hem of my coarse brown robes, and carried a familiar fresh, clean salt-sea smell. I lifted the baby's cap to my lips and whispered. "Where is the baby?"

Yolanda's fingernails of hers stung, but brought me back to the present fast. Madeline-Jeanne was happier being remembered and dying for good, maybe finding her son in heaven or some other place—but it happened because Liam had manipulated her. Played on her longing for her baby.

I swigged more of the orange juice to wash away the sour taste. "Thanks for bringing it out."

"Doesn't make much difference for you with a second remembrance hanging over your head." Yolanda shook her head, worry clear on her face.

"No one knows what Liam's talisman was, or if anyone does they aren't saying." Paulo offered, turning his hands out. "But we'll find it for you, someway."

"No need." I stroked the linen cap. "I know what it is— and where."

REMEMBRANCE

Five months later, Liam's true name echoed in my head as I watched snow fall. Thick flakes drifted through the air. A light dusting already covered the ground. Though still afternoon, lamp posts lining concrete walkways already glowed, shedding bright golden light against the looming dusk. Some of the light reflected off the shifting waters of a lake.

Three layers of glass and some special gas or other substance pumped between the panes protected me from the cold, dark, and snow even though I'd doffed coat, hat, and mittens. They hung around the corner in the coat closet near the locker holding my suitcase.

My sneaker-clad feet rested on gray-and-green industrial carpet. Instead of jeans and a uniform shirt, I wore a new burgundy turtleneck and black slacks. They made the back of my neck and waist itch despite the moderate temperature. My toes twitched within my shoes. Fingers rapped against my legs. A few drops of moisture oozed from my palms and along my brow.

Enough sunlight lingered to show the picturesque landscape of a top-rated college, one of the top colleges for sorcerers.

Such a pretty place, with snow all around. The sight triggered memory of a line from the *Ballad of Eriselda*, about ash falling thick as snow. The lyrics promised the dead Eriselda she would be remembered for herself, but those who killed her never named in the world and condemned to languish in obscurity. Her homeland cherished her talisman, while her murderers' languished in museum storage unconnected to their names.

A faint hint of leather and parchment, sweat and wood, filled the air. Suitable to the settings.

Glass-fronted maple bookcases and display cases lined the walls, all discreetly locked and likely spelled against theft. The bookcases featured runs of collegiate yearbooks and old course catalogs from the days they had to be consulted in print, plus assorted other works. Memorabilia, mostly in green-and-white—a pennant, hat, t-shirt, programs—filled the display cases.

Four long matching tables stretched across the center of the room, each with four chairs upholstered in dark green. A workstation occupied a strategic position to oversee the tables, with its back to clear glass doors leading into the depth of the Arden College Library's special collections department.

The desk sat empty. No need to have someone there as all of their valuables remained locked away and the tabletops bare save for the box I'd brought with me.

The box didn't fit at all. Recycled cardboard in white and blue, its sides and top advertised an obscure brand of diapers. Earned me at least a dozen double takes as I'd hefted it around on the train ride up to northeastern Pennsylvania. No one looked more than twice. Yolanda, Paulo, and I had covered it with a dozen protective spells.

The contents survived the trip intact. Untouched.

Ready to be turned over.

Hinges squeaked as the glass door opened and Diego entered. Glasses perched on his nose, combining with his button-down white shirt and black slacks to make for a scholarly appearance.

"It's good to see you in person." Diego held out his hand.

"Likewise." I wiped my sweaty palm on my pants before taking his.

"How are you doing?" He pulled out a chair from the table, legs scraping softly against the carpet, and gestured for me to sit.

"Not too bad." I shook my head at the chair, only to realize I shifted restlessly from one foot to the other, and my hands twitched. "I'll be better soon, I hope."

"So do I." He left the chair out and circled the table to stand so I faced him sitting or standing. Other than once when he first arrived, he hadn't glanced at the box, even though it so clearly didn't belong here. "You're certain this is what you want?"

"Don't you want them?" I stiffened and stepped back.

"Of course. It's an honor. We're happy to have your gifts. We will cherish them." He ran a hand through his hair, fingers not so shaky as mine but not completely calm either. "I only want to be sure this is your choice."

"I've thought about it a lot and this seems best to me,"—I took a deep breath—"but you have to take everything and keep them together."

"Everything?"

"I checked with Tiy to clear my plans. She approved, but asked Jay Doe to host Nimur one last time to check with them. They okayed it. So everything's in order."

"Why don't you show me?" Diego waved at the box.

Rubbing my hands against my pants again, I stepped up to

the table and tapped the sides of the box in a jazzy rhythm. Sparkles filled the air for a few moments, bringing the smells of pine and sand. The top parted, flaps flopping to either side. Hands trembling, I brought out the contents piece-by-piece. Unwrapped them and laid them on the table.

A baby's cap in blue and white, blood stains still visible on one side.

An illuminated manuscript edition of the Gospels.

A pile of printed pages.

Diego went first for the book. Simple calfskin covered the thick tome, although it had originally been intended to be decorated with gold and precious jewels. Nevertheless, the contents spoke of the investment of countless hours of labor to create a work of beauty. Vibrant colors blazed on every page. The book opened most naturally to the spot where a red-and-gold beast formed the first letter in a chapter from Luke.

Though no artist, I remembered using a quill dipped in ink to sketch the beast. Building it up through layers of color and the proper substances necessary to allow the gold leaf to adhere. Filling the pages with all manner of color and designs.

Liam had sneaked back to see the pages, once bound. Caressed the volume, guilt heavy in his belly at the depth of his desire to keep it. Hid it away, shoving it out of sight, when the first cries and shrieks announced the arrival of Vikings intent on pillage.

It remained there, unnoticed, when they left—exposed to the elements. Rain poured down even as he lay dying in the ruins. Then Ge-mimor—Moneta—Nimur appeared and offered him the chance to live and protect his work forever.

For over a thousand years, he had. Even at the last, when he worked to destroy everything, he slipped it into the display of lost books to ensure the book would be seen, admired, and cherished.

My memories now, all of them, though they'd belonged to Liam and before that to Alhred. So much of their pasts had already sunk into my brain, sinews, and bones. I'd picked up languages they'd spoken. Given the right equipment, I could illuminate a manuscript or sew a fine garment—if not with the same artistry as Liam and Madeline. Jeanne and Ahlred. After I turned over his and Madeline-Jeanne's talismans to Diego and the library, maybe that would change.

To give Diego credit, he spent equal time examining the baby's cap. Admiring the materials, the small stitches, the love and care invested into the work.

"We're not a museum or a major research center." He sighed and laid the cap back on the table. "These will be cared for and used, but I cannot guarantee how often anyone will ask to see them."

"I don't mind, as long as whoever does use them—at least if they're a sorcerer—also uses this. You don't have to share this with mundanes; they won't believe. But sorcerer students and researchers have to read it if they want access to the cap or book. I'll send you a digital copy, but I wanted these with them." I waved at the papers.

"What is it?" Diego glanced over the first lines. Then gazed up at me, brow wrinkled in puzzlement.

"It's the story of how I ended up remembering them, along with memories of theirs that I relived. Plus anecdotes and stories I got from Tiy and Silvestre and Haru and other Forgotten willing to talk to me."

Putting everything together and writing down the story of how I came to have the talismans proved harder than running away from Liam. My brain ached in recollection of the hours, weeks, months I'd spent crafting a narrative that made sense and wouldn't bore readers to tears, but grab them and make them read it all and understand some part of Madeline and Liam.

For the last time, I cradled the cap in one hand and caressed the illuminated manuscript with the other.

"If I give you only the talismans, that shapes how people will remember Madeline and Liam. If they think about them at all, Liam will only be the unknown illuminator and Madeline the seamstress." I pushed the papers closer to the manuscript and baby cap. "But they lived, loved, and hated. Almost died. Were lost and forgotten. Worked for Nimur for centuries. Madeline adored her baby so much, she became vulnerable to manipulation to the point she attacked a man and stole his baby. Liam worried about the souls of the Forgotten, fell under the influence of the witch hunter, and in the end decided Nimur had turned into Mis-gemynd, evil memory, so he tried to destroy the House of Memory.

"They were Jeanne then Madeline, Alhred then Liam." I touched the cap, then the book. "I want them remembered for more than the objects they left behind—for themselves and all they were and did. Bad and good; good and bad."

ORDINARY SORCERY

Adventure and working for magical organizations runs in the family—read on for a taste of Bea's oldest sister and *The Webmasters of Fate*

Rose soared high. Oldest daughter. Smart. Popular. A born leader ready to remake the world in the name of Truth, Justice, and Equality.

Then she fell short and crashed. Dropped out of law school. Lost confidence as the future she always expected slipped out of her hands.

Until the day an idle word uncovers a sorcerous plot to control the present and shape the future by changing the past. To stop it, Rose must power through her weaknesses—or give up her remaining ideals.

Powerful, believable characters face a high-stakes adventure in *The Webmasters of Fate*.

The discovery of the ruins of Atlantis turned my life upside down.

Boredom drove me to surf news sites that Friday afternoon, starting with the most credible and reliable newspapers. I'd already completed all necessary tasks on my plate plus a half dozen unnecessary ones, but several hours of the work day remained. My sole desire was to find something engaging to keep my eyes from glazing over.

I preferred to present visitors with a ready smile and create a welcoming impression. In short, deliver the version of Rosalind Celia—aka Rose—Williams the firm hired as a receptionist and administrative assistant in the first place.

Anyone passing through the smoky-glass front door of the Webmasters of Fate's Philadelphia office would find a calm, sedate young White woman dressed in sensible black sneakers, black jeans, and a dark green shirt, her tall, lean body poised at a pseudo-mahogany workstation, in a chair with squeaky wheels. Seashell earrings dangled from my ears, longer than my medium-brown pixie-cut. And a smile, of course, pasted on my face.

As opposed to a wild-eyed creature bored out of her skull and ready to pounce on any source of potential amusement. Or a slumped figure snoozing over her keyboard only to wake with the imprint of keys on her face. I veered between the extremes on normal Friday afternoons, but more so on slow, hot summer Fridays before three-day weekends.

I'd already used up the one piece of chocolate I allowed myself per day on a luxurious double-chocolate truffle from the bakery on the first floor. Even with the rich taste lingering on my tongue, I needed invigoration of some sort.

Especially when my direct supervisor, the second-in-charge, turned the thermostat up as soon as the senior director—webmaster—left for the weekend.

"When the cat's away, the mice will play." Geneva's

breathy alto tones rang out as she popped out of her office to give me the news. With a fist pump, she pulled off her thick, oversized cream sweater to reveal a thin red top tucked into her slacks, much more fitting for a humid summer day. A White woman a good two decades my elder, she ran a hand through short, light brown hair with only a few hints of frost at the ears. "No more freezing inside only to broil when we go out."

I smiled until she returned to her office. No sense irritating Geneva, who'd always been considerate to me . . . but she left me in a quandary.

Before, the chilly temperature ensured my fingers rattled away at my keyboard to keep warm as I shivered at the desk. Not fun, and I welcomed the first upticks as the air went from arctic-winter-day to balmy-equatorial-night, except it didn't stop. Within moments, we reached too-toasty.

My eyelids drifted downward, and my head rolled in lazy, drowsy half-circles. The residual caffeine in my bloodstream reduced the odds of my falling asleep, but I yawned and twiddled my thumbs while staring aimlessly at the images of different kinds of webs and networks decorating the pale gray walls. Founded in the 1980s as a subsidiary of Lachesis, Inc., the Webmasters of Fate produced video games and invested in art. Images from the games hung on the corridors and in the reception area and communal office spaces, along with photographs and visualizations of networks. Telephone networks, social media connections, anything web-like.

Even the custom, flat industrial carpet of light gray boasted black lines tracing spider webs and lifelike images of spiders here and there. All sorts of spiders, too, except magnified three or four times so viewers could distinguish legs, pedipalps, and spinnerets. At the start of my first day at work, all three of the local directors warned me never to kill a spider. If I found one anywhere I should to leave it be or, if brave enough, scoop it carefully up on a piece of paper and bring it to them or, if they weren't around, slip paper and spider under the door of one of their offices. I made a point of never letting my shoes step on a single spider imprinted in the carpet just in case it proved to be the real thing.

At least I had a job, and one at a firm that designed and delivered intricate games I'd regularly played—*Survive Vesuvius!*, *Long Live Palmyra,* and the grade-school-oriented *What's Under Your Feet?* The firm's products were admired for unparalleled degree of detail—helped in no small part by the owners, top executives, and at least half of the design and programming staff all being sorcerers.

Usually, work provided stimulation. As a regular matter, I got to buzz employees in and out and deal with visitors—not a lot, but some. Receive packages. Edit memos. Arrange appointments such as health, beauty, pet care, golf tee times. My title might be administrative assistant, but in point-of-fact I acted also as receptionist, concierge, and personal assistant to every employee working on site. This meant dealing with all sorts of tasks from mind-numbing number crunching to solving people's logistical problems.

Yet summer Friday afternoons stretched out, with every hour seeming to last three times as long. All around me people jumped and quivered to get time to speed up. Other Monday-Friday nine-to-five hourly workers probably spent the afternoon daydreaming about what to do with our rare paid holiday.

At least, I supposed other hourly minions daydreamed.

I didn't. The last thing I wanted was three days alone in my minuscule studio apartment. The alternatives didn't appeal either. Spend some of my very limited discretionary funds on a trip out of town to visit family and fake a smile while they worried over me? Take up an invitation from one of my few remaining friends and likewise get worried over and nagged to do something more "interesting"—in other words with better bragging rights—than my current job? Get out of my apartment and mingle with crowds of strangers at one or another of the street festivals?

Practice casting sorcerous spells even though I'd never managed to make even the smallest, most reliable spell work once, much less twice in a row?

No. No. No.

And NO.

Above all, I didn't want to dwell on magic.

The world had three kinds of people in it: billions of mundanes who didn't believe in magic, millions of sorcerers casting spells under the mundanes' noses; and the minute number with the worst of both worlds—we who believed in magic but couldn't work a spell to save our lives. I no longer fit easily in the mundane world, but neither did I belong in the sorcerous.

I needed a distraction. A challenge. A goal to accomplish that *meant* something.

Or a quest.

Considering where I worked, I should have known better than to say that out loud earlier in the day.

Because Fate most certainly provided what I'd asked for.

ATLANTIS FOUND! Inch-tall letters flashed at the top of the news site—breaking news! A five-second video clip filled the space below. A grainy brick wall half-covered with barnacles loomed in the distance. Water flowed around, along with bits of seaweed and plastic. The camera operator zoomed in, revealing a faint insignia on the wall. It resembled nothing so much as a mix of the symbol for anarchy and a stereotypical witch's hat.

Then the video clip jumped to a celebration aboard a luxe ship. People burst open champagne bottles right and left. In the middle a big, sweaty White guy in a too-tight blue sailor shirt and shorts jumped up and down. His badly dyed black combover flopped with every jerk.

"We did it! Am-I-right? Hoo-boy, we're going to paint the town red tonight. Atlantis or bust, baby!" He could barely be heard over the hoots and yells.

I hit the mute button, shaking my head. "What in holy hell?"

"What's so interesting?"

The lungs and vocal cords that produced the question came from a six-foot-tall Black man built on solid lines, dressed today in a close-fitting, midnight blue Polo shirt and matching slacks. He smiled more than frowned, although the smiles didn't always reach his light brown eyes. Black hair cut in a high top with a fade framed a long-nosed face, his skin a deep brown with sepia undertones. A hint of lavender and sandalwood hung around him, the dominant notes in his preferred scent.

I froze, my stomach turning into a lump of lead in my belly at the unmistakable growly bass of my third boss: Maksim Irving. Fifteen years my elder, he ranked as the newest director—i.e. one of the people who ran the firm versus salaried minions, or hourly peons such as me.

Such a big man should thump around, but no. Today he wore soft leather sandals, but even in hard-soled boots walking across tiled flooring he could sneak up on a cat. He regularly slipped through the treated-glass front door without setting off the discreet bells attached. Routine glances up at the door and *not* getting caught up in anything on my computer were the only defense against him and certain others slipping in or out unnoticed.

I'd come up short and he'd snuck in.

"Well? What caught your eye?" Maksim tapped the top of my monitor with a long finger complete with a ragged nail edge.

"Nothing, sir." One hand hovered over the mouse without touching. "Just checking the news."

"That's all? You certainly seemed wrapped up. I could've marched right by you without being noticed." He chuckled and stamped a foot, making at best a soft thud.

Did he really think that sounded loud? Maybe he moved so softly because he physically couldn't make much noise. Allowing myself one look-over from head to toe, I refused to believe that. He had to be capable of loudness, and just amusing himself at my expense.

Prying apart teeth that had begun to grind together—the last thing I needed was a dental bill atop the rest of my debts —I wetted my lips and managed a small smile. Tilted my head and clasped my hands against my chest.

"There's breaking news, about the discovery of Atlantis."

"Jack Smith's excavation?" His hands clenched so tight his knuckles lightened. "The man's a—"

No surprise on Maksim's face. Nothing. Only his fists showed any sign of reaction.

I'd expected much more. Shock. Astonishment. Something bigger than biting his tongue over even saying the polite version of what Smith was.

Alas, my mouth opened and I filled in the blank. "Smith's a conman. A thief making a big, flashy show about finding Atlantis in the Bermuda Triangle while he redirects at least half of the millions he's swindling into numbered accounts. Oh, he puts on a good facade, getting one of his billionaire marks to kit out a diving vessel, but the guy's a walking, talking cliché! He can't even keep his accent straight, going from pseudo-Southern redneck to pseudo-Brooklyn in a single sentence."

"Don't hold back. Lay it all out, sister." Maksim settled his fists on his hips, teeth grinding. "I hate the man myself."

"He's bad, but the people funding him are as bad or worse.

Buying into his stories of Atlantis being the pinnacle of White domination—they just want an excuse to feel superior." My jaw snapped shut so hard and fast the click reverberated along my skull. Seven months of keeping my own counsel and not sharing anything too personal at work, all blown in a moment.

"I don't disagree." The spark in Maksim's eyes and twitch of a tic in his cheek suggested much more than his words. "But walls sometimes have ears. Around here, the floors and ceilings do, too. And some of us are known to support causes others find . . . distasteful." His head tilted toward the open door leading to the senior webmaster's office.

"Point taken." I pasted a fake smile on my face. "I'm sorry, sir, but Mr. Anstruther isn't in this afternoon."

"Bounced out early, did he?" His eyes narrowed, and the tic sped up as his voice dropped. "I wonder if he's in Bermuda, celebrating with the rest." With a sharp jerk, he twisted his face in as fake a smile as mine. "So what's Smith latest find, the library? Another temple?"

I shook my head and patted my ears with my hands. "I'm sorry, I don't think I heard you right. Would you mind repeating . . ."

"What part of Atlantis has Smith uncovered now?"

"You believe this crap—" I swallowed hard and omitted other curse words, no matter the amused twitch of Maksim's lips. "I mean, that Atlantis even existed for Smith to find?"

"No one has ever been truly certain whether Atlantis existed, but to give him credit, Smith found clues the rest missed." His fisted hands banged against his thighs in a-synchronous beat. One foot tapped against the floor, sending minute vibrations that raised sympathetic resonance in the soles of my sneakers. "The man's an irritating, racist piece of . . . but he's stubborn. I doubted at first, but the artifacts he's brought up in the last three months would make a believer out of almost anyone."

Wait, three months? According to the news, Smith had only found Atlantis today.

Yet when I turned back to my computer, everything had shifted.

Hot New Atlantis Discoveries! Instead of a grainy image of a barnacled undersea wall, the video now showed a phalanx of white-legged divers swimming four-across along the remains of an ancient street. Broken walls of varying heights, none over six or seven feet, lined the way. At the end stood a jagged archway.

The camera cut away to show Smith beaming and waving his hands at tables covered with items, some cleaned and others still bearing barnacles and layers of sand. Immense pitchers, jugs, jars, and platters—both whole and in pieces, and all with elaborate decorations, some of the colors still recognizable. Youths portrayed in charcoal gray and brick red danced around and above a large bull on one platter. The artistic style reminded me of Ancient Minoan art from history class a few years earlier, but with blockier, squarer lines.

No way.

After all the changes, all the turmoil of the last year and a half, the world had finally crossed the limits of my belief. Life could crumble my plans to pieces and make me accept magic —but not the existence of Atlantis.

I refused to have my present alter as I watched.

"Atlantis never existed. Plato invented it. Everything I've ever read about Ancient Greece, before and after I discovered magic, insists on that—and it's certainly not in the Bermuda triangle." I ran a hand through my hair, yanking on threads until my head hurt, but the screen didn't change. "So how could Smith find it? And even if he did, how did he go from having found it today to finding it months ago in a matter of seconds?"

"Oh, Atlantis existed, it just . . ." Maksim blinked. Shook his head hard several times in succession as though a mosquito had flown into his ear, then rubbed his temples, although his foot kept rapping. "What did I just say?"

"Atlantis existed. Which, all due respect to you being my boss and all, it doesn't. Never did."

"No?"

"No."

"No?" He swayed as though I'd hit him. The wobbly movements increased until he rocked so hard, blinking all the while, that he toppled over. He hit the floor with a thud. No matter how soft the carpet, a body slamming against the floor made a ruckus.

He lay on his back facing up, jaw wide and tongue out and panting as though he'd run up the stairs from the first floor far below us. His arms splayed wide, hands flat against the carpet and fingers digging into the strands.

My chair wheels screeched against the rubber mat covering the carpet as I pushed back from my desk. I nearly knocked the chair over in my rush to get down next to him. Except, what could I do? I'd taken a first-aid course, once way back in high school. Most of my medical knowledge came from novels and television shows, not exactly reliable sources. If he was having a seizure of some kind, should I call 911? Put something between his teeth to make sure he didn't bite his tongue?

Or call for help and let someone else figure it out? Not my preferred deal, I liked to handle things myself when I could— which partly explained why my life had tanked the way it had.

"Help! Someone!" I knelt next to him, hands fluttering uselessly in the air above him.

"No." Little more than an aspiration. He grabbed my

hand with one of his. Calluses along the edges of his fingers scraped as he squeezed tight. His breath carried a hint of garlic. "Time. Space. Wait."

His eyes blinked rapidly, gaze distant and unfocused. Shadows danced across his face, almost under the skin. They had a flat look, as though an animated movie projected onto him. Yet a thrum of power emanated from his body, setting my wisdom teeth vibrating. I couldn't do magic, but recognized when others did . . . or had it done to them . . . This had all the hallmarks.

Unfortunately, nothing I'd learned about sorcery taught me what to do if someone else was suffering from a spell of some kind. But maybe it wasn't any different than what I'd do for anyone under other circumstances.

Prying my hand from his grasp, I dashed to the break room down the hall and around the corner. A head topped by a thick set of headphones bobbed from the corner of the big collaborative work area, but didn't turn my way. My shoes squeaked on the tiled floor as I skidded past the empty table to the mini kitchen. I grabbed a paper towel and dampened it with water chilly and straight from the tap, plus popped open the refrigerator and nabbed a cold bottle of water.

I sped back through the empty hall. He hadn't moved. Worse, his arms lay limp and head tilted back at an awkward angle. Only his heaving chest and the whistle of air escaping his lungs showed he still lived.

Dropping back onto the carpet, I laid the towel on his forehead. The water bottle slipped from my fingers and rolled until it stopped at an angle against his thigh.

He gave a sigh and the whistling sound lessened. I might've sighed myself, in relief because the whistling had hit me all the wrong ways.

"Sir? Mr. Irving? Maksim?"

He only reacted at the last.

His hands rose and clapped on either side of my face. Not pressing or hurting, just holding my head there above his. Sweat dripped down his forehead and small but visible gusts of steam wafted above the dripping paper towel.

"Rosalind Celia Williams, did Smith find Atlantis?" His gaze fixed on me. I couldn't look away.

An urge to agree rose and nearly filled my throat. The easiest thing would be to let it slide. Keep my job and not rock the boat. Not try to be a smarty-pants, know-it-all and above-it-all savior—to quote one of the first stones that had splintered my life's trajectory—especially since the matter struck him so oddly.

Too late. I'd already pushed the *no* line. Making nice would require me to take it back. Admit an error that I didn't believe in.

"How could he? Atlantis doesn't exist."

"You're right." His hands dropped away. He glared at me and snarled, a beastly sound. Shaking himself all over, he ripped the towel from his forehead. Sat up and burst into a coughing fit. He grabbed the water bottle and unscrewed the top. Drained the whole thing in a couple of long swallows. Then he slammed his hands together, crushing the bottle between them. The plastic cracked, and the remaining drops sprayed out. "More than you know. Atlantis never existed."

"Then why . . ." A couple of drops landed on me—face, neck. I wiped them off with a hand, rocking back on my heels.

"No time for whys right now." He shook his head and magicked the bottle away.

Clapping his hands together, he pulled them apart slowly. He'd held nothing, yet the air between his palms filled with an intricate tangle of strands as though he'd started playing a string game. All sorts of colors: bright greens and yellows, sullen blues and purples, flashy reds and orange, plus brown and gray and black.

I reached out a finger toward them, fascinated by the way they pulsed and seethed, glowing with light.

"Watch out." He pulled back. "Don't touch."

I recoiled as a brief flash of heat hit me. A faint stench flared in the air, as though a hair burned to a crisp. I patted my forehead, but nothing seemed wrong even though bits of ash danced in the air around the threads.

His fingers twitched this way and that, and the strands responded. Colors whipped along with rapid beats, then slowed. He studied the result for a long moment, then brought his hands together and the lines of light vanished.

Leaning over, he flattened a palm against the carpet. His fingers inched to the side until the tip of the long finger slipped under a strand of web.

I'd thought the webs printed on the carpet fiber. An artistic illusion. Yet as he pulled the filament of web away, additional lines appeared in the air outlining an intricate tangle of strands far more complex than those he'd held in his hands.

Worse, spiders appeared. Dozens after dozens surged out of the carpet to skip along the strands. Black. Orange. Brown. Tan. Gray. White. All purring. The vibrations pouring from them filled me, worse than anything else.

Creeping, leaping.

Swinging on strands from the web.

Jumping from the web to skitter along his arm. They seethed in an ever-growing mass wrapping him from fingers to shoulder. One made the leap from arm to the tip of his nose.

I hadn't a shadow of arachnophobia when I took the job, but then I hadn't lived through a mass of them seething around me. Small, medium, large, including three tarantulas as big as my hand, one of which passed a hair away from me as it crawled over to sit on Maksim's foot.

I fell over backward, inching away on my backside until I hit my desk and couldn't go any farther. Because of the spiders—and the sudden burst of magic.

Knowing the firm had a sorcerous side was one thing, experiencing it this way quite another.

Find out what happens next in The Webmasters of Fate

Be among the first to learn of new releases: sign-up for her newsletter at https://BookHip.com/PCSWMCK. Book recommendations, updates on stories, and snippets from works-in-progress—plus a free Dancing Princesses story for signing up!

ABOUT THE AUTHOR

Alea Henle writes non-fiction by day and fiction by night. Contemporary and historical fantasy, fantasy romance—and more! Check out her website www.aleahenle.com.

www.ingramcontent.com/pod-product-compliance
Lightning Source LLC
Chambersburg PA
CBHW061433210726
48287CB00007B/2190